# the perfect friend

ALSO BY BARBARA COPPERTHWAITE

*Invisible*
*Flowers for the Dead*
*The Darkest Lies*
*Her Last Secret*

BARBARA
COPPERTHWAITE

# the perfect friend

bookouture

Published by Bookouture in 2018

An imprint of StoryFire Ltd.

Carmelite House
50 Victoria Embankment
London EC4Y 0DZ

www.bookouture.com



ISBN: 978-1-78681-549-1
eBook ISBN: 978-1-78681-548-4

*For Norman Price*

# CHAPTER ONE

## NOW

From my first breath, I was destined to be a freak. The signs were there in my childhood, concerns as I grew up, narrowing down to a vanishing point of the here and now, where everyone in the room is staring, waiting for me to speak. An awkward cough here, the clearing of a throat there, a chair leg scraping over the wooden floor as someone shifts, all absorbed by the expectant silence of the small community hall.

The circle of twenty or so plastic chairs cups me as I prepare to talk. Once, that would have made me too self-conscious to speak, but instead it comforts. I know the deepest, darkest secrets of all the people looking at me, leaning forward to catch every word. They know mine, too – or a sanitised version, anyway. This is a safe space created for confession. Still, I'm trying to decide how much truth to tell. This started as little white lies. Then the white turned to a black blight that blotted out everything, running out of control.

*My name is Alex Appleby. I'm 44. I'm a dressmaker…* The words are so clichéd I can't help silently sounding them in my head before I take the plunge. A deep preparatory breath assaults my nose with the smell of Pledge and Windolene. I suppress a sneeze, then speak.

'I'm a liar. Well, a recovering anorexic, and all I did during my illness was lie to cover my tracks and keep my addiction alive.

'"I ate earlier, and I'm still stuffed."

'"I'm saving myself for my big meal tonight."

'"That was so tasty, I've scoffed the lot" – this one, incidentally, is the best: I always had the food hidden in a napkin, or my pockets, or my handbag.

'It's only just occurred to me, now I'm recovering, how many lies have been told to everyone who cares about me. I'm ashamed. I always thought of myself as an honest person. Of course, that could be a lie, too.'

My laugh is self-deprecating, and my audience take their cue, faces breaking into smiles.

The support group started out when the leader, Jackie, had been in a car accident and found it hard to cope. She'd wanted to talk to others who'd suffered a similar trauma but hadn't been able to find a group locally. Being a bustling force-of-nature type who, once she makes up her mind about something, won't let go of the idea, she started this one herself. Her second member had been Lainey, who had joined because she'd been mown down while on a pedestrian crossing and suffered flashbacks; but she was also grateful because as a result of the accident, doctors had diagnosed her pancreatic cancer early enough to save her life easily. Eventually, Lainey left, but not before recruiting first me – after we got chatting one day in the hospital café, over in Newcastle – and then Carrie, a fellow cancer sufferer, although hers was breast.

There were other members, too, who had been through all sorts, from rape to bereavement to the shock of being burgled. Jackie didn't mind that her group had morphed into support for people who had been through all manner of trauma, rather than only for accident victims. It was nice for all of us to share in the group, getting to know each other. Even though our experiences were so different, at the root of our issues were similar emotions: fear, anger, difficulty in coping, the urge to pretend to be strong as we fell apart. Dealing with the change in the way people reacted to us. The sense that our lives were split into Before and After.

In the circle, I seek out Carrie's reaction to my words. She grins, gives me a double thumbs up of encouragement, still unaware that I, her new best friend, have other lies that involve her. There's an ulterior motive in taking her under my wing.

My words are for her more than anything, warning her I'm not all that I seem.

'I haven't just fibbed to others, I've failed to be honest with myself – some of the biggest lies people tell are to themselves,' I add. 'At my lowest, even my own body tricked me. My starving carcass released endorphins, chemicals designed to make me feel good, to mask the pain it was in and help keep me going. Giving up that rush is hard, and now I'm no longer in the grip of my eating disorder it's a struggle without those endorphins. I need to find something else that can fill that hole and make me feel good about myself, but what, and how?

'At my worst, I hallucinated, my eyes literally deceiving me. After three days without food or sleep, I thought I was caged in a red and white circus tent, like something from a freak show, while an audience trailed past me, pointing and laughing. It felt so real. See how easily we can deceive ourselves into accepting an altered reality? The doctors told me it was most likely caused by an electrolyte disturbance, probably due to inadequate nutrition. Whatever it was, I was so delirious that two nurses had to hold me down. That was when I was at rock bottom.'

The memory makes me feel shame at how low I'd reached, but also pride at how far I've come. Everyone is silent, intent as priests at confession. Carrie nods at me.

'At one point, my twins appeared at my bedside to say they could no longer cope with seeing me kill myself. "Why aren't we enough for you to live for?" my son, Edward, asked. God, he looked so hurt and angry. How could I find the words to explain that he *was* enough for me to live for? That when he'd left, I'd lost my reason to live. That by trying to find my own identity again I stumbled down this rabbit hole and fell into some kind of weird other world where the only thing that mattered to me was food. I had something I could control again. Something that no one else could mess with.

'There is good news, though: I'm finally starting to climb out of this hole and see that there is more to life. I'm seeing the damage done and trying to repair it. I'm determined to get better. This week I put on another two pounds, and am feeling really proud.'

A ripple of clapping spreads and grows as I sit down. After several beats, Jackie speaks, her Belfast accent softened after years of living here in Tynemouth.

'Members, thank you so much for taking part tonight. Some of us have had a tough week.' She nods at Pat, who is dreading her birthday in a fortnight, the first since her husband, James, died. 'Others have had a more positive one. Some have spoken, some have had the strength only to listen. Together, we support and celebrate every step. Long may it continue. Have a good week, everyone.'

With murmured thanks, people stand, break into groups, drift away. Outgoing and chatty, Carrie normally stays behind after the meeting has finished. Actually, she usually persuades us all to go to the pub for a 'liquid debrief', despite it being a Monday night. She's the type of person who, at a party, dances on tables, whooping and doing shots. I'm the type who sits in the corner, watching and worrying someone will fall off the furniture and hurt themselves.

Tonight, though, Carrie's slim body slips quickly through the crowd of fellow confessors, and through the door that says 'emergency exit only' but is permanently propped open. I see her expression reflected in the glass before she passes through the opening into the car park. She is biting her lip, frowning. I'm sure she catches my eye for a moment and sees me behind her, but doesn't slow, even as I hurry to catch up.

'Carrie, fancy some company?'

She stops, turns, but as I approach it's clear to see her shoulders have risen, even if she doesn't realise it. She doesn't want to stop, but can't think of a polite way of ignoring me, obviously. I'm pushing myself in where I've no place, I know, and consider making my excuses and leaving her alone, as she so obviously wants. But I also know from bitter experience that sometimes it's when we need people that we're most likely to isolate ourselves. It can be dangerous for someone like me, an anorexic, who hides everything all the time. So many skeletons in my closet. Carrie isn't a recovering anorexic, though, I remind myself. Still, I can't help sticking my nose in and hoping it won't get bitten off.

Just in case she needs me.

My skeletons won't let me do anything else.

# CHAPTER TWO

Now I've caught up with Carrie, she's had time to plaster a smile on her face. It's not enough to remove the small line between her barely-there eyebrows that peeps below her green and white bobble hat. An arctic easterly breeze swirls round us, coming off the North Sea that is a few streets away, as we look at each other, awkward.

'You don't mind, do you? I'm going your way, so… ' I trail off.

She laughs to fill the silence.

'No, that'd be lovely.' She's a good liar, almost pulls it off. Only a professional such as myself can hear the tinkle of dishonesty.

Hands deep in pockets, bent against the nose-tingling cold, we walk swiftly in the direction of her house, exchanging chit-chat about the meeting. Although we might seem like a strange pair – she's only twenty-four – our friendship works, not least because we've unconsciously fallen into a mother-daughter role. Right now, my mother's instinct is on full alert. While I rack my brains about how to raise the subject, we leave behind us the jagged, 2,000-year-old ruin of Tynemouth Castle and Priory, which watches proudly over the east coast and town alike. To my right, and far below, the crashing sea urges me to hurry. We bullet past Percy Gardens, and I'm no closer to a solution, only half an ear on the conversation.

'Poor Pat, so I thought I'd organise something. What do you think?' Carrie asks.

'Great idea!' My enthusiasm disguises the fact that I've no idea what she's organised. 'Anniversaries can be tough, I'm sure,' I add, keeping my comment vague.

Five minutes later, having spent the entire time discussing Pat, we reach Longsands beach and take a left away from it. I'm running out of time. It's only as we are about to part ways, and stand beside her garden gate, that I find the courage to be candid.

'You know, I can tell there's something wrong. Something you haven't shared with the group. I hope you don't mind me asking, but… is everything okay? You know you can trust me.'

Can she, though? Why should she, after everything I've done? I shudder at the thought.

'You're cold,' she gasps. 'Do you want to come in for a minute to warm up before you carry on home?'

I feel a little ashamed at being handed success by her pity, but I'll take what I can get. Rubbing hands as if to warm them, I nod, and soon we're inside and she's offering to make me a cuppa. She doesn't take her hat off. She says she hates feeling a draught on her bald head, even though it's now covered in short, baby-blonde hair that looks like a stylish pixie crop. I didn't know her when she was bald, but I've seen photos and she's got such a delicate face that she still looked beautiful.

The first time I met her, she told me how she'd set fire to her NHS wig in an act of defiance against cancer. 'God, it felt good seeing that thing melt into the flames. Like I was taking control of my body again, you know, and sticking two fingers up to cancer,' she'd said, hazel eyes dancing at the memory. ''Course, I hadn't realised how cold I'd be without a covering, so started wearing hats. I never thought I had a face for them until I went bald. Every cloud has a silver lining, eh?' Then she'd given that infectious, machine-gun-fire laugh.

I lean against the kitchen counter, watching her take out the only two mugs she seems to own. Her two-bed maisonette is sparsely furnished, with no pictures on the walls, or even photographs on shelves. She seems to live on the breadline. There's a big bunch of flowers in a vase, though. Propped up beside it is a card that reads:

*Love you more than words can say, Mum and Dad xx*

'Sorry. About earlier. Putting you on the spot.' I shrug my thin shoulders apologetically, a move I'm currently well built for. But I'm putting on weight. Slowly. Surely. I've no choice, if I'm ever going to get better and stand a chance of gaining my children's forgiveness.

'No, Alex, it's fine. I just… I'm not sure I'm ready to talk about it yet, is all.'

She hangs her head, bites her lip again. She always does that when she's trying to hide something; doesn't seem to realise she's doing it, but I've studied Carrie a lot. I couldn't help myself, once I realised the terrible thing I'd done to her. Sometimes teetering on the edge of confession, standing on the precipice, but unable to make that final step forward that will send me free-falling towards the truth. I can't face seeing Carrie's expression once she knows. Or the judgement of others, the disgust of my children, even though I deserve it all.

Instead, I do what I do best. Lie.

'Carrie, please, you know you can trust me. It won't go any further, if you don't want it to, but surely sharing is better than carrying this burden alone.'

She nods, teeth clamping down on her lip until the skin goes white.

'You're worrying me now,' I add.

'Oh, Alex, it's the cancer. It's back. And there's nothing they can do this time.'

*No. She doesn't deserve to die. I do.*

The room seems to shift beneath my feet, bucking, trying to make me fall. My fingers cling to the counter edge, curling around it to steady myself.

'Are—' My voice sounds thick and scratchy. I clear it, try again. 'Are they sure?'

'They told me first thing this morning, it was a real hammer blow. I've been in shock ever since. That's why I didn't tell you earlier – you're the first person I've had to say the words to. Saying them… it's like getting the news again. I'm dying. It wasn't a bad dream.'

'What about a—'

'Second opinion? There's no point, Alex. I've seen the scans for myself. It's everywhere. Everywhere.'

She shakes her head, gives a small sigh. No tears. Her teeth clamp down on her lip so hard in her determination to be brave that a pearl of blood blooms.

Right there and then, I know what must be done. Whatever Carrie wants, Carrie gets. I will make her last days the best she will ever have. Whatever it takes to make her happy, I'll do. We'll write a bucket list together, and if I don't have enough money myself to pay for everything she wants to do, I'll start fundraising if needs be to make it come true. It is the very, very least I can do. My penance seems minuscule in comparison to my crime.

# CHAPTER THREE

'Drinks on a Sunday evening? It's not like you to be so spontaneous, Alex. I must be rubbing off on you!'

'Leading me astray, more like.'

'Well, if this is what a bad influence does, long may it continue. You look good in those jeans, by the way. Told you that you didn't look like mutton dressed as lamb in them, you idiot – glad you listened to me. Wish you'd gone for another colour, though. Is that top new, too?'

It is. I'm wearing black jeans, black boots, black suede jacket, and have just realised my new top is also…

'The label describes it as onyx,' I say.

Carrie herself is a kaleidoscope of colour in her multihued, floaty dress, which is a firm favourite from the charity shop.

'Well, the outfit matches your hair,' she laughs.

Actually, I'm a very dark brown and have pulled the frizzy mess into a ponytail.

I fake-tut and, with a gentle hand on the small of her back, propel Carrie towards The Priory pub, on the busy main street. Despite being a small town within half an hour of the city of Newcastle, Tynemouth has its own personality as a quaint seaside resort and bustling town that stares out at the North Sea. It's unique again from the busy fishing quays and more industrial feel of North Shields, down the road. Independent shops, cafés and pubs thrive along the wide streets of pretty Georgian and Victorian buildings.

From the way Carrie's pushing against my hand, she clearly fancies visiting one of the other pubs – she's certainly spoilt for choice.

'It looks dead in there. I can't hear any noise coming from it.'

'Well, that's great, means we'll have the place to ourselves.'

'Let's go somewhere livelier. How about—'

I yank open the door, shove her through.

'Hey!'

'Surprise!' a sea of faces yell.

Carrie jumps a mile, then her face lights up.

Phone calls, emails, hustling face-to-face, it's been a whirlwind thirteen days launching the fundraiser and organising this surprise party. It's taken everything out of me, but it's worth it to see the look of joy on Carrie's face.

'Oh, Alex! This is wonderful!' she gasps.

Originally my idea had been to make Carrie's dreams come true myself. It had been easy to start a conversation about things she'd have loved to have had the chance to do or see. I'd discovered that she'd always wanted to go on the Orient Express. 'No murders, though, hopefully!' she'd joked.

She'd had loads of ideas, in fact. Go to Marrakesh, meet Brad Pitt 'and snog his face off', see the Angel of the North and abseil down it, go scuba-diving. She even mentioned that when things had been particularly bad during her treatment previously, she'd made up her mind to organise a big charity run, 'to give something back', but had never got around to it.

Beams of enthusiasm had seemed to radiate from her to me, and despite her protestations that, as lovely as these dreams were, she really wouldn't want the fuss involved in them coming true, I had made an executive decision. I knew I had to make these things happen – although snogging Brad Pitt might be impossible. In fact, that night, I'd hopped onto Twitter, knowing Carrie would never find out, and tagged Mr Pitt, asking if he'd be interested in doing a favour to a dying woman, and attaching a picture of her. He hadn't replied, but the tweet had got a lot of likes, comments and retweets.

The kindness of strangers had overwhelmed me – and given me a thought. My counsellor at the eating disorder clinic I attend twice a week is always telling me that when there's a problem I should acknowledge it, and seek assistance to resolve it if necessary. It's something I generally struggle with, but looking around the buzzing room, I can't help thinking she'd be proud of me right now, because that's exactly what I've done. Inspired by the reaction on Twitter, I'd set up a Facebook page. It had been the perfect place to organise the fundraiser in secrecy. Clothes shops had donated stock, a beauty salon had given a makeover, then there were massages, chocolates, cakes, a spray tan, a meal in a restaurant, even a weekend in a luxury hotel; a deluge of incredible prizes for the raffle.

Everything was done online so Carrie wouldn't know a thing until now. The Priory pub has pulled out all the stops for us. The party was organised at such short notice that it hasn't had time to change its decorations, which are up for the next big celebration, so it's full of cotton wool cobwebs, skeletons and the occasional pumpkin.

'Sorry it's a bit inappropriate—'

'No! I bloody love Halloween!' Carrie's rapid-fire laugh sounds out. To prove her point, she shows me a pink diamanté skull ring she's wearing on her finger. I bet my daughter, Elise, would like that.

The religious men of the actual priory would have almost certainly disapproved, but as long as the guest of honour is happy, who cares? Perhaps they would have enjoyed it, I muse, as I look around at everyone's happy faces. After all, they built above the mythical Jingler's Cave, which is said to be haunted by infernal souls and demons, so they clearly weren't without a sense of irony.

Disco classics from the 1980s strike up as we move through the crowd. Carrie looks radiant. She's the centre of attention. I'm so happy my gamble paid off. Well-wishers and friends surround her, and there is so much positivity it's inspiring.

'You're the nicest person I've ever met. You don't deserve this,' says one woman. 'You're in my prayers.'

Her friend nods. 'Keep fighting, we're all here cheering you, beautiful.'

'Stay positive and kick cancer's arse!' says a third, punching the air.

'As long as I'm able to kick, I'll be doing just that,' Carrie promises.

The first woman cups my friend's face in her hand. 'If this isn't beauty, I don't know what is. Stay strong!'

As they walk away, Carrie leans over to me. 'Are your kids coming?'

I scan the room, then shake my head. 'I didn't really expect to see them here, to be honest.'

'Things no better? Surely they'll calm down eventually and start talking to you again. I thought I'd actually see them tonight.'

'They're angry with me. They blame me for their dad leaving.'

'Well, if they're old enough to abandon their mum to go and live with their dad, they're old enough for you to give them a good talking-to. Tell them the truth!'

'Reasoning with sixteen-year-olds isn't always easy. The truth is, it's my fault my family fell apart, okay? There's no one to blame but me.' I force myself to take a calming breath. 'Anyway, tonight's about you. You are enjoying yourself, aren't you?'

'Of course! It's so kind of you. Seeing all my Tynemouth friends together is all I could ask for.'

If I were dying, I'd want to get in touch with old friends and loved ones and tell them how much they meant to me. I'd want to say goodbye properly and not have any unfinished business. While thinking about that, after hearing Carrie's news, I'd had a brilliant idea – I'd organise a surprise party for Carrie, invite friends she hadn't seen since moving to the area. Doing things was nice, and a bucket list is a wonderful thing to have, but for me, life is about love and people more than anything. When sitting on my deathbed, the material things I'd gathered around me, or the places I'd visited would be lovely memories, but what gave my life meaning was my kids. They were my greatest achievement, and what life was all about: love and family.

Carrie doesn't have kids, but she has lots of love in her life. I'd tried to do some detective work and get in touch with everyone. But try as I might, I hadn't been able to find an address book to sneak a look at, and Carrie thinks social media is a waste of time, so I'd no way of finding anyone. Not at the speed things had moved, anyway. It means none of her family are at this do, but at least she's surrounded by Tynemouth pals from the support group, as well as those eager to discover if they've won a raffle prize.

Jackie comes over, squeezes my arm, interrupting my thoughts. Although she's a whisper under 5ft and barely comes up to my chin, she has the type of confidence that makes her seem taller. She almost vibrates with energy.

'What you're doing is amazing. I'm in awe of you,' she whispers. I freeze and shake my head, embarrassed.

'Organising karaoke and dance nights, or facing death? I know which I'd rather do. This isn't about me,' I protest quietly.

'Of course not, but that doesn't mean that what you're doing isn't incredible. You're a good person, Alex, feel proud of yourself.'

A good person. What would she say if she knew the truth?

As I'm worrying, the familiar face of local journalist Belinda Edwards appears across the room. She gives a thumbs up and nods to the man next to her, with a camera slung round his neck. I nod back, feeling the warmth of a smile spread inside me.

It had been one of the supermarkets that had suggested I call the local newspaper.

'We'd definitely be interested in donating. Would it be okay to invite a photographer along? Get a little write-up in the local press? It might encourage more people to donate, once they read about Carrie's story,' the manager had said.

'Brilliant idea!' I'd replied, kicking myself for not thinking of it. The more people know about how wonderful Carrie is, the more money will be donated, and we can really make her dreams come true.

Now the press is here, I can officially kick the event off. Smiling, I start towards the raised platform that will double as a stage tonight. A hush descends, electric with anticipation.

'Thank you, everyone, for coming. We're going to be announcing the prizewinners, who have been drawn at random, in an hour's time, so make sure you stick around for that.'

Some people look at their watches, but I carry on.

'Tonight is all about a truly special person who is very dear to me – to us all here: Carrie Goodwin.' Applause. I wait for it to die down. 'Before I get you up here to make a speech yourself, Carrie – yes, I'm afraid you're going to have to – I wanted to say a few words myself. Carrie, we haven't known each other long, just six months, but in that time we've become great friends, because you're such a special person. You've been through a hell of a lot, but you've never complained, and always make time for others. Well, now we want to make sure you put yourself first for once. We want to make your dreams come true, so tonight we're raising money to do just that. So far, donations have reached £18,250! Can you believe it?'

Everyone whoops. Carrie looks absolutely stunned. I really wanted one of those big cheques to present to her, but the bank was a bit funny about it because the account is in my name. Not ideal, but opening an account for a single fundraiser had been, though not complex, not as straightforward as I'd anticipated. As the clerk had started talking about private trusts, unincorporated bodies, paperwork, my impatience had kicked in, and I'd just opened an account in my name instead. Then arranged for the JustGiving page I set up to pay directly into it. I wanted to concentrate on getting as much money for Carrie in as short a time as possible, not messing about with tedious money management. Shame, though, as a giant cheque would look great in the pictures. Still, the photographer captures everything, his flash making my friend jump and cover her face in surprise.

'Come on up, Carrie, this is all for you! You might not kiss a film star, but tomorrow I'm booking the Orient Express for you.'

All eyes are on her. My smile is sliding away as I look. She's shaking her head, hands over her face. Backing away. Running from the room, a trail of shocked silence left behind her.

# CHAPTER FOUR

I close the door to the ladies' loo and lean against it to stop anyone else entering. Carrie is dabbing at her eyes with a piece of screwed-up loo paper, a stall door swinging closed slowly. She looks at me in the reflection and gives a shaky laugh.

'I'm sorry. It's so lovely of you, but it's all too much. A photographer? A story in the newspaper? I don't want this kind of attention, Alex.'

Carrie smiles a tight little line that barely lifts the corners of her mouth and doesn't get rid of the frown around her eyes. She must be in pain. She never cries – or if she does, she doesn't show it, instead always radiating peace. Not tonight.

It was stupid of me to hope my surprise would help her forget about her terminal cancer. I should have listened to her. She didn't want this fuss, but I'd ignored her, thinking I knew best. In trying so hard to please, I'm making things worse. But I can't seem to stop myself. Somehow I need to make things right.

'Do you want me to get rid of them?'

Carrie nods, eyes shining with tears. Her hands are loose fists, fingers rubbing against one another. She's worrying. And angry. With me.

Guilt rips through me. I've done this to her.

'Don't worry, I'll sort it.'

Her relief is an audible sigh and a whispered 'thank you', before she turns the taps on and starts splashing cold water onto her face.

❁

It doesn't take long to find Belinda, the reporter, who is working the room getting quotes from people. With a jerk of my head, I motion her to one side as George Michael starts singing about how he'd like someone to wake him up before they go-go. The crowd starts to join in, party atmosphere restored. Not among everyone, though; some are throwing me curious glances, wondering what the gossip is, while others look full of pity that Carrie's been taken ill.

'Is she okay?' asks Belinda.

'Look, would you mind not running this story, please? This is too much for her, she's overwhelmed.'

'Ah, thing is, we've left a space in the paper. I've got to write it up now so we can go to print tonight. It's too late to pull it.' She seems to be thinking. 'Listen, this is a lovely feel-good story. The community rallying round, local businesses getting involved. Carrie's probably a bit embarrassed about all the attention, and I understand that, but it's no harm to anyone to run it, is it?'

I chew on my nail, don't know what to say. The reporter lowers her voice further.

'Thing is, if I don't come up with a story, my editor will skin me alive. We've literally nothing to replace it with. We can't run with a hole in the paper – I'm going to lose my job over this.'

She looks really worried. Her photographer pal keeps glancing over, aware something is going on. I feel backed into a corner.

'It's such a positive piece.' Her hope hangs in the air, virtually grabs me by the lapels.

'It's really too late for you to find something else?' I check.

'Definitely.'

'Well… okay, I've got no choice, have I?'

'I know Carrie feels shy about it, but we'll make sure everyone comes out of this looking good. Promise. Besides, when people read about this, they'll donate too – you'll make loads of money, and think of all the wonderful things Carrie can do then. I'd love to think I helped a dying woman get her wish.'

Of course. That's what this is about. Carrie might feel overwhelmed right now, but when her dreams start coming true, she'll be back to her usual self, loving the attention. I keep on chewing my nail, my finger giving a warning throb I ignore.

Despite the earlier disaster, the night has turned into a success. I've announced the prizewinners, and Carrie is out of the loo and has hit the dance floor that's been spontaneously created near the back of the bar. She's shimmying – actually shimmying – like a disco diva alongside Jackie, Patricia, Anthony and Parvina. Judging from their wide-open mouths and the way their veins are standing out on their necks, they're singing at the tops of their voices as they 'Ride on Time'.

I hang back, longing to join in but unsure of what to do. All evening I've successfully avoided Carrie, so it would be stupid to undo that good work now. If I go near her, she'll ask me if my mission to stop the article has been successful. It's one fib I can't face telling, not right now. Instead, I lie by omission, easing on my black suede jacket and slipping away before anyone can notice. Only Jackie glances over, raising an eyebrow that she quickly hides. No one else sees me glide out the door.

The coverage in the newspaper the next day couldn't be better. Everyone is smiling in the photograph, although Carrie's head is turned to the side, as if trying to look away. The write-up is perfect. Hopefully more donors will be in touch. A quick check using Internet banking shows my account's balance has increased by almost another thousand pounds. I sit at my dining table, staring through the French doors and out across the garden, smiling as hope fills me up. Birds flit at the feeders, but I don't see them; instead I'm imagining all the wonderful things Carrie can do with that money.

My mood fades when she calls, though. Her voice is clipped.

'The front page, Alex! Really? It's lovely of you to care so much, but I don't need money or bucket lists or anything, okay? All I want is to be left in peace.'

'But the money is there, it's been raised, so… Well, you might as well enjoy it. It's what people want.'

The only sound to fill the silence is a sigh. Finally, she speaks. 'Okay. Maybe. There's something else, anyway: I've made a decision. I'm moving back to my parents in Plymouth.'

'I thought they were somewhere in Derbyshire?'

'Yet more proof that you never listen to me. Don't try to change the subject, Alex. Just promise me this is the last bit of stupid publicity you've organised. My life – and death – are no one's business but my own.'

'Of course. You're right. I'm so sorry.'

An insignificant word for the damage I've done. The better I try to make things, the worse they become. I've never before heard Carrie sound so annoyed.

'I'll see you tonight at group?' I ask.

She confirms and says her goodbyes, leaving me feeling heavy, as if I've swallowed a stone. She's wrong, though: her death isn't just her business. It's mine, too.

Whether she likes it or not.

# CHAPTER FIVE

## THEN

Milk dribbled down my chin. Head thrown back, I finished my drink with a gasp. Wiped my face, then filled up the glass. At the gentle thunk of the fridge door closing yet again, followed by the glug, glug, glug of liquid, Mum came in.

'We're going to have to buy a cow to keep up with you, you're drinking that much,' she laughed. 'Reckon we can fit one on our lawn?'

A shrug was my reply. I was too busy swallowing down more.

'Why are you drinking so much, anyway?'

Finally I put down my glass. 'Because milk makes you stronger, Mum, and I want to make sure he never hurts you again.'

Her fingers flew to the choker of bruises peeping guiltily above her turtleneck top.

'It's complicated, Sophie. Sometimes adults do things they don't intend, but that doesn't mean they don't love each other really. Dad's sorry for what he's done… and I shouldn't have goaded him by arguing back.'

My seven-year-old brain tried to make sense of the excuse. If adults did things they didn't mean, then that meant they were liars. But telling fibs was wrong. Dad was always telling whoppers, the biggest being that he was sorry. After beating Mum black, blue and multicoloured, he'd sometimes cry, saying the word over and over and over, but it never stopped him from being mean again.

He never learned his lesson.

Mum lied all the time, too. She said she was fine even when she was bleeding. She said Dad didn't mean the things he said; words I didn't understand, but which made his eyes go hard and mean, as if he wanted to hurt us with a look. *Bitch, slut, whore.* She said he needed our love. But he never seemed to want it.

Being in the same room as him made me want to hide inside the walls. One day that wouldn't be enough, though. Young as I was, something told me that one day I'd be too big to hide, and then Dad would come for me as well as Mum.

Well, I'd be ready for him. I'd get him before he could get me. I'd grow big and strong and protect my mum.

# CHAPTER SIX

## NOW

For the first time, I'm dreading the support group. I lurk outside the building, almost turn around, but in the end can't keep away. I'm too weak. Late as I am, the meeting doesn't seem to have started yet, thank goodness.

Carrie is already there, of course. She's wearing her favourite striped beanie hat, sporting all the colours of the rainbow, but even without it I'd be able to tell where she is immediately because she's surrounded by a crowd. Presumably everyone is making a fuss of her after last night.

Although slender as a whip, her skin is glowing, eyes so bright and clear that it's hard to imagine cancer is eating her alive. As I look on, time is no longer linear; it seems to concertina, so that I can see through its folds all that has been, all that is to come. This time yesterday Carrie and I were friends, about to enter the pub for her surprise do. This time two weeks ago I had no idea she was dying. In two months' time, she'll no longer be here.

My innards turn to liquid mercury at the thought.

'Happy birthday to you,' everyone strikes up. Of course, that's why they've all gathered: it's Patricia's birthday. Exactly as she'd told me she would on our walk to her house a fortnight ago, Carrie surreptitiously organised a whip-round at the last meeting and got everyone to sign a card for her. I join in the last few words: 'And many more!'

Patricia's all tears and happiness as she opens her present of a stack of five crime thrillers.

'They're the ones you like, aren't they?' Carrie checks. Patricia's a nervy lady who loves to terrify herself by reading gangland tales of hard-faced criminals and glamorous women. 'Um, and this is a little something just from me. It's not much.'

Even though she's barely got two pennies to rub together, she's bought Patricia a beautiful metal bookmark. Adorning it are three delicate lilies.

'Oh, how lovely! How did you know they're my favourite flower?'

'You mentioned the other week that they were what you like to lay on your husband's grave.'

Patricia hugs her. 'Typical of you to remember such a personal detail. You're a one-off, Carrie Goodwin.'

Over her shoulder, Carrie notices me for the first time. As soon as she's free she comes over, shoes clicking on the wooden floor. 'I'm sorry for being such an ungrateful cow. It's no excuse, but I'm a bit all over the place at the moment, and—'

'Don't say another word. I'm the one who should be apologising,' I gasp.

The meeting gets started, and as usual it whizzes by. I tell them the latest about the twins.

'Elise won't even call me "Mum" any more. She insists on calling me by my name instead. She's so angry, and I've no idea how to get through to her. As for Edward, when I see him he's always calm and polite – like I'm a stranger.' My arms ache to hold them, and the pain of loss makes it hard for me to breathe. 'Things seem to be getting worse, not better. Although we didn't see each other often, we used to talk, despite everything. Not now. We should be going on shopping trips together, cuddling up to watch films, going on day trips. You know? Just a normal family. I'd love to give them advice on their lives, but they've made it clear they don't want me.'

Tears escape. Many of the group are mothers, and their faces are full of sympathy.

'Have you tried talking to Owen about it? Would he be willing to help you? It would be for the good of the children. He needs to put them first,' says Parvina.

Sniffing, wiping at my face, I shake my head. 'There's no getting through to them. I'll just have to be patient. Even though they hurt me, seeing them... ' I put my hand on my heart and gasp, unable to continue. Finally, I catch my breath. 'Seeing them even for five minutes with them telling me they hate me is better than nothing. We'll get through this. Things will get better.'

Talking is always exhausting, but I feel so much better for sharing what's going on in my life.

Finally, Carrie stands. She's the last of the group to take a turn.

'When I was about four, in art class one day I got all the colours of paint lined up and felt so excited because I was going to paint a huge rainbow. I painted the thick bands, one after the other: red, orange, yellow, green, blue, indigo, violet, and threw a couple of others in, too.

'Impatient, I didn't wait for each one to dry. The wet paint ran, one into another, and instead of the smiling colours I wanted to hang over my bed, all I had to show for my efforts was a sludge-brown mess smeared across the page.

'It broke my heart. How could something so pretty end up looking so miserable?

'But now I think of it another way. Now I see all the crap in life, and know that if I look hard enough I can see the good in it, something beautiful. I can find the rainbow in the sludge brown of everyday life. If I just try hard enough.

'That's everyone's challenge. We've each of us got our reasons to be miserable, but we can't let the clouds win. Instead, let's create our own rainbow.'

She gets a standing ovation.

❁

Afterwards we all go to the pub for our liquid debrief. Everyone's chattering.

'You smell nice,' Jackie says to Carrie. 'It's not Straight to Heaven, by Kilian, is it? My sister works on a perfume counter and gave me a tiny sample of it. She was telling me it's over two hundred pounds a bottle!'

'Is it? I rubbed myself with a magazine before I came out. I'd have to sell a kidney before I could afford a bottle – who'd pay that for fragrance!'

'James always used to get me J'adore, every birthday,' says Pat sadly.

Honestly, I just want to give her a big hug; she looks so heartbroken, picking at the brown cardigan she's teamed with a brown corduroy skirt. Instead, I distract her by asking about the books she's been given, and she's soon talking enthusiastically about drugs, gangland lovers and gunrunning. An elbow digging in my side distracts me, minutes later.

'Hey, fancy getting out of here?' Carrie whispers out of the corner of her mouth, holding her glass in front of her so people don't see a hint of her lips moving.

I cover my own to reply. 'So soon? What's going on?'

'Explain later.'

She's already scrabbling her things together, saying her good-byes, so I follow suit.

Outside, she groans in relief.

'Eurgh, Jackie was giving me the third degree about palliative treatment. Boring! Like I want to spend my dying days talking about that. I want to have fun! She'll probably start asking Pat about James's funeral next. Honestly, for someone who runs a support group she can be a bit insensitive sometimes.'

My reply is a snort. It's true. Jackie's well intentioned, but she can be a bull in a china shop, emotionally, at times.

'Oh, and then she started banging on about how much time we spend together.'

'Us?' My heart hitches. Jackie's noticed how overeager I am to be with Carrie. She's suspicious. She'll discover the truth. If she does, I may have to take steps to stop her talking.

# CHAPTER SEVEN

Carrie doesn't seem to notice my panic; instead she turns it into a joke, wiggling her eyebrows up and down suggestively. 'Yeah, I think Jackie might be jealous.' She links arms with me. 'Come on, I've a bottle of wine back at mine with our name on it.'

'I'm not sure.'

'What else will you do? Sit at home, alone, worrying about your children? You can do that with me, too – or even better, I can take your mind off it by forcing booze down your throat and making you watch bad films with me.'

I laugh. 'Okay, that sounds good, actually.' She does a little dance of glee. 'How do you do it, Carrie? You're always so upbeat and positive.'

'Dying just means I appreciate every single thing about every single day, and I don't even have to worry about pensions, or eating healthily, or exercise. It's great!' As she speaks, she opens up the box of doughnuts a member of the group has bought for her and takes a big bite out of one. 'Mmm, custard cream. And the best thing? There are no calories in anything when you're dying – fact.'

When we reach her house, she goes straight to the loo. The sound of her vomiting is a reminder of the reality behind her brave words. She can't keep much down these days. Still, she comes out smiling, as if nothing has happened, and opens a bottle of wine.

'Are you sure you should be drinking?'

'Oh, one little drink isn't going to kill me,' she winks. She fills a tumbler and a mug because she doesn't own any wine glasses. 'Low-ball glass for you, as you're the guest. You know your problem, Alex? You worry too much. Live each day like it's your last. Seriously, you're not just "glass half-empty", you're like, "oh, if what's in the glass is so great, why's it been left by someone? And it's probably been left for so long that it's gone rancid now, so I'm not even going to bother trying it". You need to lighten up.'

'Well, if my glass is half-empty, I reckon it's because you've nicked some of it – you think your glass is so full it's overflowing,' I joke.

'That's me, I'm brimming over – and why not! Anyway, fancy watching a film? Something sloppy, like *The Time Traveler's Wife*, or what's that one with Keanu Reeves, *The Lake House*?'

'Huh, actually, I've just remembered I've got an urgent appointment to wash my hair. I'm off – oy!' The purple fur cushion she chucks bounces off my head.

'Come on, misery guts, live a little! We can dissect how books are so much better than the films. You love that.'

'Ha, you know I can't resist book talk.'

'Top up your glass, sit down and we'll have a gossip.'

But as she flops down beside me on the sofa, her face changes, mouth pulling downwards. 'Everyone's been so kind to me. I'll miss you all so much. You especially, Alex. It's unbelievable what you've done for me. No one has ever done anything like that for me before.'

The look on her face reminds me of the expression Edward pulled as a child when he wanted a hug but hadn't dared ask in case Elise laughed at him. So I give Carrie a cuddle. She's shivering.

'I'm getting your duvet, you're not right,' I worry.

'I'll be all right in a minute,' she calls.

Too late, I'm already upstairs. When I return and wrap it around her shoulders, she melts into it, pulling it closer to her until she's cocooned.

'I'll be all right,' she repeats, despite her lip trembling. 'I'm just being silly.'

'Er, no, you're not. It'd be silly not to react like this. You're in shock, Carrie, still coming to terms with everything. Don't you dare apologise to me.'

'I just don't want to go, not really. I'm not ready. I thought I was – oh, I really thought I was – but I'm not.'

'Then fight, Carrie.' I take her hand. 'We'll fight together. I love your positivity, but you don't always have to put a brave face on things.'

'Sometimes… sometimes I do feel scared,' she confesses.

I put my arm around her, duvet and all. 'That's why I'm here. I'll be with you every step of the way. Promise.'

To try to cheer up, we end up watching both films. I'm glad I insisted on subscribing to Netflix for her, a gift that had made her burst into tears. The movies are all so sloppy that they flow into one for me, as do the constantly topped-up glasses of wine.

'I've never found love, never settled down. Always moved around a lot,' Carrie slurs as the credits roll. 'Always had to.' A tear trickles down her face. She rubs at it with her sleeve, leaving her cheek red. 'I've just always been so alone. I wish I weren't.'

'That's my fault,' I say. The room is starting to spin. Or perhaps it's my head. I'm not sure if I said that out loud. Carrie doesn't pick up on it. My thoughts are rolling round, too, light with the clarity of alcohol, creating a tornado of regret that my best friend doesn't realise I'm to blame for her biggest fear as she faces death.

'You know who some of the most dishonest people in the world are?' I announce. 'Nice people. They'll say anything rather than hurt someone's feelings. They'll tell you that you haven't hurt them. That they know you're a good person who is only lashing out because you're in pain. That of course they know you didn't mean the awful things you said and did. They're too nice to tell you the truth.'

Carrie's reply is a barely discernible snore.

Probably for the best, because I'm saying too much, letting slip things I need to hold tight.

Prodding her awake, I manage to herd her stumbling form up to bed. Pop a bowl beside her, with a dash of disinfectant, just in case.

When I next open my eyes, it's morning, and I've got a crick in my neck from sleeping on the sofa. Carrie presents me with a mug of coffee and some toast, then settles beside me. She's brought the duvet back down and goes to put it over both of us and turn the telly on.

'No, no, I can't stay. I've got a client arriving in, urgh, in twenty minutes. Don't worry about seeing me out,' I add.

Carrie has been making to stand, but sinks back onto the sofa. 'You sure?'

'Think I can find the door on my own, thanks.' I wink.

'Just feels a bit rude… '

'Rubbish! I can see myself out. You look too comfy to shift.'

'You've got a point.' She hugs the duvet to her belly, giving it a squeeze, eyes half-closed, then opens them and grins. 'Do you know, I might treat myself to a bit of a duvet day. Thanks, Alex, for, you know, everything.'

'Don't be daft, I've done nothing. See you tomorrow. And don't forget what I said: if you need me, call. Any time. I mean it.' The last was said almost as a threat, my finger wagging in her direction, eyes stern.

'Yes, Mum.'

A warm glow spreads across my face, my whole body. Like I've come alive. It's just a silly tease, a throwaway phrase, but it's been so long since anyone called me 'Mum'. I don't like to admit even to myself how much I like it. To hide it, I pass her the remotes for the television.

In the hallway, I zip up my coat and step outside while still fiddling with my gloves – almost tripping over a parcel left on the doorstep. It's about the size of a shoebox. I turn to call to Carrie, but the words die as I notice the message scrawled in red pen.

*I'm watching you*

# CHAPTER EIGHT

*I'm watching you*

It looks threatening, screamed in big red capitals. I check over my shoulder to make sure Carrie hasn't got up and followed me, then pull the door closed. Kneel down and scoop up the box before I can change my mind. It's incredibly light. Perhaps it's empty? Some kind of practical joke?

The parcel has nothing to do with me. But those words scrawled in scarlet capitals across the top of the box seem off. I'll take it home, check inside, then tape it up again and pop it back on the step before anyone can notice it's disappeared.

The whole walk home, I regret my decision. The spire of St George's Church reaches up to the clouds in all its Gothic glory, pointing out how they frown their judgement down on me. Still, I hurry on, my thoughts moving as fast as my feet.

I'm being overprotective of Carrie, I know. Mothering her. Smothering her. It's because I'm not allowed to be there for my children any more. My fault. All my fault. The thought depresses me. I don't want to act out of selfish reasons, instead I want finally to be doing the right thing by people, making amends for pain caused. My counsellor, Rosie Knight, has warned me that anorexia takes good personality traits such as perfectionism, attention to detail, determination, and twists them into something destructive. Perhaps it's happening again. Perhaps I should back off and leave Carrie alone.

Alone, to face death? No, that's never going to happen. I need to atone, and if I don't do it now then it will be too late. She'll be gone. The urgency, the sense of time and life slipping away, makes my footsteps faster… then I slow… The houses all have pumpkins, cobwebs, witches adorning windows and gardens. Halloween, of course.

This box is a silly Halloween prank. It's supposed to sound menacing!

I'm almost home, though, and can't be bothered to turn around and return it. I'll do it tomorrow.

Once inside, I drop it on the coffee table and stare, indecision gripping me once more.

*I'm watching you*

Well, now it's here, might as well go ahead and open it.

It's taped up with standard brown tape. I have a roll somewhere, and dig it out, along with the sharpest knife in my kitchen, a filleting knife that has never been used. Checking my tape against the one used on the box, I'm relieved it's the same width. Great, I can cover exactly over the tape and return it, without it obviously having been tampered with.

Precise as a surgeon, I slice the tape. The release of its tension is audible. Using the tip of the knife, I ease up a flap. Peer inside. There's a lemon-yellow cotton jumper, balled up. It looks like one Carrie sometimes wears. Perhaps someone borrowed it and is now returning it. The message on the outside doesn't make sense, though; although it could be some kind of odd inside joke between Carrie and a friend.

Relieved, I start to fold up the jumper, but notice there's something else at the bottom of the box.

A photograph. Of Carrie and me. We're outside the community hall, leaving the support group, presumably. I peer closer. Yes,

Carrie has her striped beanie on, so it was taken at our meeting last night. The person who took the snap was to our left, and the photo is fuzzy, as though taken with a poor camera, or possibly because the image has been blown up because the photographer was some distance away. We're clearly identifiable, though, and both smiling and relaxed as we talk.

I sit back and stare at the image. Why would someone take a picture of the two of us? What do they mean, they're watching her? Are they spying on me, too? A ghost walks over my grave.

Paranoid, I go to draw the curtains, despite it being daytime. The neighbours' Halloween decorations catch my eye again. This whole thing with the box and the photograph is a bit melodramatic. It's just a wind-up, something to put fear into Carrie, in the same way people wear *Scream* masks at this time of year, or dress up like Freddy Krueger.

I'm sure of it.

It's a pretty twisted practical joke, though. Definitely not the sort of thing a woman struggling to come to terms with dying will appreciate. I won't pass it on. After all, if it's just a practical joke, there's no harm in keeping it to myself.

# CHAPTER NINE

That night, anxiety gnaws at my stomach. Unable to eat the steak casserole I've made, I pop it into a container – Carrie might like it. She is all I can think of. In bed, I leave my mobile on rather than switching off like usual. Just in case Carrie needs me for anything. Restless, I text her.

*We're going to attack this cancer. We'll fight it & win!*

She soon replies.

*Bless you, there's no winning, but I appreciate the thought. Don't worry about me, lovely. Look after yourself. Sleep tight x*

All through the night my sleep is disturbed by worries about Carrie, cancer and that bloody box. Each time I wake, I check my phone, fearing my friend has fallen ill and I've missed her cry for help. Scared that someone is watching her, waiting to pounce.

By the next day, I've changed my mind so many times about what to do with the box and photograph that I feel dizzy with indecision. Finally, I've no choice but to keep it to myself, because I've undone and repacked it so many times that the flaps are floppy, the tape in thick layers. It's obvious it's been tampered with repeatedly.

As I eat my breakfast of scrambled egg, I glare at it.

*I'm watching you*

This worry isn't doing me any good, and I only eat half my breakfast before pushing it to one side, feeling sick. I try to lose myself in my work as a seamstress, taking people's ideas and making their visions come true to create bespoke gowns. I'm working on a prom dress at the moment. Usually there's comfort in the rustle of the fabric, the snip of the scissors, the hum of the sewing machine, but today I jump at every innocuous sound, and almost slice the delicate, pistachio-green material at the sharp snap of my letterbox closing.

Before I know it, it's lunchtime, which means I've missed my eleven o'clock snack as well as barely eating breakfast. But I'm not hungry. Not even a little bit.

Recognising the danger in that feeling, I contact my daughter, asking if she and her twin brother want to join me for lunch at The View. The restaurant has floor-to-ceiling windows than run its length and breadth, making the most of the stunning panorama of Longsands beach, the sea and sky.

I wait and wait for Elise and Edward, taking my time to read and reread a menu I know off by heart. I even pull out a mini book of sudoku puzzles, to pass the time, as numbers and puzzles often soothe me.

After half an hour of putting the waitress off, I finally order scampi and chips, feeling pleased at the achievement. Just a year ago, I'd have had the corner of a cracker for lunch, then walked for an hour to burn it off. A boiled sweet could last a month: I'd suck it for blissful seconds, let the sugar surge into my bloodstream then spit it out and pop it on a shelf for another day.

But I am winning the battle against anorexia – touch wood. I knock on the table.

The portion of food I've been given is gigantic, but I eat every piece of scampi bar one and almost all of the chips. With every mouthful, I wonder if the twins will appear. There's no sign of them through the huge windows.

I miss the kids so much. The four of us playing chess, boys against girls. Or messing about on the beach, jumping waves. Elise is bohemian and independent. I can imagine her running a market stall one day, selling clothes and handmade jewellery, belts with bright, sparkly buckles and the like, before setting up a shop. Edward's creative outlet is playing the piano, but he'll follow his dad's footsteps into accountancy.

How I long to see them. But it's my fault they aren't speaking to me, and I've got to somehow prove I'm worthy of their trust. That I won't let them down ever again.

Then last night flies into my mind, and how I've failed even Carrie. I've got to do better. For everyone's sake.

A swirl of auburn catches my attention. It's Elise, her waist-length hair fanning around her as she looks this way and that before spotting me. Her expression is difficult to read, and it breaks my heart. Her brother is nowhere to be seen.

'You look like you're feeling sorry for yourself,' she says, sliding into the seat across the table from me.

'Do you want anything to eat?' I ask, trying to avoid a row.

'Do you?' she snaps.

'Already have.' To prove my point, I nudge the almost empty plate towards her.

'Anorexia has the highest mortality rate of all psychiatric conditions, Alex. You need to start being honest with yourself.'

It's hard to know what hurts more, her refusal to call me 'Mum', or her criticism. I open my mouth to protest, but the words slope away, confused, because the food has barely been touched.

There's a mountain of chips and almost half the scampi left. I thought I'd eaten almost all of it.

But I am a liar. There isn't a single aspect of my life that isn't ruled by deceit. It seeps into everything, a poison that weakens, taints, kills all it comes into contact with. The biggest distortions are those I tell myself.

'So what's the excuse this time, Alex?'

'I don't – I didn't – I—'

'You trying to kill yourself? Is that it? Give me your hand.'

I should argue, should remind her that I'm the parent, not her. Instead, I find myself holding my hands out in front of me. As she takes them, I can't help noticing she's got a pink diamanté ring, identical to Carrie's. Those two are alike in a lot of ways.

'Hmm, not too cold, that's something, so your heart's not packing up yet. And your nails haven't started to pit and go purple.' It's one of the signs of heart failure I was warned to look out for at the clinic. Heart failure can be common in anorexics. 'But you need to watch yourself, Alex. I won't watch you starve yourself to death.'

'I'm not! I'm eating. See!' I push a handful of chips into my mouth. A passing waitress gives me a wide berth.

'And another thing. I've noticed how much time you're spending with Carrie. Is it really healthy? It's like some sort of weird infatuation.'

'What? No!' I hiss, trying to avoid getting another dirty look from the waitress. 'I just owe her, that's all.'

Despite Elise's demands to know why, I refuse to go into detail. She won't give up now she's in full flow, though, her words a torrent of disappointment sweeping past me. No matter what I say, I won't get through to her when she's in this mood.

I stare resolutely at the beach and imagine her eight-year-old incarnation running along on one of our many holidays here, before the permanent move. Her legs were long, skinny, almost luminous white strings, but her face was determined, her arms pumping hard to reach her little brother.

'Don't eat your ice cream too quickly or you'll be sick,' she warned.

'I'm not going to!' He rolled his eyes but gobbled the treat anyway. Then they raced into the waves together, leaping over the gentle rollers… until Edward was sick, as predicted.

Edward hated being eleven minutes younger than his sister. Elise loved it. The bossy big sister, constantly wagging her finger at her reserved twin. As she's grown older, she has taken to nagging me.

I emerge from the memory and look around. My daughter is nowhere to be seen. She left without me even realising, her empty chair an accusation.

*Bad mother.*

Perhaps Elise has a point, and my desire to make things up to Carrie has become a new obsession. But the photograph was of the two of us – Carrie and me – so I'm involved whether I like it or not.

Why send a picture of us?

Maybe I should show the box to Carrie after all. She'll probably laugh, instantly knowing who's sent it. Then I can stop worrying about that and get on with booking the Orient Express for my dying friend.

Yes, deal with reality, not imagined bogeymen. With renewed determination, I decide to take the box round right now.

# CHAPTER TEN

When I pull up Carrie appears at the front door. She's hanging onto the door frame as though it's the only thing keeping her upright, and seems to be looking around with a lost expression. Concerned, all thoughts of the reason for my errand flit from my mind as I get out of the car – after walking from The View to home to fetch the box, I couldn't be bothered to virtually retrace my steps to Carrie's, so had driven instead. Now I'm glad of the faster journey, because by the look of it, she needs me.

'Are you okay? Has something happened?' I call.

As I run up the garden path towards her, she shakes a box of cat treats. The sound takes me back to my childhood and school productions, where the only thing I'd been trusted with was shaking the maracas.

More shaking, accompanied by kissing noises.

'Smudge!' Carrie stretches her neck, looking this way and that. 'He's been gone all night. It's not like him.'

The grey tabby, with piercing yellow irises and fur markings that make him look as though he is wearing smudged charcoal eyeliner, has barely left Carrie's side since she adopted him a handful of months ago. I look around, up and down the road. There's no sign of him.

'I'm sure he'll turn up. Come on, let's go inside. See, this is why I could never have a cat, I'd worry too much about them not coming home, imagining all sorts when actually they're out having a whale of a time. I'm sure he's just found something that's captured his interest, or is being fed by someone else and having a cheeky snooze on their bed, before coming home to you to get fed again.'

'You think?'

'Definitely! And you've not seen anyone lurking around, looking suspicious, have you?'

'I don't understand—'

'Just thinking that if someone had, um, run Smudge over, they might have come to your house to let you know, or something. But no strange people have been around here that you've noticed?'

Her eyes narrow. I'm babbling, trying to get to the bottom of the box rather than the mystery of the missing pet. The last thing I want is to scare her or make her suspicious, so I try to steer the conversation back on track.

'I once took in a cat just before Christmas one year. Found him near the bins, searching around for food and looking up at me with big, sad eyes. After that, he came round every night for a week, so I decided he couldn't possibly belong to anyone and took him in. For a month he stayed on my bed all night, then every morning when I went to work I'd let him out. Each evening when I came home, there he was, waiting for me. He was a lovely little thing, black and white, so I called him Felix.'

'After the advert.'

'That's right. Anyway, I was going away for a couple of days, so I checked Felix into a cattery. Had to pay for his injections to be done beforehand, mind, so it cost me a few quid. When I got back after three days, there were posters up: "Have you seen this cat?"

'Turned out Felix belonged to a woman a couple of streets over. Every night, she'd let him out, and he'd come to mine and spend the night. Then while I was at work, he went back to his owner. What a life of Riley – and being fed by us both, too! After that, "Felix" sported a collar so people would know he was called Raffles and wasn't a stray.

'My point is, Smudge could easily be doing something like that. That's cats, isn't it – they're independent, get up to all sorts while they're out of sight. So don't worry about him.'

Carrie's shoulders relax. She gives a sigh that's almost a laugh. 'You're right.'

''Course I'm right. Now, shall I put the kettle on? Oh, and I've brought you some steak casserole I made last night but then couldn't face eating, thought you could have it tonight.'

'Trying to keep my strength up? Thank you! You sit down, I'll make a cuppa for us.'

After getting the casserole from the car, and studiously ignoring the box on the back seat, I find Carrie in her kitchen. She's still glancing out of the window. I do, too, and once again spot the neighbour's decorations. They've even got a glowing cauldron on the roof. It gives me an idea about the box.

'The kids used to love Halloween. They'd apple-bob, just like I did when I was little. Loved to get dressed up, too. Do you have any Halloween traditions?' I'm fishing – and hoping it's not obvious.

'Funnily enough, Mum and I were talking about that last night.' She and her parents are incredibly close and speak most days. 'We'd always get really dressed up and go around the neighbourhood, trick-or-treating. Every house pulled out all the stops – in fact, people used to drive over to see the displays. Yeah, our street was quite famous in the town. Afterwards, Mum and Dad would get everyone round to ours for a Halloween party. It was brilliant fun. They'd always buy me a silly gift, too.' She shakes her head, lost in memories, then carries on fishing a teabag out of a mug.

The relief! The box isn't a sinister message at all, just part of some weird family tradition. 'Did you used to play practical jokes on each other?' I check, eager.

'Ooh, no. I don't like practical jokes, they always seem a bit cruel to me.'

'Not silly photographs, or funny little messages, or… um, I don't know… '

'Is that something you do with Elise and Edward? Hey, are you seeing them over Halloween?'

I fiddle with the steaming mug Carrie has handed me seconds before, uncomfortable with the turn the conversation is taking.

'Oh, Alex, are things still bad between you all? I don't understand how your husband got custody of the children.'

'He – I – it's complicated. When he left me four and a half years ago, they decided they wanted to be with him. They had their reasons. I'm – well, I'm just not good enough. For any of them. I'm a bad wife, bad mother.'

'Rubbish! You're the loveliest person I've ever met. Look at everything you've done for me. We've only known each other six months or so, and you're like a second mum to me. You're amazing.'

'Now you're the one talking rubbish.' I sip my tea. The water's still scalding. It doesn't burn away the bitter taste of betrayal, secrets and lies. 'The kids like being with Owen, so what choice do I have?'

'It's selfish of him to keep them away from you.'

'He's a good man. He'd never intentionally hurt me.'

'Sounds to me like you're still in love with him.'

Another swallow of too-hot tea. It gives me an excuse to have tears in my eyes. There isn't a single day that I don't think of Owen. That I don't wake up and miss his head on the pillow beside me. That I don't fall asleep pretending his arms are around me. I miss the person he was before we fell apart.

'Don't be silly. We're well and truly over.'

Carrie folds her arms, looking at me with one eyebrow raised. 'If you insist. But when was the last time you went on a date? You need to move on.'

I close my eyes, knowing that the one time I'd tried to do that I've regretted ever since. Then force my eyes open and a smile on my face.

'Oh yeah? Seen any tall, dark, handsome strangers hanging around lately? Or short, blond, ugly blokes? Anyone who might be interested in a middle-aged woman with a freight train's worth of baggage?'

'Sadly not.'

'No one unusual hanging around? Random strangers?'

She gives me a funny look. 'Er, no. Why?'

'No reason, just desperate,' I joke.

Desperate to get to the bottom of that photograph. Carrie hasn't seen anyone out of place, as far as I can tell. The puzzle of who sent the box remains. The writing on it seems to blaze in the air before me: *I'm watching you.*

Carrie peers anxiously out of the window again, taking advantage of the lull in conversation. Grabs the cat treats and opens the back door.

'Smudge! Come on!' Shake, shake, shake.

The mystery box lies where I left it, on the back seat, and I'm so glad I didn't show it to Carrie after all, because I can't help wondering… Is Smudge's disappearance a coincidence, or another step in a campaign to scare a dying woman?

# CHAPTER ELEVEN

## THEN

Last night Mum turned the music up extra loud to cover the arguing, but it hadn't barricaded out her shrieks of pain. I'd put my hands over my ears and tried to sing along, like I always did, mute tears streaming. When silence had finally descended, it had been scarier than the shouts, and sleep had refused to come so that I could escape into it. I dreaded getting up for school, but hadn't dared risk Dad's rage if I was late, either, so when the alarm went off, I crept downstairs for breakfast. Terrified of what I'd find, I imagined a steel cage wrapped around me for protection.

After a lifetime of walking on eggshells, I'd developed a hunched tiptoe to my gait, perfect for going unnoticed as I crept past Dad, who sat at the rickety breakfast bar. While I helped myself to a huge glass of milk from the fridge, Dad took another swig from his 'special water bottle'. He started most mornings by pouring himself a vodka from it. I was ten, old enough now to realise when Dad was drunk – which was most of the time.

He cut into the fry-up Mum had made for him.

Spat it out.

'It's cold! Can't you even get this right, you stupid cow?'

Mum seemed glued to the cooker, all big eyes and biting lip, with no reply, no movement. It was the kind of stillness only people who have spent years living in fear can achieve. We both watched silently as Dad picked up his plate and hurled it at the wall. I crouched down. Too slow. A stray shard of ceramic nicked my cheek. Exploded fried eggs and a massacre of tomatoes slid down the pale pink walls to join the sausages rolling on the floor.

Dad took a gulp from his water bottle and spat another incoherent insult, making Mum wince. She absorbed the abuse, not saying a word. Mum never said anything to criticise Dad, too scared of him to ever risk confrontation.

Silence goaded him as much as arguing back, though. His chair screeched over the terracotta tiles as he pushed it back and stood. He lurched forward a step, swayed, stumbled. Only saved himself from falling flat on his stupid, ugly face by bracing against the wall.

'Do you hear me? I'm watching you, you little bitch.'

Another step forward, momentum propelling him at Mum until he loomed over her, nose pushed against hers. 'One of these days you'll push me too far. I'll kill you. And your brat.'

Spit flew from his mouth as he spoke, landing on Mum's chin. The veins on his nose and cheeks reminded me of the crazy paving we'd got in the backyard. But it was his bloodshot eyes that scared me. They made me think of a picture of the Devil I'd seen in a book at school, where fire spewed from his mouth. All that was missing from the man standing in front of me were the horns.

His hands twitched, ready for action.

No! I squeezed between him and Mum, her last and only line of defence. Hands on my hips, I pulled myself up as tall as I could. I barely reached his chest.

'Leave her alone! I hate you! Go away!'

Iron fingers in my hair. Head slammed back against the wall, rat-tat-tat, quick as machine-gun fire. Stars blazed, dizzying, no gravity until I hit the floor. Dad stepped over me, foot catching my side, then stumbled from the room, leaving me in a heap on the floor like a scrunched-up piece of paper. Discarded, unwanted, thrown away. The story of my short life. I sat up. Something sticky was dribbling down my face. Blood? No, egg.

The tiniest whimper came from Mum, counting itself lucky to escape. She didn't move until a window-rattling snore came from the living room. She helped me stand up, dusted off my clothes, wiped my face clean with a cloth.

'You all right?' she checked. I nodded, and her mouth faked a smile. 'Where there's no sense, there's no feeling, eh? Right, off you go to school. And you know the rules, let's keep this in the family.'

Keep it in the family. As though it was something special to be guarded. But my insides felt hot with rebellion. I wasn't going to keep quiet and take it any more, not after the talk we'd had at school the other day all about secrets.

'Find someone you trust, ideally an adult, and talk to them. Never be afraid to tell your problems to somebody, and it will be okay,' that's what my teacher had told us.

I'd only got one friend at school. Not even a friend, really, but Jessica didn't seem to mind too much if I sat next to her in some of the classes, and sometimes, when no one was looking, we whispered to each other. It was nice having somebody to talk to even if it could only be in secret. So as soon as I escaped the house, I ran as hard and fast as I could to my friend's house, and knocked on the door, breathless.

Jessica's mum answered. I liked her mum. She had a big, beaming smile, nothing like my mum's, which only lived on the corners of her mouth, ready to switch back down into a timid line if Dad appeared.

My teacher's words ringing in my ears, and my head ringing from the blows, I didn't even wait to find Jessica. Instead, I grabbed hold of both Mrs Norbury's hands and let the words pour from me. Her mouth dropped open as she listened. At some point she must have led me into the kitchen, but I barely noticed as I emptied out the truth of my life. Jessica peered into the room, giving me a funny look, but her mum shooed her away and made me a hot chocolate with milk, not just water like I got at home.

Finally, the words slowed to a trickle, then a drop, until they stopped. Mrs Norbury hugged me.

'You've been a very brave girl,' she said. 'Thank you for trusting me.'

The heat I'd felt before returned, but now it felt comforting, not angry. Everything was going to be okay, because I'd done exactly like teacher said and told somebody my problem. They were going to help me, and I'd never have to be afraid in my own home again. When she dropped Jessica and me off at school, I almost floated.

Concentrating on lessons was hard when my head was full of pictures of Dad being arrested and led away in handcuffs from my home. I itched to be there to see it, fidgeting in my seat in impatience.

At home time, I ran until I got a stitch and walked the rest of the way as fast as I could, holding my side. There were no police cars in my street, not a hint of flashing lights or uniforms. Perhaps Dad had already been taken.

There was a car I didn't recognise, though. Maybe it was CID, like on telly. Cool.

When I let myself into the kitchen, voices mumbled through the walls of the living room, sliding through the cracks of the closed door. Dad's deep boom was among them. I crept up to the door, my heart feeling like it was beating so fast it might escape up into my mouth and pop out. I pressed my ear against the flaking cream paint. It was enough to make out the occasional word.

Dad apologising. Mrs Norbury's voice, higher than normal but still recognisable. *So that was whose car was parked outside.* Her husband telling Dad to 'make sure it doesn't happen again' and saying something about 'being put in a difficult position'.

What did it mean? Dad was in trouble, right? He had to be. He'd been really, really bad.

The voices were getting louder, closer. Before the door could open I ran back into the kitchen.

By the time the four adults trooped into the kitchen I was sat at the breakfast bar, head resting on folded arms, legs swinging pendulum-like as if I'd been sitting there, bored, the whole time.

'Here's the little tyke,' said Dad, ruffling my hair. 'The kid's got one hell of an imagination – hey, one day she might make a living out of it, become a bestseller. I'm sorry you got dragged into her stories, though.'

He shook his head in mock despair. Around me the adults swirled with awkward jokes and expansive gestures, laughing a little too loud, a little too keen. The corners of Mum's mouth mutinied into a smile that didn't reach her anxious eyes.

'Apologise to the Norburys, sweetheart,' Dad added. 'You almost got your dad in a load of trouble.'

'I didn't do anything wrong.' My jaw stuck out, as stubborn as my crossed arms. The adults gave an uncomfortable chuckle.

'You mustn't tell tall tales,' Dad said.

Mum finally chipped in, looking at Jessica's parents. 'You can see what we have to deal with.' Her hands moved as if washing each other, anxious.

Mrs Norbury didn't seem to know where to look. Her eyes slid over me as if I wasn't there. There was no sign of the beaming smile that had made me feel so safe earlier.

'Well, we must be going. We need to collect Jessica from her gran's house,' she said.

At the doorway, Dad's arm wrapped round Mum's shoulder, imprisoning her.

'Great to see you,' he called one last time, waving his new friends off. They waved back through their open windows.

We all watched them reverse off our drive and trundle away, growing smaller. Indicated left and disappeared. Then Dad closed the door. His smile melted into a glower that made my stomach curdle and a warm sensation trickle down the inside of my leg.

It had been a mistake to say anything. A mistake to hope.

Honesty had got me absolutely nowhere.

# CHAPTER TWELVE

## NOW

*An evil, targeted campaign. Or two coincidences.* That's the choice facing me. My hands open and close to a slow imaginary beat, as I vacillate between the two while simultaneously trying to ease my mild arthritis. At this time of year the cold often makes my fingers ache, thanks to the amount of breaks the bones have suffered. Good job my ribs don't do the same.

Open: has Smudge been taken by the same person who is sending Carrie threatening messages? Close: has he wandered off, at the exact same time as someone's pranked my friend?

I'm in my usual seat in the corner of the waiting room at the eating disorder clinic which I have to attend every Wednesday and Friday. I've come here straight from Carrie's, and it's a relief to get away – already I can feel my racing mind calming into coherence. The clinic is a sort of home from home in many ways, particularly as I've been an inpatient several times, the longest period a year. The nose-tingling smell of antiseptic feels safe and comforting. The way the hard-wearing buff carpet tiles are laid so the nap alternates its direction, north-south, east-west, is as familiar as my own carpet. The crack above the nurse's door that runs up to the ceiling; the tinny radio playing jingly-jangly music from decades ago; they are like old friends.

I know the nurses, too. The ones with strident voices and businesslike attitude who are soft as brushed cotton. Maria is my favourite. A short, round woman with a smile as brilliant as her postbox-red hair.

There are no posters in the waiting room, which is a blessing. No repeat reading until the messages become like Chinese water torture of the eyeballs, the words dripping into the brain. Still, my eyes slide over 'no patients beyond this point' for the millionth time, and stare blindly at the magnolia wall as I return to the puzzle in my mind. Generally, I enjoy a mental challenge, but this is several levels above a cryptic crossword or brain-teaser.

The more I think about it, the more I decide I'm letting emotion override logic. Some bored kids have almost certainly decided to bait a vulnerable, lone woman, which is horrible, but nothing too much to worry about.

More concerning has been my own reaction. The fact that I made links that don't exist and allowed myself to get so stressed out means I'm letting my imagination get the better of me.

I've always had an inventive mind, losing myself in stories I make up and drawing pictures of fantastical creatures. It's one of the reasons I'm so good at my job, listening to what people want in their ideal dress, then taking the best bits and creating something wonderful for them. Making people's dreams come true and seeing the look on their faces is incredibly rewarding. But my imagination can also be a curse; I must not get carried away. Instead, my scattered energies need to be focused on practical help for Carrie, sorting her bucket list, while simultaneously making sure I stay healthy.

I'm looking forward to talking it all through with my counsellor, the lovely Rosie, although it's tempting to leave bits out. It's been drummed into me that omission is destructive in therapy, though. The problem is that in Rosie's opinion, many of my problems are stemming from the support group – and she's never approved of me going there. It's something we've discussed a number of times. Mixed messages, she says, warning of confusion, and there being a price to pay later, in regrets. I should listen. But I don't. The group fills a void in my life left by the loss of my children and husband, allowing me to speak exclusively about them with no anorexia-driven agenda. Unlike here.

A door opens near me, and a nurse pops her head round it. I don't need to look at her name badge to know she is Ruth.

'Twenty-three,' she calls. Like bingo. A thrill runs through the seated people, a murmur of interest. Another person seen; a little closer to my own number being up.

The first time I entered through those doors I'd been convinced I wasn't ill. I'd only agreed to come to the clinic to shut people up, convinced as I was that I was too fat and too old to have an eating disorder. According to my therapist, although most people think of anorexia as a teenage condition, it's not uncommon for it to develop in women in midlife, often triggered by trauma of one kind or another – most frequently divorce, bereavement or empty nest syndrome. My husband was gone, along with my kids, and that definitely coincided with the start of my eating disorder.

It's been a long, hard road to recovery, with several nasty setbacks, but this time I'm doing much better. The team give me realistic goals to achieve, saying a full recovery would be the ideal but that not everyone can get there. Instead, any level of improvement is to be celebrated – and even something as simple as maintaining weight rather than losing it is a big step for many of us. They also realise that, like me, eating disorder sufferers often have several relapses before recovery. Knowing they understand my everyday struggles has removed a lot of my pressure.

Recovery can be a scary thing to contemplate for people like me. Even now, I sometimes catch myself viewing it with ambivalence, and there are times when it takes more strength to eat than not. But every day I fight. So far, for the last ten months, I've been winning.

Finally, I'm called into a side room. The nurse quickly makes a note of the digital readout on the scale. Looks up from the clipboard, smiling.

'Okay, it's the same as last weigh-in, so well done.'

She listens to my heart, takes my blood pressure and then I'm done. Time to sit down to speak with my counsellor.

'How did the fundraiser go?' asks Rosie.

'Good, yeah, really good.'

'You seem tense. What's been happening.'

'It's Carrie. You know, that girl who… ' I trail off.

Suddenly I feel nervous about admitting what's been happening. Even with the most positive spin it sounds crazy now I'm about to say it out loud. Rosie isn't in the mood to let me off lightly today, though. Instead of filling in the blanks of who Carrie is, she gives me a look. A look that says, *come on, finish the sentence.*

When I don't, she gives me a verbal nudge.

'Remind me how the two of you first met.'

She knows, but I know better than to argue.

I like Rosie. Her office seems chaotic, her desk a mess of notebooks and Post-it notes and pens and half-full mugs of coffee left so long they've developed a scum on top. Her hair never seems to be brushed, and her tops tend to be half tucked in, half hanging out, as if she's been interrupted while dressing and had to run from the house. It's comforting, and always makes me feel relaxed. But for all the seeming disorder, she's as sharp and precise as a pin when it comes to analysing emotions. There's an agenda here as to why she wants me to tell the story of my complex history with Carrie, and all I can do is spill and let it play out.

'I hadn't realised when I met Carrie just how she was connected to me. She came to the support group and something about her vulnerability made me feel for her almost immediately. There's twenty years' age difference between us, and I wanted to mother her. Take her home and look after her,' I say.

Rosie's gaze is steady. It doesn't flicker away to her notebook once, or to the pen resting lightly between finger and thumb.

'What was it about her that made you feel that way?'

My fingers run over my lips, trying to find the right words. 'She was new to the area, and I remembered what that was like. I think she reminded me of Claire a little.'

'Claire Paver? In what way?'

'A young, lost girl. Someone who needed help.'

Claire was nineteen when I met her, during my second enforced stint at the clinic, after I'd been sectioned. She was already an old hand, having been sectioned herself innumerable times since she turned twelve. Her teenage years had been as structured as a prisoner's: breakfast, 8 to 8.30 a.m.; snack, 10.10 to 10.25 a.m.; lunch, 12.15 to 1 p.m.; afternoon snack, 3.10 p.m.; supper, 6 to 6.30 p.m.; final snack, 9.30 p.m. Our meals and snacks were supervised, and the toilet locked until half an hour after we'd all eaten, to ensure we didn't deliberately throw up.

'Keeping my food down isn't the problem – it's getting it down me in the first place,' Claire always joked.

While others her age were gaining freedoms and learning to make decisions for themselves, everything about Claire's life was decided, of necessity, by others.

There was comfort as well as need in its familiarity, but it also meant that she became institutionalised. Every time she was well enough to be allowed home, the world seemed a scary place and she'd fall straight back into her routine of stopping eating. She admitted as much to me one day.

'I like it here,' she'd told me, as she dug out the glitter-covered nameplate she'd made for her room and hung it once more on the bedroom door at the clinic. 'It's all I've ever known. I don't like it out there in the world. Suddenly I have to make decisions for myself – I feel all this pressure. If I could just live here for ever, I'd be happy.'

In some ways she reminded me of an old lag who keeps stealing so he can get back to the routine of prison, which is all he's know his entire life, his one constant. Without the routines and protections in place, though, she'd have starved herself anyway, so what was the alternative?

'There was a hideous inevitability to her death,' I tell Rosie. 'She was only three days away from her twentieth birthday, you know. That was when I knew I couldn't carry on like this. I had to get better. I had to stop lying to myself and everyone else. So here I am, a recovering liar, slowly leaving behind adult-onset anorexia, a condition that's controlled my life for years. And, I don't know, maybe I recognised that fragility in Carrie, too. Maybe I could see death closing in on her—'

'That's very sad, but it's not the whole story and I think you know it. You wanted to mother them both, would you say? Yet you're deliberately leaving something out.'

'I'm—' My whole body shakes, not just my head. 'We're not talking about that. We're… there's something else I need to tell you.'

Eyes prickle in protest; Rosie's face blurs as she drowns in my tears. The reprieve is purely visual.

'You know, at some point you're going to have to be honest and face the truth,' she says. No accusation, no judgement, simply a statement.

'I am honest! I'm—'

'You won't truly begin to get better until you accept reality. Stop lying to yourself.'

'You know nothing about me. You don't even listen to me. Call yourself a counsellor? I talk to you and you refuse to listen. You just see me as someone to be fixed, when I'm not broken any more.'

A stupid lie that doesn't even fool me. I sound like a sullen teenager, not a forty-something. But why has Rosie chosen today of all days to push me? I haven't had a chance to talk about what I have on my mind.

She's been leaning forward, but sits back again and nods as she runs a hand through her hair from the neck up to the crown. That's why her hair's always messy.

'Okay… Let's go back to Carrie and the first time you met her.'

'Good, well, at that first support group meeting she talked about moving to a new area and having trouble making friends at work, but that she'd met someone and fallen in love. She'd thought she'd finally met a good man, someone to settle down with, maybe even have children. She kept saying he'd made her feel safe – I got the impression that was very important to her, and that it wasn't something she'd ever had before. But then she'd got cancer, a very aggressive form of breast cancer, that starts with a rash. She told us all that her cancer was what had pushed a wedge between herself and Simon. She blamed herself for them splitting up.'

I look anywhere but at my counsellor as I speak. Shame is a neon sign, lighting me up for the world to see.

'That wasn't the truth, though. As she described her "perfect" boyfriend, I realised I was the reason he'd disappeared on her during her treatment. I was the reason she was alone. I stole her boyfriend.'

# CHAPTER THIRTEEN

There's sweat on my forehead and my heart is pounding. I want to run, fast and far, to distance myself from the admission, even though Rosie has heard it before. The shame never lessens. I used Carrie's boyfriend, and she was the one who paid the price, being left alone to face the biggest fight of her life. She'd managed to beat the cancer, but now, just a couple of months on, it's back, worse than ever. That's why nothing on earth will make me step away from her, because it's my fault she's alone.

My breaths are deep and shaky as I try to calm down enough to speak again. Rosie doesn't say anything, simply leans over and grabs a box of tissues which she then proffers.

'I'm responsible for Carrie's situation,' I gasp, dabbing at my face.

'Responsible.'

The word drops like a lead weight between us.

'Alex, you use that word a lot when talking about your friend. Let's explore that a little. Why do you think that you should be culpable for what happens to her, simply because you slept with her partner?

'You didn't give her cancer. You didn't encourage Simon to leave her. And we've discussed before the fact that you wouldn't have slept with him in the first place if you'd known he was with someone already. Correct?'

No matter how many times we go over it, Rosie never understands my point.

'I owe her. Besides, she's all alone, fighting for her life. She's close to her parents, yet they aren't here with her. If one of my kids had cancer, I'd drop everything and be by their side battling it with them. Why aren't they?'

Rosie opens her mouth to speak, but I bulldoze over her.

'They've never visited, as far as I know. She makes excuses for them. It makes me furious.'

'Why do her parents' actions annoy you so much?'

My arms fold firmly across my chest, barring that line of questioning. There's an awkward silence before Rosie tries a different tack.

'Tell me what you were feeling about yourself when you decided to sleep with Simon that first time.'

I shrug, confused. Loath to explore.

'Let me ask another question, then. When you were at your lightest weight, did you feel attractive? Did you become anorexic in order to feel beautiful?'

'It's never been about being attractive, not for me. I know I don't look good being skeletal. I know I look better being a normal weight. That's not the point. I don't really know what the point is. Perhaps if I did, I'd be able to get better.'

My eyes dart this way and that, trying to herd my thoughts.

'It's not about attention-seeking, either. It's more about punishment. I don't deserve to eat, I don't deserve nice things, I don't deserve to enjoy myself.

'It's a form of self-harm, like cutting, only this is more internalised. I want to tear my skin off, and the fat beneath it, I feel so disgusted with myself.'

My fingers flex against the skin on my forearm. Three red welts are left behind. Hiding them under my hand, I tumble on.

'Simon was only meant to be a one-night stand. That was the initial idea. It was something wild and out of character because I wanted to feel womanly again. I'd put on some weight and felt conflicted about it. Everyone told me it was a good thing – I knew it was a good thing – but I didn't *feel* it.

'There'd been no denying the extra calories I'd been eating had boosted my energy, though. The lethargy that had dragged me down previously had disappeared by that point, and I'd felt—' I search for the right word, brushing against various descriptions and tossing them to one side. *Normal.* That was the one.

'It had been such a long time since I'd felt normal that it took a while to identify.' I give a little smile, remembering. Emotions that had lain dormant had started to stir. One that grew was curiosity… Was I desirable? It had been a long time since I'd been with a man.

'I wanted to feel the weight of a man on me again. To feel sexy. To be seen as a woman, rather than a genderless, invisible forty-something. It seemed impossible to imagine anyone looking at me and feeling passion,' I explain. 'It wasn't just about someone wanting me, though. It was that I couldn't remember what it was like to see a man myself and want him.'

To play the game of flirtation, the push and pull of looks, of longing and lingering touches that grow into heat and action.

I shrug my slender shoulders. 'My life had narrowed down until it was all about food, and I wanted to expand it.'

'What attracted you to Simon?'

'This might sound counter-intuitive, but it had to be someone who didn't matter to me. Sex was such a big deal already, the thought of exposing myself physically to rejection was bad enough. Add in the complication of emotional attachment and it was more than I could cope with.' A shudder quakes my body. 'It needed to be an experiment, a chance to rediscover myself sexually. If it went well, then perhaps, one day in the distant future, I could think about risking a relationship.'

*Although who would want me with all my baggage, anyway?*

'One day I'd stopped for a hot chocolate from Crusoe's – you know, the café on Longsands beach, near the abandoned Victorian outdoor swimming pool?'

Before speaking again I think, sending myself back in time. In my mind's eye I can see the rocks, the golden crescent of sand. Nearby, children are at the half-term Surf School, their cheeks red with excitement as much as the cold. I sit beneath the fairy lights strung across Crusoe's patio, on a bench made from silvered and salted driftwood that's smoother than silk beneath my fingertips. Waves, clouds, families at play, ebb and flow as I eat the mountain of cream on my hot chocolate, using the Flake as a spoon. Decadent and challenging. When just the right amount of cream is left, I stir it into the steaming drink with the Flake, which melts deliciously until only the nub is left, which I then pop into my mouth.

I can still taste it, my mouth filling with saliva even as I sit in my counsellor's office. It's such a simple thing – and the perfect illustration of how much I'd achieved. At one point, the thought of being in the same room as that hot chocolate would have had me literally shaking with fear, as though I could somehow absorb the calories from the air. While it wasn't quite correct that I'd eaten it without a second thought, it was true that I'd enjoyed it. Just as I'd been celebrating internally, I'd seen Simon. *Choice made.*

'What it was about him that drew my eye, I don't know,' I tell Rosie. 'He'd got a fit body in his wetsuit, and a confident ease about him – he smiled with the children a lot, laughing with them. I liked that. But honestly? I don't know why I chose him, apart from the fact that he was there. Right place, right time.'

I'd cracked out rusty flirtation skills that hadn't been used since my husband and I got together. A smile and a lingering look. Wandering over to make small talk. Laughing. A hand on his bicep. Brushing a line of sand from beside his eye. All the time talking myself into what I was about to do.

*Why not? Why shouldn't I do something silly?*

As soon as the children left, I'd taken him to my house. His tanned skin smelled of salt and fresh air ozone, with a tang of musk. His hands were rough as driftwood, but tender. The sex was better than I'd thought it would be, but afterwards I'd felt ridiculous and ashamed. Still, when he'd suggested meeting up again, I'd found myself agreeing. My libido had been woken and refused to go back to sleep.

'I hadn't thought the fling was hurting anyone. But after about a fortnight, we were lying in bed together when he announced that he loved me and was going to leave his girlfriend for me.

'It was the first time he'd ever mentioned being with someone else. I was bloody furious with him. I'd thought this was a harmless shag, that it didn't hurt anyone – us included. I'd had no idea he was in a relationship, or that he'd developed feelings for me. I'm shouting at him, telling him all this, when he drops the bombshell that this woman has cancer. What a shit! I told him to get out, that I didn't want anything more to do with him.

'But the damage had been done by then. The following week Carrie joined the support group, and as she talked about battling cancer and losing the love of her life, it became obvious she was Simon's ex.'

The memory envelops me. Once again, the guilt is a physical blow, making my stomach throb. Words dam my throat, unable to escape, leaving me gasping for air. It's several moments before I can speak again.

'She's so hurt by the break-up. Yet another person I've damaged without even trying. I jinx everything.'

'So you befriended her to somehow make amends. Alex, how has your eating been since the news that her condition is untreatable?'

'Fine.' Then I remember the barely touched scampi and chips. 'Well, maybe a bit less than usual.'

'How are you coping emotionally?'

It's tempting to say 'fine' again.

'Umm, Carrie's my top priority. I'm devastated she's dying, and worried for her, obviously. I'm upset that I'll never really get the chance to make amends to her. And… ' I'm unsure whether to continue. My therapist is watching me carefully, pen poised. 'I think someone is messing her around, as well. Maybe picking on her because they know she's vulnerable. So I'm going to have to keep a close eye on her.'

'What makes you think someone is picking on her?'

The constant questions were once annoying, but I'm used to them now. Still, I feel a niggle of irritation at having to explain every tiny detail of my life. Locking down my tears, I update Rosie on what's been happening with Carrie in the last few days. I swear she's looking at me strangely. It makes me stutter and stumble over my words and fiddle with a button on my top as I speak.

She makes some notes, shaking her head almost imperceptibly as she does.

'This has all happened since she told you she's dying?' Rosie checks. 'Alex, you need to be careful, you're taking on responsibilities that aren't yours. I'm concerned this could trigger another relapse.

'In my opinion, Carrie's terminal illness is reminding you of your other losses. Even if this doesn't prompt a setback in your recovery, I'm concerned that you may be replacing your reliance on controlling food with a dependency on Carrie. Once she's gone, I'm unsure how you're going to cope. We need to address this, Alex. You need to consider pulling away slightly from her.'

'You're making it sound weird, like it's something dark between Carrie and me. All I want to do is look after her and make things better.'

'And in trying to do that you may be imagining things you can fix that aren't there. You need to start dealing with reality.'

The pen is put down on her desk and rolls under the remains of a paperwork avalanche. I wish I could hide along with it as Rosie continues towards her inevitable conclusion.

'I'm not just talking about Carrie. You know what I'm referring to, Alex. I don't think you're ever going to truly recover until you admit and confront your past. Are we ever going to address what really happened with your children and your husband and you?'

# CHAPTER FOURTEEN

You know that saying, saved by the bell? Well, that's what saved me from that nightmare session with Rosie, because even as her stare demanded answers, her electronic timer dinged to say our time together was up. I almost sprinted out, relief lending me wings.

I spend the afternoon and early evening alone, tucked away in the largest of my three bedrooms, which I've converted into a sewing room. Working on the prom dress I'm making, and letting the swish of taffeta soothe my fevered thoughts as I go over what she said. She'll never convince me to back off from Carrie. I love that young woman like a daughter now, and I'll see through to the bitter end my promise to be there for her.

Time has flown by; I hadn't realised it was so late, especially as I've had to have the light on since 2 p.m. It's been one of those murky winter days where the sun barely seems to come up. I'm drawing the curtains when I see the twins heading for my front door.

'What a lovely surprise,' I grin, hustling them inside before they can knock.

They bring the cold in with them, that sweet, sharp smell, so I immediately fuss around, making hot drinks and wittering about them 'catching their death of cold'. I can feel Elise growing impatient with me, but Edward soaks it all up, smiling patiently. My sunshine boy. Talking of which…

'Is that new? I love it!' I run his scarf through my fingers. It's soft, probably cashmere, and has yellow, burnt orange and charcoal-grey stripes. 'It's good to see you in something a bit brighter – suits you!'

'Cheers, Mum.' He blushes to the tips of his ears, at that age where he seems permanently embarrassed by me.

'We actually came over for a reason,' Elise cuts in. Straight to the point as ever, she puts her hot chocolate down on the coffee table with a clunk. Her eyes challenge me. 'We want to talk about what happened between you and Dad.'

'It's adult stuff.' I regret the phrase as soon as it's out of my mouth. The shutters have slammed shut, my daughter's face closing down in an instant. 'Okay, hands up, that's an excuse, and I'm sorry for trying to fob you off.'

Two pairs of folded arms confront me. I try again. 'What I mean is, it's complicated, like relationships always are. There's no simple answer I can give you. All I can say is that we both had flaws in our personalities that meant the marriage didn't work out. But it's not all bad – cracks are what let the light in, too. You're our light.'

The truth would destroy all their illusions and plunge them into darkness. I can't let that happen, even if they do get angry with me. Two red spots have appeared on Elise's cheeks, and they're growing, a clear indicator of her annoyance. Edward remains calm as he chimes in.

'You never tell us what happened. It would be helpful if you'd open up about the past.'

'There's no point going over it.'

Elise scoffs. 'Yeah, why bother being honest with your family when you can distract yourself with puzzles and your surrogate daughter? You don't need your real kids.' She stands, throws my sudoku book across the room. 'Look at you. Starving yourself, using diversions and superstitions to pretend to be in control when you're too weak to actually be honest and really take control of your life, Alex.'

'I wish you'd call me Mum—'

'Earn the title!'

Edward gets between us as I try to explain.

'I know I've made a lot of mistakes. Give me a little more time and I promise I'll do better.'

'Dad says—'

'You shouldn't believe everything your father says.' My voice is sharp. Scared of what may have been revealed. 'Sorry, I shouldn't have snapped. I don't want to speak ill of—'

'You don't speak at all. You don't do anything. What did you eat tonight?'

'I... Damn, I forgot. I'll get something now.'

'I'll do it,' offers Edward. 'How about pasta and veg?'

The move to the kitchen brings the argument to a close, for which I thank my lucky stars. It's so wonderful to see the twins, but lately our meetings are so fraught, and I'm at my wit's end as to what best to do. I know what Rosie would say, of course, about guilt, honesty, facing up to reality, and so on. For now I'm choosing to ignore. Instead, I keep the conversation light while the food is cooked, but there is no laughter or fun between us. They stay long enough to make sure I eat every mouthful, then return to their father.

❖

The house is so empty without them. Pulling the warm woollen throw from the back of the sofa, I hunker inside it, wishing I could hold the children instead.

A noise outside. Have they come back? There's no sign when I peer round the curtains on to the tree-lined street, flooded with light from a street lamp. It must have been my imagination. Unless... The memory of the photograph of Carrie and me ambushes me. My heart thuds harder, imagining someone outside, watching me, waiting. Skin prickling, I rush round the house checking every door and window is locked. They are, of course. But after that each noise seems to give me goosebumps, and sleep is hard to find when at last I go to bed.

The next day I get up bright and early, the sunshine banishing paranoid thoughts of people trying to break into my home, or standing outside watching me. I start decorating the bodice of the dress. Each tiny, glittering bugle bead has to be hand-sewn, and after a couple of hours my sore eyes need a break. Perfect timing, because Carrie should be back from her cleaning job.

I text her.

*Fancy going for a walk or something?*

*Sounds good! If I don't answer the door, let yourself in with your key, cos I might be in the shower still.*

She'd given me her spare key in case she ever got locked out, and often tells me to let myself in.

It takes me fifteen minutes to wander to her house, walking slowly to make the most of the brilliant winter sun on my skin, despite the biting breeze. Above, chiffon clouds easily overtake me as they race one another in a cerulean sky. It's the sort of day that makes me feel good to be alive.

Carrie lives in a cul-de-sac, and at its entrance a group of mainly pre-teen kids are hanging about. They lean on their bikes, ribbing one another and cracking up. Every now and then one breaks away and rides a slow circle, or speeds across the road to a low wall and jumps their wheels onto it to cycle along the top, before returning. One of them is wearing a balaclava that looks like a screaming skull, the mouth wide open to show horrific teeth. He's only about thirteen, but there's a tingle of intimidation at the base of my skull, as if someone has placed an ice cube there, and I walk that little bit faster. The huddle pause and watch me go by, nudging each other. Whispering. I can feel their eyes on me still as I approach Carrie's cherry-red front door, calling her name as I push it open.

'Down in a minute!' the reply floats from upstairs.

But I'm not looking for Carrie. I'm staring straight down at the doormat. A manila envelope lies on it, with Carrie's name written in red capitals.

The same handwriting as the box. I'd recognise it anywhere.

Floorboards creak upstairs. Carrie is coming. Quickly, I pick up the envelope, look around for somewhere to hide it, to retrieve later. There isn't anywhere.

Footsteps above me approach the stairs. She's coming! I undo my jacket and shove the envelope inside, clamping it awkwardly against my body with my arm and slamming a rictus smile on my face just as Carrie appears at the top.

She pauses, head on one side. 'You okay?'

'Fine! Yeah, fine. Can I use your loo? Thanks!'

Not waiting for a reply, I scurry past her and bang the lock in place.

My pale reflection, framed by dull, dark hair, stares back at me from the mirror over the sink. Fever-bright brown eyes, flushed cheeks. Should I tell Carrie about the envelope, or once again keep it to myself? I don't know what to do for the best. Perhaps it's a card, making it clear the last message was a weird joke. Or perhaps there's something even more sinister inside.

A gentle knock plays on the door.

'You got a dodgy stomach? You've been ages. Sure you want to go for that walk?'

I don't answer. Instead, I flush the loo and fold up the envelope so it fits in my inside jacket pocket and quickly zip it up. Wash my hands, then open the door.

'Sorry. Period pain,' I grimace. 'But I've necked some painkillers, so I'll be fine. Come on, let's go.'

The boys are still wheeling like bored seagulls at the mouth of the cul-de-sac. I keep my eye on them as we walk by, a cloak of guilt over me as I wonder at what age children change in people's eyes from cute to something to be approached with caution, fear even.

'Smile!' laughs one, a cheeky grin on his face as he holds his empty hands up as though framing us for a photograph. His friends snigger. Join in.

'Say cheese.'

'Click, click.'

Realisation dawns, slow as a sunrise.

He's the one who took the picture of Carrie and me, and his little group of friends think he's hilarious. Stealing one of her tops from the washing line is just the sort of stupid thing a kid would do, too. Relief and annoyance swirl into a ball of fire. Of all the idiotic pranks. He could have scared Carrie to death thinking she'd got a stalker after her. But I can't confront him like I want to while my clueless friend is here, otherwise she'll know I've been keeping things from her.

We stroll on, ignoring the catcalls. Soon we've turned the corner and are heading to the beach. I pull up short, start patting my pockets.

'Ooh, I've forgotten my purse. Took it out of my pocket when I went to the loo,' I tell Carrie. 'I'll run back and fetch it.'

As I round the corner, the adrenaline is thumping through me. They might only be scrawny kids, but there's about ten of them and only one of me. I can't keep quiet, though. In and out quick, before I can change my mind.

'Oy! You lot!' I shout.

They freeze in confusion as I get closer. In my pocket, my gloved hands are balled into fists, making me feel braver, despite the throb of nails bitten down so low they're painful. The screaming skull mask balaclava seems to leer at me.

'Listen to me. The stupid practical jokes, the photographs, everything, it all stops right now. You hear me?'

'What? It wasn't me,' whines the nearest lad. A reminder they're more children than adults.

'I don't care which of you it was. You do it again, you so much as look at that house in the wrong way, let alone go near my friend, and I'll go straight to your parents. They'll make your lives a living hell.'

Each of them gets a glare that I hope shows I mean business. Then I march off, before their shock can turn into something else. By the time I'm out of their sight, I'm trembling at the thought of what I've done, but elation lifts my steps, too. Just as promised, I've protected Carrie.

# CHAPTER FIFTEEN

'Cor, it might be sunny, but there's a nip to that wind. It's cutting straight through my holy of holies.'

'What's that mean?' I laugh.

'My nickname for these jeans. Put it this way, if I bend over in them, someone might get blinded by the terrible sight they see. The knees aren't the only place these babies are ripped.' Carrie cackles, bending her knees to expose white kneecaps.

By silent agreement, as usual we've bypassed the side road that sweeps down to Longsands and would bring us out beside the Surf School where Simon works. Instead, we've gone further along the main road until we reach a smaller walkway and steep steps to the beach.

Marching across the soft golden crescent of sand is giving me a rosy glow, but the wind seems to have grown knives that slice through the relative warmth of the sun. Carrie must be really feeling the chill, despite the sunshine-yellow padded jacket.

'We need to buy you some clothes – you can't be going around in rags. Maybe we could spend some of the bucket list money on that. And we need to book your trip on the Orient Express – sorry, I've not got round to it yet, I really must.'

'I've been thinking, and honestly, it's a lovely thought, but I'd rather the money went to charity.'

'What? No, you deserve this.'

'So do loads of other cancer sufferers. I'd far rather the money went towards stopping anyone else having to go through this. It's not even having to deal with the cancer itself, though, that's hard enough; no, it's everything. No one but doctors should have to know the names of drugs like Herceptin, epirubicin, cyclophosphamide, Taxotere. My hair fell out, my toenails turned black, I got "chemo cough" and even developed nosebleeds. Because my eyelashes fell out, I got loads of styes, too.'

The coward in me is so glad I didn't witness this, as it all happened before I knew her; the mother in me wishes I'd been there to take care of her.

'I'm not complaining,' she adds. 'The treatment may not have saved my life, but it bought me extra time. I've made new friends, met you…'

I make a comment about how amazing she is, but she dismisses it by blowing a raspberry. We always have a giggle together. Despite our age gap and being total opposites, we've become firm friends. She seems to like older people and feels more comfortable with them, though. Simon's thirty-nine.

Carrie links her arm with mine as we continue walking.

'Enough about me – how are you doing? Any news? Have Elise and Edward realised they're being daft buggers yet and started talking to you like you're an actual human being?'

'They're not that bad.' Sadness leaks through my smile. 'Eating disorders are tough on families. The children said they felt they were treading on eggshells, scared of saying the wrong thing and triggering something in me that would stop me eating again. It's hardly surprising they find it easier to avoid me. Knowing they're tiptoeing around me makes me so angry for what I've put them through.'

'Er, you do know that what you've got is an illness, not a lifestyle choice, right? No one chooses to be this way. We've all got stuff that makes us do crazy shit sometimes, stuff that doesn't always make sense. But the people who claim to love us are supposed to understand, not hurt us. They can't use our problems as a weapon to beat us with.'

'I know, but I'm their mother.'

'They're lucky to have you. I'd have given anything to have a mum like you when I was growing up.'

'Thought your mum was great?'

'Well, yeah. But you can't have too many brilliant mums in your corner.'

'Daft beggar.'

For the next minute neither of us speaks, as we climb the steep steps taking us from Tynemouth towards Cullercoats Bay. At the top, I enjoy the view across the wide, battleship-grey sea. The spray at the top of the waves makes brief rainbows in the sun; gone in the call of a gull.

'Anyway, I thought your kids left before you got your eating disorder.' Carrie has a habit of picking up conversations minutes after they've ended and continuing them as though there's been no pause.

'Uh-huh. I was feeling low after the kids and Owen had left, and I was suddenly all alone, and… the rest is history.'

'No offence, but I always thought it was teenagers that developed eating disorders.'

'According to my therapist, it's more common than you'd think in women my age. She says that, in some ways, we're not unlike teenagers: our bodies are changing, our hormones are all over the place and it can be hard to deal with. We're bombarded by pictures of women older than us who look about twenty years younger. It's exhausting trying to have the body of Elle Macpherson. Especially when I didn't have a figure like that my entire life. Of course, the reality is often far, far more complex than looking at too many doctored photographs of supermodels. It was for me, anyway.'

'But you nearly died, Alex. Surely your kids realise they should be making the most of you, not making life harder.'

'People tell me I almost died,' I agree. 'For a long time I'd roll my eyes and think they were being melodramatic. Even when I was in hospital I felt it was rubbish and begged to be allowed to leave. I thought I looked fine. Now, despite accepting it as the truth, it's still hard to get my head around. Knowing they almost lost me is the bit the children struggle with – and let's not forget, they are only teenagers, so it's second nature for them to hide fear in anger. They've had a lot to deal with, and Owen is always there for them.'

'He never leaves their bloody side,' Carrie grumbles. 'It's suffocating, that's what it is.'

'Everything that's gone wrong in this family is my fault.' My answer is prim but honest, but my young friend instantly tenses.

'What do you want your gravestone to say, Alex? "Here lies a doormat"? Fight for what you want, because no one is simply going to hand it over because you're a good girl who plays by the rules. If you're not doing something every day that you'd be proud to put on your gravestone, then you're not living right.'

Currently my gravestone definitely feels blank.

As we reach the end of the path, we pause at the top of the stairs down into Cullercoats Bay. I use the excuse of being breathless to not reply to Carrie's goading. Below us, a group of children are darting in and out of one of the caves below, laughing at the pigeons they scare out. Other families play on the curve of sand, which is wide at the moment because the tide is low. Dogs splash joyfully in a shallow lagoon created by two piers which stretch out from either side of the beach like arms trying to hug the sea to land.

'I had been thinking of asking for my ashes to be scattered somewhere hot, like the Cayman Islands,' Carrie says suddenly. 'But I think I want to stay here, where I've been happiest. I want friends, family and loved ones to get together and have a party. There should be laughter and fun when I'm sprinkled.'

'You might have to allow us the odd tear, too.'

Grief inflates my chest, making it hard to breathe. I sniff, clear my throat. I can't think about the world being without this bright, inspirational young woman. Instead, I stare down at the piers covered in multicoloured seaweed. Then I point to the far side of the bay, and the buildings above it.

'Fancy a drink at the Queen's Head?' Anything to change the subject.

❁

Freshly motivated, we quickly reach our destination. It's only 11.30 a.m., so the pub is almost empty, apart from two women leaning against the bar.

'Two pints is fine, but make your excuses after that. You hit six pints with her and you don't know which way she'll go. She can get nasty,' I overhear, as I order a couple of orange juices. The laughter of the two women is a hoot of joy in the cavernous room, softened only when it hits the pool table.

'Ooh, slot machine!' grins Carrie. She shoves in a couple of quid, but gets nothing in return apart from brilliant pulses and glows of light and crazy noises as she pushes buttons.

'Not my lucky day,' she says finally, sitting beside me at one of the small round tables. 'Hey, I better sit with my legs crossed or people will see my holy of holies!'

'You didn't mean what you said about not wanting the money, did you? We raised it for you.'

'Don't need money where I'm going.' A shadow of sadness flits across her face, a cloud covering the sun. Then she smiles and blasts the cloud away. It gives me the courage to try again.

'But I was thinking about setting up a website and putting stuff on social media to get more money coming in. Enough for you to go on the trip of a lifetime—'

'I don't want it. And I definitely don't want to go on social media.'

It's happening again. Carrie looks nervous, just like she did at the do the other night. I can't help feeling she's keeping something from me. I try to tell myself it's okay, because I'm hiding something from her, too. Something big. It's so awful that she'd never speak to me again if she knew, so bad that probably no one would ever speak to me again. Whatever she's hiding, it can't possibly be as bad as my own secret.

'What's your bugbear with social media, anyway?' I ask. 'Isn't everyone your age on everything these days?'

'I just don't see a reason to publicise my every move to the entire world. I'm a private person.'

'You just announced that you've got a hole in your jeans that virtually shows off your backside, and you're claiming to be private?'

'Well, maybe I'm old-fashioned, then. Taking pictures and sharing them all over Facebook or whatever isn't my style. Besides, there are some weird people out there, trolls and troublemakers.'

It makes me think of the envelope digging into my ribs. I haven't dared take off my jacket, in case it falls out. But Carrie's right, most younger people would head online if they wanted to play a prank on someone or bully them. They almost certainly wouldn't print off a picture and post it through a person's letterbox. It's too much effort for kids.

I remember the bemused looks on the boys' faces. Their whining protest of, 'It wasn't me'.

What if they were telling the truth?

The more I think about their reaction, the greater my horror grows that they weren't simply covering their tracks. They seemed genuinely at a loss.

Heat rises over my skin, emanating from the envelope. I need to know what's in it. Carrie is talking, and I nod, make noises of agreement, but I've no idea what she's on about. I have to be alone. I have to get a look at the contents.

'I need the loo.'

Jumping up, I bang my knee on the table and make our drinks jump.

'Is it your stomach again?' asks Carrie, but she's talking to my back.

# CHAPTER SIXTEEN

The walls of the cubicle are claustrophobically close and seem to breathe against me, sucking air from my lungs. I struggle to pull the envelope from my inner pocket in the confined space. It yanks free suddenly.

'Ow!' My elbow throbs where it hit the door. I cradle it, but only for a second, because the brown paper and glaring red lettering are calling me.

What's inside this time? Another photograph? Or something worse? No point putting the moment off any longer.

Counting slowly to twenty, I try to calm myself then flush the loo, just in case Carrie decides to come into the ladies' to check on me. The rushing water disguises the tearing open of the envelope, the rip of the picture being liberated from its paper prison.

Once again, the photo is fuzzy, as if taken from a distance. But there's no mistaking who it is: tousled hair, bright smile shining from tanned skin – it's Simon. It's impossible to make out where he is as the picture is cropped closely to his face.

I turn it over and see a message in the same red pen.

*There are no secrets from me*

My stomach lurches. I lean over the bowl gasping and spitting out the saliva that fills my mouth. The feeling passes as quickly as it comes, but I'm still light-headed as the implications of the image spin around my mind.

The boys wouldn't be behind this. Whoever it is must know about Simon and me and is warning Carrie. They think I'll betray her again, either with Simon or some other way. Once a cheat, always a cheat.

Carrie wouldn't be able to piece together what's happened just from this photograph, though. I don't understand why this person doesn't simply come out with the bald truth. There's nothing to gain from playing games.

Unless they don't want to help her. The perpetrator could be someone whose ultimate goal is to goad and hurt her with the truth, rather than warn her.

Either way, I'm too involved in what's going on to show Carrie this message. I've got to act to protect myself as much as her, so I'll get to the bottom of who is behind it and put them straight. Hopefully before Carrie discovers what a cow I've been.

It's all well and good declaring to myself that I'll track down the message-sender, but I've no idea how. What I need to do is come up with a plan – and in order to do that, I need some time alone to think. So after one orange juice, I make my excuses to my friend, pleading workload.

'Deadline is looming, and those beads aren't going to attach themselves. Plus, I'm kind of toying with the idea of adding some asymmetrical iridescent metallic fringing across the bodice and to the back of the dress.' To illustrate, I stand and motion diagonally from my waist across my body and over my shoulder.

'Woah! Sounds lush!' Carrie gasps. 'Your dresses are so colourful and sparkly. I'll never understand why you spend your whole time in boring black.'

'Flattering, easy black, which goes with anything.'

'Dull, unimaginative, depressing black. You want to get some brighter colours going on in your wardrobe – I'm telling you, it's impossible not to feel happier when you're wearing something vibrant. It's my fashion Prozac.'

With that, she zips up her yellow coat over her clashing lime-green jumper and we're on our way. She keeps going on about my clothes, though.

'Go on, borrow some of my things. We've got a similar build, similar colouring. We could be sisters.'

'I've got twenty years on you. I'd look ridiculous in half the stuff you wear.'

She pulls a despairing face. As we reach her house and I say goodbye, I ask her if she fancies coming to mine tonight.

'I'll cook a curry, and we can watch some more of your terrible choice in films,' I try to tease, to cover my desperation to get away. 'You might as well stay over, too.'

'Who could resist an offer like that? Six o'clock?'

'Perfect.'

She knows I don't like to eat late, it messes up my routine.

When I leave, the group of boys are over the other side of the main road, away from the cul-de-sac. They eye me warily as I walk over. The smile on my face doesn't seem to reassure them.

'Hey! How you doing? Look, I wanted to apologise for earlier. I completely got the wrong end of the stick and should never have blamed you guys for something you hadn't done. I'm so, so sorry. No hard feelings, eh?'

A wall of silence absorbs my apologies. I swing my arms, clap my hands together. Awkward.

'So, umm, actually, I wondered if you'd seen anyone hanging around here? Anyone a bit odd or out of place?'

'Yeah.' *Great!* 'You.'

'Ah, I probably deserve that. I shouldn't have had a go at you all. I really am sorry. I'll be honest, I'm worried about my friend. If you do see anyone suspicious, especially if it's anything to do with that house there, that I just came out of – the one with the red door, see? – I'd be really grateful if you'd let me know.'

Blank looks all round.

'Here, to show I'm not completely insane, have twenty quid for your trouble.'

The leader of the gang, the cheeky one who pretended to take my photo with his hands, snatches the crisp note from me so quickly the friction warms my fingertips. He doesn't speak, though. None of them does. They all continue to stare, giving nothing away. I've no idea if I'm getting through or not, but I can't blame them for not trusting the apologies of a woman who shouts at them one minute and bribes them the next. I feel terrible for tearing a strip off them, and even worse now for trying to ask a favour, but I've no choice.

'The money's yours either way, but could you do that for me, do you think? I promise I'm not mad.' The smile I give is genuine.

The one with the horrible skull balaclava leans on his handlebars and shrugs. 'Whatever.' Then the leader wheels away, and his little gang follow behind. They almost certainly won't be doing me any favours, but hopefully they've accepted my apology enough not to tell their parents about me.

Back at home, I feel better for knowing those kids might keep an eye on Carrie, but obviously I need a better solution than that – apart from anything else, they'll be back at school when half-term ends. Over the years I've discovered that my best ideas tend to sneak up on me when I'm relaxed and not actually thinking about the problem, so after I've checked and double-checked the locks, admonishing myself for the prickling unease I feel that someone is out to get me, I start to work.

First I pull out the notes from a meeting with a fifty-something woman I had the other night and look over the sketches. This will be her second wedding to the same man, and she wants a real showstopper. My background in costume design comes in handy, as people seem more and more inspired by shows such as *Strictly Come Dancing*, and want something classy but theatrical. One preliminary sketch was a real favourite, and I make annotations as my imagination fills in the blanks to bring it to life. Flock lace with a V-neck slashed to the waist for sex appeal, but a fan insert in velvet to keep it demure. Broad strips of contrasting haematite and crystal rhinestones which will catch the light beautifully for that first dance, while a panelled skirt will flare out during the turns.

Satisfied, I put it to one side. The rest of the day is spent peacefully creating swirling, glittering patterns reminiscent of the sway of the sea over the bodice of a prom dress. It's slow work, as each of the 8,000 beads must be hand-stitched in place, but it will be worth it in the end. This is probably my favourite part of dressmaking: there is real joy in seeing the details of a plan come together and putting those finishing touches to it that make it truly special. The absolute best bit, though? Seeing the expression on the client's face. There is always a nerve-racking moment of queasy anticipation that they might hate it, I'm studying their face… and then when it breaks into a smile, a wave of joy crashes over me. There's nothing like it.

Operation Protect Carrie is still without a plan when I finally put the outfit away. There's just time for me to sneak in a quick call to the kids before I start to cook. Feeling cowardly, I opt for Edward, and he answers almost immediately.

'I wanted to apologise for earlier,' I explain. 'You're right, I haven't explained myself at all, and you and your sister deserve to know the truth about everything. It's just going to take me a little while to work up to it, but I'll get there, I promise. I've no right to ask, but I'd be so grateful if you could give me a bit more time.'

'We've been patient this long, Mum, we can wait a little longer.'

*Mum. He called me Mum!*

'You sure?' I check.

'As long as it is a little, and not a lot.'

Fingers crossed, the grimace on my face at that dig doesn't show in my voice. 'Of course. It'll be soon. I'm psyching myself up for it.'

A soft chuckle. 'No matter what you tell us, we won't bite.' A pause. 'And don't worry about Elise, I'll talk to her. She'll soon calm down.'

'I hope so.' It's a fervent wish.

With a handful of 'I love you's, I say a reluctant goodbye and get chopping vegetables. I'm giving the curry a final stir when my phone rings.

'Hey, could I park on your drive, please? Your road is chock-a-block. I'd drive home and walk to yours, but I've got chemo tomorrow first thing, so… '

'No problem! Drive round the block, and by the time you get back I'll have moved my car into the garage.'

I do just that, reversing my Audi in, closing the garage door and running to the bottom of the driveway to open the gates so my friend's ancient Golf can get in. Then I sprint back inside, just in time to stop the rice from boiling over. Perfect timing!

When Carrie walks in she's brandishing a bottle of fizzy apple juice, as neither of us is a big drinker. Minutes later, she's tucking into the food and waxes lyrical about the curry, which is always her favourite meal of mine. Pleasure mingles with sadness that my own children aren't here to enjoy my home cooking, but I push away the impossible thought and focus, instead, on enjoying the company of the young woman I've come to think of as a surrogate daughter.

'I don't know how you do it. It's better than any takeaway, hands down,' she grins as she eats.

'It's easy to make – I'll have to teach you.'

The words make us both stall momentarily as realisation sinks in. Carrie won't have time to learn new skills and use them. She's so young, only twenty-four, and already her life is slipping away from beneath her like shifting sand.

❁

Morning is a flurry as we both have to be at our appointments early. I'm feeling brighter and more refreshed after a better night's sleep knowing someone else was in the house with me. It's also a relief to know that I don't need to worry about Carrie discovering any nasty presents today, because we've arranged to meet up for coffee after we're both done. My 'plan', such as it is, is to get to her place before her and check for anything untoward before she arrives. It's not much, but it's the best I've come up with so far.

I'm trying to chivvy Carrie out of the front door, but she's busy attempting to give me tips on how to chat up men, despite my protests that I'm not interested.

'… and I said, "if you think my name is pretty, wait until you hear my number". Smooth, eh?' She steps out of the door and falls silent. I almost bump into her.

'What's up?' My question is answered as I look over her shoulder. 'What the… ?'

Someone has smashed the windscreen of her car. The shattered glass sparkles over the seats as if someone has scattered a handful of diamonds. The tyres have been shredded, the rubber reduced to ribbons.

Carrie doesn't move. I push around her to get a better look. A glance at the cars parked along both sides of the street show they are all intact. Carrie's Volkswagen is the only one that's been vandalised.

Someone has deliberately chosen Carrie's car. This is personal. Someone's targeting her.

It has to be the person behind the sinister messages.

*I'm watching you*
*There are no secrets from me*

Who is doing this? Why would anyone pick on a dying woman?

Beside me, Carrie stands as still as a dressmaker's mannequin. Hands hanging loose at her sides, the only movement coming from the tears running down her face. Then she sinks to the floor, covering her face with her hands, whispering to herself. I can barely make out the words.

'I can't take any more. When will it be over?'

# CHAPTER SEVENTEEN

## THEN

I didn't have friends, so I created them. Unlike Jessica, who no longer spoke to me since her parents told her I made up stories, my imaginary friends were loyal and always there for me. There was a whole gang of us in my bedroom sometimes, and we'd talk about all the mean people at school. Who cares? We didn't need them anyway.

Sometimes I had imaginary parents, too. They were quite old, spent years trying and failing to have kids of their own, and then they adopted me. They called me their little miracle and showered me with love and presents. They were perfect.

'Sweetheart, how about a game of football with your old man, eh?' make-believe Dad asked. He liked to play with me in our huge garden, which didn't have empty beer cans sown across the overgrown lawn as if hoping they'd magically sprout more. The fence surrounding it didn't look like broken teeth; it was perfectly straight, no holes, and painted a pristine white.

'I'm not sure, Daddy, it's starting to get dark,' I reluctantly decided.

'How about a bedtime story instead?'

'That would be lovely!'

It would drown out the sounds of shouting that punched through the floor from below. I should have run downstairs and got between Mum and Dad. I should have protected Mum. I wanted to, but my own hurt held me in place, after last time, when she sided with Dad's lies about me, making out I was a telltale fibber to Mr and Mrs Norbury. All I'd wanted was to get rid of Dad so that he'd never hit her again, and she'd been too scared to back me up.

I'd learned an important lesson, though: I was the only person who would look out for me.

Now I put my hands over my ears so that I could hear make-believe Dad better.

'Tell me a happy story,' I begged. Sometimes I'd tell him I was too old for bedtime stories, but he always replied that nobody was ever too old for fairy tales.

A bang of something heavy being knocked over. A shriek. I pressed my hands tighter against my head and started rocking. My useless real parents were ruining my fantasy. Dad was in an even worse mood than usual at the moment because he'd split up with his other woman, Mum had told me this morning. She'd whispered the news to me before he got up, so that I knew to be extra careful. We needn't have worried, as the morning had actually been easier than usual, because he'd called Mum on his mobile, from upstairs, demanding that she bring him breakfast in bed.

Dad had had a whole day and evening to get worked up, though. It sounded as if he was taking it out on Mum. Although…

I took my hands away from my ears. Strained to hear.

What I made out was scarier than any screams.

It was silent as the grave. *Mum's grave?*

Heavy footsteps. The front door slammed so hard the house trembled. I didn't dare move, too scared of what I might find. Was that a groan? I stood. Took a step. Edged to the door. Darted down the stairs so fast I almost tripped.

Mum lay on the floor, the coffee table on top of her. Blood covered her face.

She was dead.

My muscles strained as I picked up the solid wooden coffee table and moved it off her body.

Her fingers twitched.

Her right arm flapped.

*Thank you, thank you, thank you!*

It took me a moment to work out that she was trying to sit up, but together we managed it.

'I'll call an ambulance,' I panted, once she was propped up against the sofa.

Her nose was strangely flattened, and blood gushed from it like a tap, turning her clothes sticky red.

'No, no. I'll be fine in a minute. No need for a fuss.'

A cough made her wince. One arm wrapped itself instinctively around her ribs.

'Please, Mum.'

'It looks worse than it is.'

That was one of her favourite phrases. I knew better than to argue. Instead I got a bowl of water and a cloth and started cleaning her up. It was something I was good at. A glass of water and some painkillers were swallowed down with a grateful nod from her.

Once I was sure that she wasn't going to die, I started to tidy up. The last thing we needed was Dad coming home and kicking off because the place was a mess, even if he was the one who had made it. Mum still sat on the floor, trying to get her strength back.

Something sliced my foot, making me gasp. The shattered remains of a glass tankard engraved with the words 'World's Best Mum'. I'd bought it a couple of years before, while at a school outing to York to see the Jorvik Centre and learn about olden days when there were Vikings. Mum had had to save up the money sneakily to afford the trip – if Dad had found the money, he'd have drunk it away. I'd been so grateful to her. Not now. It seemed right the words were shattered, because she didn't deserve the title. I chucked them in the bin and covered them over with newspaper.

Finally, the room appeared as though nothing had happened. Mum was a different matter. She still looked like a puppet with the strings cut.

'Run and get a roll of bandage, the wide kind, from the first aid box, there's a good girl.' She winced.

Minutes later, Mum's head was resting heavily on my shoulder as I took her weight and wrapped the bandage round and round her tender ribs.

'What happened this time, Mum?' I asked.

'He wanted a foot rub to cheer him up. Then he complained my hands were like sandpaper.' Her eyes were fixed on some distant point past my ear as she spoke. 'Sometimes when he hits me I think, "Come on, carry on, kill me, because I can't take any more".'

'Don't say that, Mum!'

Her gaze snapped back into focus. Wiping at her face, she gave a shivering laugh.

'Ignore me. Sometimes adults do and say things they don't mean.'

Sometimes they lied, cheated, hurt – and apparently that was okay.

# CHAPTER EIGHTEEN

## NOW

She keeps insisting she's fine, but Carrie's still shaking as she sits on my sofa, sipping a hot cup of tea. The happy-go-lucky young woman I know seems to have disappeared since seeing her vandalised vehicle. She's hunched over, pulling at her hat – she must be thinking of when she had hair long enough to hide behind.

For a moment, hearing her asking 'when will it end', I'd wondered if she knew who was behind the stalking – there's really no other word for it now. Momentarily, I'd considered telling her everything that's been going on, but changed my mind fast as a whip crack. Of course, Carrie must have meant the constant attrition of problem after problem for her: breast cancer, breaking up with her boyfriend, a terminal diagnosis and now her car smashed up. When will it end, indeed. She has enough to deal with already; it's better for her health if she believes this is a random act of violence.

Safe in the knowledge I've done the right thing, and will continue to shield her, I've still got the problem of how to turn detective and discover who's behind this disgusting campaign.

*Hold on a minute...*

A thought occurs that sends ice dousing through my body. The mystery messenger may not have realised this was Carrie's car. There's every chance they thought they were attacking my vehicle; after all, it was parked on my driveway and my own car was hidden in the garage.

*This could be revenge for the hurt I've inflicted on my friend.*

The photograph of Carrie and me, the picture of Simon and now this vandalism outside my house – Carrie and I are both at the epicentre of this. I can't walk away even if I want to.

When I get hold of the person who's done this, I'll throw myself on their mercy to make them stop. Even if my secret has to come out to end this misery, so be it; my only priority is Carrie.

I wish they were in this room right now, to see what they've reduced her to. I've never heard her sound defeated before, but her words earlier scared me: *I can't take any more*. She'd sounded as if she were giving up, wishing for death to take her.

My hands feel cool against her warm skin as I lay a palm on her forehead.

'How are you feeling? Should I call the doctor?'

'I'm fine now.' Her head shakes firmly, but her hands are trembling enough to show her lie.

'Okay, well, in that case, I'll call the police.'

Fingers close on my forearm. 'No, it's horrible, but it's not worth bothering them with.'

'But they'll give you an incident number so you can claim on your insurance for new tyres and a windscreen. Otherwise the cost is really going to add up.'

'Um, okay, don't have a go, but... ' She takes a sip, stalling. The hot liquid seems to make the words flow easier. 'I don't have insurance. Don't pull that face! I can't afford it, and it's not like I'm going to be around much longer anyway, so I thought I'd spend the money on food and heating instead of handing it over to a big company.'

'You can't drive around uninsured!'

'I can't drive around full stop. Not now.'

'Here's an idea – use some of the bucket list money to get the car fixed and cover anything else you need to get mobile again.'

'Alex, I've told you, that money should be donated to a cancer charity. I don't want it.'

'You're so stubborn!'

Another sip to steady herself, the tea's surface rippling at her tremble. 'That's what's got me this far in life, against all the odds. Oh, heck! Look at the time, I've got to get going or I'll be late.' Liquid slops everywhere as she jumps up.

'I'll give you a lift, it's faster than you catching the Metro.'

She sags with relief, but double-checks that I'm definitely okay with it.

'No arguments,' I say. 'The Freeman Hospital's a fifteen-minute walk from the Metro station; I don't want you doing that when you're feeling weak.'

'I'll be fine – I don't want to put you out.'

'You're not,' I say, in a voice that brooks no more argument.

❖

Between the two of us, we somehow manage to push her car onto the street, where parking is freed up now that people have left for work. Then we both get into my car and twenty-five minutes later I drop her off at the Freeman Hospital.

'Sure you don't want me to come in with you?'

'Don't be daft, you're due at the clinic any minute.'

'Yes, but they'll understand if I miss a day. It's only a weigh-in and a bit of talking, not life and death.' Actually, they'll give me merry hell, but she doesn't need to know that.

'Tell you what, let's meet for a coffee afterwards. I—' She hangs her head as she speaks. 'I don't fancy being alone today. Though if you're busy, don't worry about it – I'm being silly.'

'Coffee sounds great. I'll pick you up here when you're done.'

Have my weigh-in and therapy session; zoom to Carrie's house and check it out; drive back to the hospital – it's going to be an exhausting morning. I'm twenty minutes late when I reach the clinic, which kick-starts a lecture on how I must take my treatment seriously. I take it meekly, knowing it's deserved, but also knowing that sometimes life isn't about putting yourself first, it's about prioritising other things.

Rosie seems keen to pick up where we've left off, and much as I'd love to refuse, I'm really not in combative mood. My energy must be saved for the battle ahead with the mystery messenger.

'Have you taken a step back from Carrie, as we discussed in the last session?' she asks.

At the shake of my head a small sigh of impatience escapes her lips, apparently keen to flee the room's tension. I wish I could join it. Instead, I gaze resolutely at a stain on Rosie's desk, trying to work out what it is. It's dark brown and seems to be flaking at the edges.

'You need to concentrate on your own well-being, or I'm concerned you'll start to slide back.'

'I'm eating fine, though. I eat better when I'm with someone, so spending time with Carrie is positive for me.'

'Really? Today's weigh-in shows you've dropped a pound since Wednesday – and on Wednesday you'd only maintained your weight, rather than gaining. You've got to stick with the programme, Alex, and not let up. How are you going to tackle this?'

'I'm – I don't – I mean, a pound's nothing. It's no big deal, you don't have to keep going on about it.'

Rosie's slopped coffee onto her desk at some point before I came in. I stare at the brown meniscus clinging to the bottom of the mug and the fake wooden desktop. Put two and two together and realise the other stain I'd been staring at is very old milky coffee.

'You mentioned before that you were concerned for Carrie. Is that still the case?'

My nod is minuscule. Hiding won't do me any good, though, so I update Rosie on what's been happening, as well as my thoughts and fears on the subject. I know I have to be honest about this;

after all, she's my counsellor. Today, though, it doesn't seem to be enough for her.

'Alex, we need to address the underlying causes of your illness. I really think it's time to push through.'

'I have issues with food. End of story.'

'Yes, but why? You've said before that you don't eat because you don't feel you deserve food.'

'You know why. We don't need to "explore" this.' I make sarcastic rabbit ear motions as I say the words.

'We can't ignore this any more.'

I don't reply. This is something I refuse to speak about, and Rosie knows it. She's always respected that and kept her distance from the subject, but recently she's started challenging me, and I don't like it one bit.

The low murmur of voices outside leaks into the dead atmosphere of our room. I clear my throat. Rub my hands on my thighs, just to make a swishing sound to cut through the air. The silence is getting to me.

'Give me something,' Rosie urges.

Silence.

'Tell me why you don't believe you deserve the food. Tell me why you're punishing yourself. Tell me about your children.'

I stand, fists balled. 'Don't talk about my children.'

'Please sit down, Alex. I understand this is a difficult subject, and revisiting your loss must be terrible, but you need to do it at some point. Let me help you.'

Can't breathe. Head dizzy. Ends of fingers tingling. 'Don't. Don't do this.'

'Just tell me one thing.'

She won't give up. She won't leave me alone – so I throw her the easiest thing I can think of that's related to what she wants.

'If I eat, I've lost control. The starving can physically hurt but it helps because it stops me thinking properly. It means I don't feel the emotional pain. I'm numb thanks to being so hungry, my brain in a fog that can't dwell on everything I've lost because it's too preoccupied with food. Food I don't deserve.'

It's not enough. I can see it on her face. 'It's time to accept, Alex.'

*Don't say it. Please don't.*

Though low, her voice slices through the leaden lull of the consulting room. It severs the careful construction of my alternative reality. Cleaves truth from lie. All I can do is watch, helpless, as the inevitable is spoken out loud.

*Please.*

'It's time to accept the fact your husband and children are dead.'

# CHAPTER NINETEEN

A vacuum has formed in the room, sucking air from my lungs, thoughts from my head, lies from my lips. This is the truth I spend my life running from.

'I do accept. I also choose not to speak about it—'

'You're in denial, in my opinion. Let's talk about your insistence on going to group therapy as well as coming here.'

A guilty groan slinks from my lips. 'Okay, I know you're right, and I shouldn't, but—'

'It's not attending it that's the problem, Alex, it's the fact that you're lying to everyone there by pretending your family is alive and well.'

Bile is rising up my throat, burning my oesophagus. Finally, words follow.

'I just... There, I can talk about the twins and actually feel the pride a mother feels in her children. It's like I get a taste of the life I've missed out on. Everyone at the group accepts that I'm a mother, even if, as far as they're concerned, the twins no longer talk to me – and hey, that's not really a lie, is it, because they don't talk to me... because they can't.'

*Of course it's a lie*, her look replies.

'I get to share how much I miss Elise and Edward,' I continue, voice edged with desperation. 'How it's my fault they aren't in my life any more, and that I feel I need to make restitution. But I also get to be a mum.'

'It isn't a true version of events, though. If you really want the group to support you, you should be honest.'

She's right, but it's an addiction I'm unable to give up right now. 'Well, I don't want the looks the truth will lead to. All the comments and questions and… '

*And judgements*, I add silently. I'm responsible for their deaths, and Owen's, too. I wiped out my whole family.

*I'm sorry, I'm so, so sorry. Please forgive me.*

Guilt is the reason why I developed anorexia. I tell people it's empty nest syndrome because it's the closest to the truth I can bear to get – after all, the children and my husband are gone, so it's technically correct. In a way.

I'd been facing my first Christmas since their loss and, with magazines full of diets to get ready for party season, I'd decided to drop some weight. Now I know it was just a stupid excuse I gave myself, a little white lie to get my punishment started, because I'd no intention of going out anywhere – I'd been in no fit state emotionally for that.

I'd got a thrill out of skipping those first meals, though. I was good at it. This wasn't about trying to get people to compliment my new slimline figure, it went deeper than that. Skipping meals meant I was punishing myself for all the bad choices I'd ever made. I didn't deserve that treat, I didn't deserve that meal, and being able to make that decision gave me a feeling of control over my out-of-control life.

By Christmas I was addicted, the restriction something I couldn't let go of now I'd learned the trick. I stopped seeing friends, annoyed by them constantly pressuring me to eat. Besides, having no social life made it easier to control my food intake.

In the new year I moved away from old friends and memories, to make a fresh start in Tynemouth. While telling the removal men which room I wanted some boxes to go in, I had a funny turn, my heart fluttering, and one of the men called a doctor. The GP said it was palpitations, most likely due to my extremely low weight, and referred me to the eating disorder clinic.

That first time, I felt so confident going there because I didn't really think there was a problem. I thought it would just get people off my back. It was a shock when the team at the clinic said I needed to continue attending, but I figured they were being overly cautious. It was their job to be. When I looked around, I saw people who were so much thinner than me. I was far too big to be there. I felt, wrongly, that people were looking at me and thinking: *Fraud. She's too fat to be here.*

Too old, too. Aside from one other woman going through the mother of all divorces, I was the only person over twenty-five.

It was decided I needed to be monitored and weighed twice a week. It was so over the top, I thought. Still, my weight continued to drop until, after a long chat with my case worker, I agreed to admit myself voluntarily.

Talk about a shock to the system. It was like joining the army: every meal planned out and timed, plus three snacks a day. Three! My heart sank, then shot back up with anger. I wasn't a child that needed everything done for me. This was patronising, unnecessary, utterly ridiculous. I forced myself to put on weight – even during the first anniversary of my losses, when all I wanted to do was curl up in a ball and die. As Christmas approached once more, I was finally signed off.

Left to my own devices, I was free to punish myself again. I wanted to die, no doubt about it, but simply slashing my wrists would be too easy – something slow and painful was required; a punishment to fit the crime. Twisted logic answered my anorexia's siren call.

By February, my weight had crashed once more. I had to crawl up the stairs. I couldn't walk further than a few steps. At the end of that month I lost my sight, then my hearing, due to malnutrition, and started to hallucinate. Doctors warned me that I was at the point of death and my heart would give out any moment. They insisted I return to the clinic. When I refused, I was sectioned.

Imprisoned, I had no control over my life, was told when to get up, what to do, when to eat. The toilets were locked until half an hour after I'd eaten, to make sure I didn't vomit up my meals, and someone often accompanied me to the loo.

Slowly, so painfully slowly, my weight increased, monitored with twice-weekly weigh-ins. I thought I was better. So did the clinic, and they let me become an outpatient. But anorexia, much like grief and guilt, hates to let go once it has its claws embedded in someone's body.

On my relapse, I was terrified, remembering the feeling of being unable to move. So I started to walk a lot to prove I could. Then I realised it was burning calories, so I walked more. People began to comment on it, and after being sectioned for a second time, I was banned from long walks.

What I needed was something I could do without people realising – star jumps in my room were my solution. Every single day I did two thousand, to my secret pride and shame.

That third stay in the clinic was my lowest ebb. People tell me I almost died. For a long time I'd roll my eyes and think they were being melodramatic. Even when in hospital, I begged to be allowed to leave. I thought I looked fine. Frustrated at the walking ban, and too closely monitored even to get away with star jumps, I started to stand all the time instead. It burns more calories than sitting. But the clinic noticed that, too.

Being confronted didn't help. Instead, I was furious at the tone, as though I'd done something wrong, when in my head there was nothing unhealthy in my activities. Even when I knew it was a problem, there was still an unnameable fear that stalked me. Something stopped me from wanting to put on weight, to get better again.

Why? Why was I lying to myself about wanting to get better?

I'm a perfectionist. I've always tried so hard to get things right. I wanted to be the perfect wife, perfect mother, and failed at both.

But I'm brilliant at starving my body and punishing myself for my mistakes. Anorexia is a form of self-flagellation, for me.

It's been a long, hard slog to get myself to stop. I'm finally eating again and am in control of my life. I understand Rosie's concerned that the group isn't helping, but I'll give it up soon. I need to cling on for a tiny bit longer while I continue to build my strength and make restitution for the way I've hurt people. One day I'll share everything with them, right down to what happened to Elise, Edward and Owen, and everything I did wrong that resulted in their deaths over four years ago. One day.

# CHAPTER TWENTY

When I get out of the clinic, my steps slow as I walk towards my car. The last people I need to see right now are waiting for me, leaning on the car. I suppose I shouldn't really be surprised.

'Mum. We need to talk,' says Elise.

I should clarify here. I don't actually see the kids. I'm not mad, or hallucinating, and I fully realise the difference between reality and my lies. I just imagine them as chubby-cheeked toddlers, or cheeky ten-year-olds, or babes in arms. Most often they're teenagers, and pretending they're speaking to me is a huge comfort. Because I miss them. Because I'm lonely. Because they should be here with me.

But I know they're not.

So now, I'm imagining the disapproval my children would feel if they were alive here and now. They'd give me a stern talking-to, no doubt. I get in the car with a sigh and start the engine before I speak.

'I know, I know. You agree with Rosie,' I say aloud. There's no one in the car park to see me talking to myself, and I feel less lonely when I do. I drive away, still speaking.

'There's no time for prevaricating. Before I pick Carrie up, I've got to nip to her place and check it out for any more messages. I can intercept them before bringing her home. You think I'm getting too wrapped up in her and should concentrate on my health. But it's thanks to her that I haven't had a relapse, not one since meeting her. Finally, I've got someone to look after and mother again.

'Besides, let's say I do stop seeing her. Then what? There's no saying that the messages targeting us both would stop.'

Another sigh as I imagine Elise arguing back. In my mind, she's always been the feisty one who tells it like it is and uses tough love. She's always dressed boho, but since I met Carrie her clothes have been brighter, and she wears a lot of jewellery identical to my friend's. Sometimes I feel guilty that in my mind's eye my daughter is morphing into my friend. Edward has inherited not just his father's kind eyes but the same humour that made me laugh at myself when I was being an idiot. He doesn't have his father's quick temper, though.

'Okay, I admit, I'm a little worried for my own sanity,' I add. 'The pressure of keeping quiet is already making me skip meals, but I've got to honour my vow to be there for her and do everything possible to help her. You know what I did to her, you know I owe her.'

'You didn't know Simon was with someone else, let alone a woman with cancer,' says Elise, taking on the voice of my head, while my heart argues back.

'My guilt aside, I can't leave a dying woman to be persecuted by some weirdo. I'm sorry, but that's my final word on the matter. I do promise I'll look after myself better, though.'

The children melt away as I pull up outside Carrie's house. Pulling the spare key from my purse, I let myself in.

Oh, crap.

❖

Heart racing, pulse stamping in my neck, I hunch over the steering wheel. Houses blur by. The car dodges through traffic lights as amber turns red, speeds over a roundabout and flies over a speed bump at a tooth-rattling pace. I'm racing against the clock to get to the Freeman Hospital, where Carrie will be waiting for me.

All the time I'm driving, I keep glancing at the glove compartment as if I can see its contents still. That's where I shoved the latest message sent to Carrie, but out of sight is not out of mind.

The photograph of a woman I don't recognise. The message scrawled across the back.

*Losing patience. Give me what I want, or me telling everyone what you've done will be the least of your worries.*

Abrupt. Terse. The impatience obvious. I shiver and turn up the heat in the car. Once again, I wrestle with whether or not to tell Carrie what's happening, but I've covered up so much now that it feels too late to turn back. This is becoming more serious, though, the person seeming to take their anger out on both Carrie and me.

Who is behind this? And why? It can't only be about me sleeping with Simon and threatening to tell Carrie. There's clearly more going on, but I can't figure out what.

A car beeps as I switch lanes at the last minute. Swear words spill from my lips, and I grip the steering wheel a little tighter, but my mind doesn't stop tumbling through the clues so far.

Carrie's top, along with a picture of the two of us coming out of the support group.

*I'm watching you.*

The photo of Simon, my lover and Carrie's boyfriend.

*There are no secrets from me.*

Now this. I wonder who the woman is and how she's linked to us. Thinking of her face again, no memories are stirred.

Smudge is still missing, too. Has his disappearance got something to do with this?

No matter which way I turn, there seems to be nothing but blind alleys for me to explore. I'm at an impasse.

Carrie is waiting near the multistorey car park. I slow and wave before entering the building and finding a free space. As I reverse in, I have a thought. *Could it be someone from the support group who's targeting us?*

They know us well; perhaps they've taken my betrayal of Carrie as duplicity against the whole group. These messages definitely feel personal as well as angry. Any right-thinking person would be annoyed with me for breaking the heart of a dying woman – I stole the love of her life, all for the sake of a quick fling to boost my flagging ego.

Jackie seems to have had a slight edge the last few times we've seen her, but nothing to write home about. I go through each member, suspecting, examining, casting aside, even as my enthusiasm for the idea wanes because it makes absolutely no sense: if someone were angry with me for hurting Carrie, they wouldn't be sending her the messages.

The only consolation in all of this is that she hasn't a clue what's happening. She's leaning against the wall beside the hospital entrance, her head lolling back as if trying to catch the sun's winter rays, though none peek through the slab of slate clouds that have rapidly gathered. The position exposes her neck, where black dots can be clearly seen on it, and the skin is red and sore-looking. She catches me staring and pulls her scarf up higher, to cover the area.

'Burns from the radiotherapy,' she mutters.

'I thought it was chemo today. Are they still giving you radio, too?'

'Palliative radiotherapy, to try to buy me a couple of extra months. Don't know why they're bothering with any of it, they're fighting a losing battle. Honestly, I'm thinking of jacking it all in – the treatments make me feel like crap, and we all know the outcome will be the same.'

'Come on, don't—'

'Eurgh, you know what, it's bad enough having all this stuff without talking about it. Let's change the subject – how did you do today at the clinic?'

My laugh is uncomfortable. 'Nice weather we're having.'

'Wow, that bad, eh? Okay, so that's your illness and mine off the table. Let's decide where we're going for coffee, instead.'

We link arms as we walk and chat. The fear of death is getting to her. The calm acceptance has been replaced by twitchy fear. I can almost smell it pouring from her. If there was a way for us to swap places, I'd do it gladly.

After losing Elise and Edward I'd felt a painful emptiness at first. But then something worse had happened: all the love that should have been poured into them had nowhere to go. It filled me up until I felt like an overinflated balloon ready to pop with a bang. Starvation helped fog my brain enough to numb it, but it was always there, an endless, painful love with nowhere to go.

Nowhere until I found Carrie, a person who, despite appearing so fun-loving and confident, seems to soak up love like a sponge. We suit each other perfectly.

She pulls me out of my thoughts now by stopping suddenly. A man is sitting on the pavement, a small plastic tray in front of him to collect money from passers-by.

'Sorry it's not much. Take care of yourself,' she says as she bends down and hands over a couple of quid. She receives a grateful nod.

Feeling bad for almost sweeping by without noticing, I do the same. He's only in his late teens or early twenties, but the eyes that flick up to meet mine in gratitude are dark-circled and world weary.

Two minutes later Carrie and I settle in a cosy café, just as it's starting to spot with rain outside. A chatty waitress takes our order, and we laugh when she mistakes us for mother and daughter. That happens a lot – we do have similar features and build.

'Doesn't the treatment make you feel sick?' I ask, watching Carrie enthusiastically putting away her chicken salad.

'I've a few hours before it hits. Around 7 p.m. tonight, I'll be as limp as a dead tulip.'

'Want me to come round, then? Keep an eye on you?'

'I'll be fine. I'm getting my strength up now, eating this.'

'Well, it's my treat.' I grab my purse, won't take no for an answer. 'I feel responsible for what happened to your car.'

'You shouldn't.'

She's hiding something from me. Her annoyance. I understand Carrie's urge to mask everything, despite the frustration of being on the receiving end of it. I've hidden my whole life, apologising. Still, I can't help wishing she'd let rip with her anger, rather than squirrelling it away. She does blame me for the car; she must do, because it happened on my driveway. The only good thing now is that giving her lifts means I've got an excuse to spend more time with her and keep a close eye out for whoever is doing this.

Next time they come for her, they'll have to get through me first.

At the thought, the desire to keep her close flips on its head. Of course! There's a way to keep everyone happy, apart from this troublemaker. Although it requires sacrifice on my part.

# CHAPTER TWENTY-ONE

The world has turned upside down for me, the solution so obvious it's amazing I didn't see it before. All this time I've been selfishly trying to keep my friend with me, but the best thing for her is to send her away. If I can get Carrie to move back in with her parents, then I'll know she's well looked after and safe from our tormentor. Rosie will be pleased, too; she'll say it will free me to concentrate on myself.

There's no time like the present to put the plan into action, so I lean on the wooden café table and am about to speak when someone beside me flaps open their umbrella. I glare. Don't they know it's bad luck to do that inside? Shaking off the bad omen, I try again.

'You mentioned the other day that you're going to live with your parents. Is that happening soon?'

Carrie stops chewing her chicken salad and puts her head on one side. 'Keen to get rid of me?'

'Not at all… but I can't help thinking it might be for the best if you go sooner rather than later.'

'I'll have to leave fairly pronto, I suppose, but,' she toys with a rocket leaf, thinking, then stabs it decisively with her fork, 'I can probably risk staying a bit longer. Maybe another month or so.'

'You think that's wise?'

'Wow, you really are keen.'

'You're like a daughter to me – and no, don't protest that I'm not old enough, because I am. That's the thing, Carrie, I keep thinking about your parents and, well, you should all spend as much time together as possible, don't you think?'

She looks at her plate. Wipes at her eyes before nodding. 'People dying should be with the people they love, you're right. But I love Tynemouth so much, there's something really special about it that's made me feel at home right away. I'm going to make the most of it while I can, because I'll really miss it when I'm gone.

'And I'll tell you something else. I'm going to miss you like mad. You're right, you've made me feel cherished, like part of your family, and you'll never understand what that means to me.'

Much as I try, no words will come. My heart's full to bursting with all the love I've longed to give a child, but now it has somewhere to go. It flows straight towards that young woman. Trying to stop it is like trying to stop loving Elise and Edward.

But she isn't Little Orphan Annie, and I'm no Daddy Warbucks. There will be no happy adoption ending for us.

She doesn't speak again until she's cleared her plate. Instead I chat about how much fun she'll have with her actual parents. Nuggets of information she's given me about her idyllic childhood are dredged up. Building sandcastles together, playing games, she even had a treehouse. When she got older, her mum was on hand and her dad always kept a firm but fair eye on boyfriends, ready in case they stepped out of line. And apparently she and her mum love shopping together. It's all the sort of thing I should have done with my own children, if only… I shut the thought down and force myself to smile.

'Maybe you'll get the chance to revisit some of your favourite childhood haunts, recreate some holiday memories together. Didn't you say your parents wanted to throw you an early Christmas? That'll be fun!'

'It's going to be amazing,' she says, but her eyes are reddening, sparkling with tears. She clears her throat. 'Excuse me, need the loo.'

Head down, she scurries away, leaving me to stare after her. What an idiot I am for upsetting her.

Feeling guilty, I decide to go after her rather than wait. Gather up our things and struggle into the loos. The toilet flushes, but not fast enough to cover the sound of vomiting.

'Carrie, are you okay? Is it your treatment kicking in? Let me get you home.'

'Erm, okay, that sounds good.'

The lock audibly snicks across, door swinging open to reveal my friend's pale face. In the minutes since last seeing her, the colour has disappeared from her cheeks, her eyes are red and there are shadows under her eyes. Rushing to the basin, she runs the tap and splashes water on her face, rinses out her mouth repeatedly, making little gasping noises.

When she's done, I put her coat over her shoulders and rub her back.

'I knew I shouldn't have taken that extra biscuit the tea lady sneaked onto the ward for me.' Her smile is weak, but her eyes beg me to laugh. I do my best but I can't help adding a sigh.

'You're such a good person. You don't deserve this.'

'Eurgh, I hate all this talk of good and bad guys, when actually everyone has a bit of both. Really, there are only survivors and the beaten. If I had the chance to save my own life, knowing it would cost someone else's, would I take it? Okay, probably not. But if someone else were mildly maimed in order for me to survive, say, lost a leg, would I allow that to happen? Honestly? Maybe. Yeah, maybe.'

When I still say nothing, she scoffs. 'You're telling me you wouldn't be willing to see someone hurt to save yourself? Or, okay, if not yourself, someone you love?'

With an attempt at a laugh, I take my hands off her back and slide them inside my pockets to hide their shaking. She's no idea how close she is to the truth.

'Are you strong enough to get to the car?' I check. 'If you're not, I can go and get it, it's no trouble.'

'I do feel a bit wobbly.' She nods, hanging onto the edge of the basin for a second.

'Stay here. I'll speak to the manager, get a seat for you at the window so you can see me when I get back. Oh, and you're staying at mine tonight.'

'No, I don't want to take advantage.'

'Then I'm happy to stay at yours instead. Come on, even before this you said you didn't want to be on your own after the car business, and now your nausea has kicked in early. If you really want to be alone, I won't be offended, but if you don't… well, don't feel guilty, that's all I'm saying. Because I'll let you into a secret: I don't much fancy being alone, either.'

A smile hangs on her face. 'In that case… !'

❖

We head back to Carrie's, so that she can pick up a change of clothes for tomorrow. As we get closer, my tension builds. Jaw tight, hands gripping the steering wheel. If there is another message, I need to get to it first.

When we pull up outside, I offer to run in for her, but she won't hear of it.

'I want to see if Smudge is home.'

'Well, let me open the door for you.' I dodge in front of her and race up the path, probably looking like a lunatic. My skin is prickling with apprehension as I turn the key in the lock. The door swings open…

The doormat is empty.

Carrie walks past me and heads for the kitchen, oblivious to my relief. The food she left out for Smudge is untouched.

'He'll come back.' I squeeze her shoulder, trying to soothe her, but I can feel the tension even through her jumper. She pulls fretfully at her hat.

'Tomorrow I'm going to put up posters.'

'I'll help. You've got to slow down—'

'Honestly, I think about him out there alone and my stomach churns.'

'He'll be enjoying a little holiday with someone, you just watch.'

Even as I say the words, my own stomach flips. Getting rid of Carrie to her parents' home is definitely the best thing to do. She needs to get away from this nutter.

'While you get some overnight stuff, I'll have a look for Smudge,' I offer.

Despite her delicate frame, Carrie's steps are heavy as she goes upstairs. The moment she's out of sight, I start searching – not for her cat but her address book. I looked before, when I was organising the party, but now there's a new urgency. If Carrie doesn't want to go to her parents yet, then I'll willingly risk a spot of busybody interfering for the greater good. I'll contact them, tell them to come over, because despite the brave face she's got plastered in place, their daughter needs them. They might not welcome me sticking my nose in, and Carrie might be annoyed, too, but I don't care because they'd all thank me if they knew the truth.

The only flaw in the plan is that I can't find an address book. Drawers are quietly opened, items moved around, shelves searched; I even peer under the sofa in case it's fallen there. No luck. There's not much to look around in, and once again I'm struck by how little Carrie owns. The furniture came with the maisonette; none of it is hers. It's strange, because her parents sound like they're reasonably well off, with her father a head teacher and her mother a solicitor. I know Carrie's only work is as a cleaner, along with some shifts behind a bar at weekends that now seem to have dropped away to nothing, so she's barely making ends meet, but I'm surprised her parents don't help out a bit more.

Perhaps they don't realise how broke she is, and that the poor girl is wearing jeans that are more hole than material. It would be typical of Carrie to put a brave face on it.

A thought strikes. Her solicitor mum is in a perfect position to know how to tackle the troublemaking messenger. I should talk to her. The thought urges me on, the search becoming even more determined.

Eventually I stand in the middle of the living room, hands on hips, slightly out of breath. Perhaps it's old-fashioned to have an address book, and no one younger than me has one. How on earth am I going to contact Carrie's parents, then? She's not on social media, so it's not as though I can make friends with them that way.

There's only one option, then. Somehow, I'm going to have to get hold of her phone.

I'll do it tonight.

# CHAPTER TWENTY-TWO

I shift awkwardly, crossing my arms. Uncross them. Rest my hands on my lap. They feel strange. What would I normally do with them?

I've spent the whole evening like this, posing, like a poor impersonator pretending to be me. Conversation has been just as stilted. With every subject Carrie and I cover, I try to steer it round to her parents, and when it arrives there I panic and think it sounds obvious what I'm attempting to do – so then change the subject away from it. Knowing her wrecked car is outside doesn't help. Its presence accuses me of failure, and there's no argument I can give to the contrary.

Someone is after her, or me, or us both. The thought sends me to the doors again, surreptitiously checking they're locked. Turning the key as far as it will go. Definitely locked. Another push against the key. It won't go any further.

It's locked. But I still don't feel secure.

My stomach is heavy as a rock, and I only eat because I have to make something for my friend, who also seems quieter than usual. The chemo or radiotherapy or whatever seems to have taken a toll today.

But now, at last, I have a real opportunity. Carrie has just nipped to the loo and left her mobile phone on the side of the sofa. It seems to fill my vision, my heart rate rising along with my fear.

What I'm about to do isn't right; I can't spy on a friend. Guilt is like a shattered mirror, reflecting my own pain back at me. Showing me that I must do this.

Hardening my heart, I lunge forward – just as Carrie walks back into the room. Yanking my hand back, I make a big show of scratching my head, horribly aware that I'm a bad actress.

'Can I get you a drink?' I say, then scurry from the room, feeling hot and stupid. I come back, brandishing two cups of lemon and ginger tea as though they're prizes.

'If you don't mind me saying, it seems like it was a rough day at the clinic. I wish you'd talk to me about it,' says Carrie.

With everything she's going through, she still notices I'm not myself.

'Everything's fine, I'm just not gaining weight as quickly as they'd hoped. But it's all good.'

'You've barely eaten tonight.' She points to my plate. 'You only gave yourself a child's serving, and you left half of it. Do you still have that stomach bug from yesterday?'

My forehead crinkles, until realisation dawns. She's thinking of me hiding in the toilets when the second message arrived. Yesterday seems like a lifetime ago.

'Yeah, it's still not right.' Fingers lace over my stomach to reinforce the words.

'You need to look after yourself. And, well, I know you don't want to hear it, but you should join a dating site,' Carrie announces.

'Where did that come from? No way. It's not very me.'

'Falling in love and living happily ever after isn't very you? Don't be daft. A nice fella would look after you, make you eat more. I want to see you settled and sorted before I shuffle off this mortal coil.'

'You know I hate you talking like that.'

'Don't change the subject—'

'I'm not, I just, well, I'm not interested in being with anyone right now.' Not after the repercussions of last time's disastrous foray. 'Maybe I'm meant to be alone.'

'Don't give me that. "Meant to be" is something smug people hide behind when life works out well for them and they get exactly what they want. It's right up there with "everything happens for a reason". What a load of bull!

'What about people who live and die in war zones? What's "meant to be" about that? Or a baby that dies in the womb before it's even had a chance to take a breath?

'If you want something, don't sit and wait for fate to step in and make it happen for you – get out there and grab it. And if you do sit on your backside twiddling your thumbs, don't blame anything or anyone but yourself for your failure. Don't hide behind "meant to be". You've got an incredible life, Alex, so make the most of it.'

The speech has made her breathless. She glares at me, panting, knowing that I have choices and opportunities she'll never have herself.

'You're right,' I nod, chastened. 'I'm sorry for being so negative. I whinge in group meetings about having no husband, children who don't speak to me, no friends or social life, being in a body owned by anorexia. But they're because of decisions I've made. It's slow, but I'm starting to become myself again, and once I am, then I can work out what I want – and make sure it happens.'

Carrie smiles. Reaches out and gently forces my hand away from my mouth, where it had flown as soon as I stopped speaking.

'First things first: you could try not gnawing on your nails constantly.' Eyes flick up – ping – she's got an idea. 'You got any nail varnish? I'll give you a manicure.'

For the rest of the evening, we gossip while Carrie tries to transform my chewed stumps into something pretty. Even painted, they look dreadful. She sits back, appraising.

'Hmm, maybe we could get you some false nails instead.'

'That's so not me.'

'That's the point.' There's no arguing with that grin, so I give in. It might be nice to pretend to be someone else for a while.

The stress of the last few days is making me exhausted, though. I spend the rest of the evening fighting heavy lids and the desire to go to bed and never wake up. I am a Russian doll of secrets, so many cradled one inside the other, all looking like me but diminishing until what is left is so tiny I fear I'm disappearing.

'Bloody hell, that was a big yawn. I'm surprised you didn't turn yourself inside out,' Carrie says, but then yawns herself. Gets up, stretching. 'Time for bed.'

'It's a chilly night, want a hot water bottle?'

'Oooh, go on then.'

She's in the bathroom when I take the hot water bottle up. Enter the room – and hold my breath. There, beside the bed, is her beaten-up old phone, the screen cracked from when she dropped it a couple of weeks back.

I hug the hot water bottle to me to stop nervous goosebumps forming. Here's my chance… again.

This time I move quickly towards it, pushing thoughts of guilt and betrayal to the back of my mind. I'll grab her parents' number, call them and get my pal whisked safely away from Tynemouth.

Luckily, the phone is so cheap and basic there's no security number or password required to open it. Working quickly, I find her contacts list. Frown, confused, come out and click on it again. The same result. I come out of it again, looking for another list, because I must surely be in the wrong place.

A cough comes from the next room, then the taps come on. She won't be much longer. I'm fumbling the keys in my haste. Once again I try the contacts list, but my eyes haven't deceived me. There are only two on it: mine and 'work'.

Okay, they'll be in 'called numbers'. Only my number is listed there. Next door, the taps turn off. She's coming! Desperation births inspiration. Received calls. Carrie's skint, so probably relies on her parents getting in touch with her.

Once again, my name and number is the only one in there.

The bathroom door opens. Time's running out. Glancing at the 'work' number, I memorise it – I've always been good with numbers, sums, accounting, that kind of thing. Trembling hands almost fling the phone back onto the bedside table. Then I yank back the duvet, shove the hot water bottle into the bed.

'Oh! Hi!' Carrie's voice comes from behind me.

I slowly smooth the comforter back in place, forcing my breathing to calm, fighting to look normal. Turn and smile. 'Just making sure you're cosy tonight. Sleep well.'

'You too. Good night.'

But as I walk from the room, I can't hide my frown. Why is there no sign of Carrie's parents' number in her phone when she speaks to them all the time?

# CHAPTER TWENTY-THREE

Sleep refuses to come. Instead, I lie on my back, sick with exhaustion, staring into the blackness. Listening out for someone breaking in. Churning over what's just happened. It's odd that there are no friends or family listed in Carrie's phone. She's always talking about them and how brilliant they are. Her childhood friends have sent her flowers and cards constantly to support her. She and her mum are particularly close, talking at least three times a week and often every day, from what I've heard. Only the other day she was telling me about how she and her dad had been reminiscing about the blanket fort he'd built for her in the corner of her bedroom as a child, playing board games together and reading to each other. It was the sort of thing I'd wanted to do with my kids.

My own father wouldn't have been able to do something like that, bless him. He and Mum had been in their fifties before they successfully adopted me as a baby, and although older parents may be more the norm now, my childhood was dominated by friends from school asking if they were my grandparents. My reply had always been fiercely protective – as far as I was concerned, I had the best parents in the world, showering me with love and constantly telling me how lucky they were to have been able to choose me. I'd always felt lucky, too.

I'd stayed close to my parents until their deaths a few years ago. Dad went first, of a heart attack, and just months later, Mum fell asleep and never woke up. A post-mortem discovered she'd suffered a catastrophic stroke that would have killed her almost instantaneously. Their being together, and neither of them suffering, was a huge comfort to me, but it means I truly am alone in the world now.

Which brings me back to thinking of Carrie and her parents. She's dying, so why wouldn't they be in touch more? Why aren't their numbers listed in her phone? Unless she's memorised them. It's a possibility, despite Carrie, unlike me, not being good with numbers.

The hospital isn't listed either. Or her doctors. Memorising her entire address book seems a little odd.

I shake my head, sending the thoughts scattering into the black void of the bedroom. Turn my pillow to the cool side, pull the duvet up around my neck and try to relax.

A noise outside. My eyes fly open. I clamber out of bed and peer round the curtain, but I can see nothing in the orange glow of the street lamps. Carrie's car is still parked on the street, cardboard and masking tape covering the gaping hole to stop the elements getting in. We'll have to arrange for it to be fixed, but with no insurance to cover the tyres and windscreen replacements, it's going to be expensive. I'll have to have another word with Carrie about using some of the money we raised for her. She's worried about what people will think, I'm sure, but no one will mind once we explain the situation.

One more look up and down the street, then I go back to bed with a sigh.

Voices. Soft laughter. A door slamming shut. Every noise outside has my heart doing a samba. How I wish Owen were here to give me a hug and tell me everything is going to be okay. I'm so, so lonely. Memories rear up, snapping and snarling like rabid dogs, threatening to rip apart the paper-thin protective walls I've built around me over the years. The tears grow fatter, until I can see the past replaying through them…

❁

Owen's face was glowing from his cheeks to the tips of his auburn hair. He always had a smiley face, but that day he looked fit to explode.

'You're sure?' he checked. I waved the pregnancy test in the air.

'The IVF worked! I don't know anyone it's worked first time for!' I grinned. He lifted me up, then put me straight back down, as if worried I'd break.

'We're going to be parents,' he breathed. 'First time lucky. It's meant to be. Told you.'

He had, too, never letting me doubt it would happen eventually, or allowing me to get depressed when my period had arrived every month, regular as an unwelcome alarm. Finally, we were going to have a baby.

He'd run into the spare room, beckoning me to follow. 'Hey, we need to get this place decorated.'

'We've loads of time yet,' I laughed. 'But... well, I was thinking maybe we could have a mural. I could paint tree tops at the bottom, as a border, then have clouds and sunshine, and birds flying over the top, along with all kinds of magical creatures.'

'Like a fairy-tale kingdom – ooh, like at the top of the beanstalk.'

'Exactly!' We stood hand in hand gazing around the room, imagining a perfect future...

I turn over now, hugging the pillow tight and squeezing my eyes closed. My eyelids can't shut out the pictures in my mind, though, which flit to my twelve-week scan.

The gel the sonographer squeezed over my stomach was cold, making me shiver and giggle. The funny wand swept across my skin. The sonographer stared at the screen, seemed almost to frown.

'Is everything okay?' Owen took my hand.

'Just a moment… Yes, there we go.' She pointed. 'Can you see? There's one baby – and there's another. You're having twins!'

For a second I was speechless. Owen and I kept looking at the screen, then looking at each other and back again, each time more excited, more stunned, fuller with laughter and tears.

'A family in one hit,' I gasped. 'Ooh, imagine if it's a boy and a girl, that would be perfect!'

'It's too early to tell right now, but we should be able to see at your next scan.'

'That's at, what, twenty weeks?' Owen checked.

I elbowed him. 'Don't pretend you don't know, you've been reading even more baby books than I have.'

There'd never been a more enthusiastic father-to-be, I swear. After that scan, he'd started talking to my stomach every night about fresh starts and how much he was looking forward to meeting his children. After so many years of trying, neither of us could stop grinning. Even my constant vomiting didn't knock my enthusiasm, although it did exhaust me.

'I can't wait for our peanuts to be born,' I'd sighed. 'And I certainly won't miss being sick every day.'

As the memories overwhelm me, tears escape. They drip across my face, make a damp patch on the pillow. I'm too lost to wipe them. I'm remembering the colour draining from Owen's face at the next hospital visit. The way he wrapped an arm around my shoulders as he reacted to the sonographer's latest news.

'All our dreams are coming true. We're the luckiest people in the entire world,' he said, shaking his head in disbelief.

'Which is the boy again?'

The sonographer chuckled and pointed. 'See, there's his—'

'Oh, yes, I see it now! And the other peanut is definitely a girl.'

'She's lying a little awkwardly for me to be one hundred per cent certain, but I'm confident enough to say you're having one of each.'

*One of each. It was all we'd ever wanted; our family complete in one hit.*

After we left hospital, Owen had got a sneaky look on his face, claimed he needed to be somewhere. When I quizzed him he'd insisted it was some appointment or other that he couldn't get out of. I hadn't believed him. But I also hadn't imagined in my wildest nightmares that by the end of the day he'd be dead.

I turn over again in bed, fling off the duvet, panic making me sweat. The urge to escape is almost overwhelming, but I know from bitter experience that there is no outrunning memories. Goodness knows I've run far enough and hard enough, but never managed to escape. My eyes are wide open to the darkness, yet I can still see the memories graffitied across my brain in glorious technicolour. I try to stop them from appearing and trashing what little peace I'm attempting to cling to. They refuse to listen to my silent pleas.

*No, no, no…*

There was something about the knock on the door, all those years ago; its weight seeming to convey doom. Two policemen had stood awkward and solemn on my doorstep. I already knew, without them having to tell me. But still I needed them to say the words. Then they did, and my world collapsed.

Owen had been so excited by discovering we were having a boy and a girl. He'd rushed out straight afterwards to collect a necklace he'd ordered for me from a jeweller. It was engraved with the words 'Forever Mine'. For the twins, he'd ordered a pair of matching Liverpool FC sleepsuits, with our last name emblazoned across the backs. He'd been too excited and distracted by the news, though. At the train station there was an unmanned level crossing, where he had to cross the tracks in order to get to the correct platform. The warning that a train was coming had sounded, lights flashing, and Owen had waited impatiently. The moment the train passed, he went through the unlocked wicket gate, thinking it was safe, even though the warnings were still going, because he thought they were for the train that had just passed. When he stepped onto the tracks, he was hit by a train coming from the opposite direction and was killed instantly.

I'd been so lost in grief I'd felt like I was losing my mind. My mum and dad had died the year before, so I was all alone, apart from Owen's parents. They cared for me so much I felt I was suffocating. I hadn't meant what happened next, but it was all my fault.

But I can't think of those terrible days, and the horror that had been yet to come for me. Instead, I kick off what little of the duvet still covers me and creep downstairs, trying to break the haunting bonds that still imprison me. I'll concentrate on trying to solve Carrie's puzzle – anything rather than remember how, still reeling from Owen's death, I killed my children.

# CHAPTER TWENTY-FOUR

THEN

I had become Mum's accomplice in covering for Dad's violence. Together we tiptoed through life, being careful not to say the wrong thing, walk the wrong way, wear the wrong clothes or give the wrong look. Still Dad found excuses to detonate, safe in the knowledge that his victims would protect him. Sometimes part of me even felt proud, because my lies must mean I was a grown-up too, now. At other times I felt ashamed for my part in the big cover-up. Most of the time, though, I didn't even give it a thought. This was my life now, and falsehood was second nature.

When I was twelve, everything changed.

The night started the same as usual. Dad was dead drunk and in a mood. I was watching *Hollyoaks*, and he started ranting about what a crap soap it was. Mum rushed over and turned the television off, and I moaned or made a sarcastic comment or did something I can't even remember.

Dad went nuclear.

Picking up the telly, he held it over his head as Mum begged him to put it down, then threw it across the room. An almighty crack as it hit the wall. The soft thud and muffled scream of flesh being pummelled as he started on Mum. Before I could stop myself, I ran forward, lunging at him. Threw myself onto his back, legs flailing.

'Get off her! Leave her alone!'

He was a bucking bronco, and this was my first rodeo. Within seconds, I flew off, landing in a heap on the floor. Stars seemed to burst before my eyes. I tried to stand. Stumbled. Knees sagging, I sank to the floor.

Dad had never really hit me before, not more than the odd slap or that time he'd banged my head against the wall. Nothing too major. It had always been Mum who bore the brunt of his anger. She pulled at his arm, trying to stop him from reaching me. Begging, pleading. A shove sent her reeling back, then she was on the floor, too.

Instinctively I curled into a ball as blows and kicks rained down on me. My nose exploded as Dad stamped on my head. I had to get up, had to find the drive, otherwise he might kill me.

Gathering all my strength, I leapt to my feet. But he was too quick, his fingers knotting in my hair, holding me in place.

'No! Let me go!' I screamed. I surged forward, feeling a massive clump of hair yank free as I ran from the house, into the road.

Footsteps pelted behind me. Where was Mum? Had she escaped, too? I didn't know – all I knew was that I was running for my life.

'Help me! Someone help me!' I screamed. It was too much to expect a stranger to step in. I was going to get caught and beaten to a pulp.

The footsteps were getting closer. I could hear gasping breath…

'Get in, quick!' yelled a woman, holding her front door open.

*Thank God, oh thank God!* I didn't break stride as I dashed inside her house, hearing the door slam behind me.

Dad started hammering on the door.

As the woman called the police, her hand trembling, I noticed scarlet blood dripping onto her carpet.

'Oh, I'm so sorry,' I gasped, pulling a tissue from my pocket and trying to mop it up.

There was so much, though, the puddle getting bigger and bigger, the room fading away…

❁

Everything seemed disconnected. There were blue lights outside… I was in an ambulance… Now I was in hospital, a police officer by my side.

'You've got a broken nose and cracked ribs,' she said. 'There's a nasty gash on your leg too.'

'How's Mum?'

'She's just down the corridor being treated. She's concussed and has a badly bruised neck. When officers arrived on the scene they had to pull your dad off her because he was strangling her.'

I nodded, every inch of my body pounding with pain but emotionally numb. The officer held up a mirror, and I recoiled in shock. I didn't even look like me, my face was so swollen and bruised.

'I want to press charges,' I said without hesitation.

Dad pleaded guilty to assault and was jailed for nine months. During that time I had surgery on my nose to straighten it, as I couldn't breathe properly. It seemed a small price to pay for finally being free of Dad.

Mum and I had fun together for the first time, laughing at TV programmes, wearing what we liked, eating any food we fancied, whenever we wanted. It was bliss.

But within weeks of his release, Mum announced he was moving back in.

'He's really sorry for what he's done. Going to prison was the short, sharp shock he needed. Now it's time to give him a second chance.'

'He could have killed us! I don't want him anywhere near me.'

'Just listen to what he's got to say and I'm sure you'll forgive him. He really loves us.'

'Yeah – to death. My jaw still clicks from being punched by that bastard—'

'I don't want to hear that language.'

There was no talking sense to her. She'd made up her mind. Fine; so had I.

I contacted Social Services and was put into care, where I was passed around from foster home to foster home.

Desperate to fit in and be liked, I'd change myself to become whatever I thought people wanted me to be, even stealing people's identities to make me feel better. It was as though I'd got rid of my imaginary friends, only to become one myself.

When not using other people's lives for inspiration, I came up with tall tales of my own. My favourite fabrication was that until recently I'd had the perfect life, with loving, kind, normal parents.

'So why are you in foster care, then?' I'd be asked by prospective friends at yet another new school.

'Because my mum's too poorly to look after me, and Dad's too busy looking after her. But once he's sorted himself out he'll be coming for me and we'll all be together again.'

Sometimes I tried for the sympathy vote, building a more elaborate tale of woe. 'My mum never wanted me – she was intellectually disabled and fell pregnant when someone took advantage of her,' I'd claim. 'She decided to put me up for adoption, but then my gran offered to help raise me – she'd always dreamed of having a grandchild. But when I was seven, Gran was diagnosed with Alzheimer's. She couldn't look after me any more, and Mum wasn't capable, and that's how I ended up in care.'

Another favourite was to talk about the baby brother I missed so much.

'Sometimes I play tennis against a wall and imagine I'm playing with him. Nicholas loved to play tennis with me,' I'd cry.

Sometimes I was believed. Until I tripped myself up, contradicting myself. Then I'd be shunned. Again.

Practice made perfect, though.

# CHAPTER TWENTY-FIVE

## NOW

While Carrie sleeps peacefully upstairs, I creep downstairs, chased by memories of Owen and my babies, and determined to block them out by concentrating on the puzzle of my present.

The most pressing are the messages. I pull them from their hiding place. If Carrie gets up, I'll hear her movements and be able to hide everything before she comes downstairs. I line them up. If there is a pattern to the cloth of my life, then it is one of manipulation and lies. Perhaps I can use that to my advantage to solve this conundrum.

A picture of Carrie and me; a picture of Simon; then one of an unknown woman. I stare at her face, rack my brains, but don't recognise her. No familiarity in the curve of a heart-shaped face or the lines of her shy smile. She has thick, white-blonde hair that's pulled back into a low ponytail and a blunt fringe. After an hour, despite knowing her image well enough to be able to draw it from memory, I'm no closer to discovering who she is. She's a complete stranger.

The writing taunts me.

*I'm watching you*

*There are no secrets from me*

*Losing patience. Give me what I want, or me telling everyone what you've done will be the least of your worries*

The last message is definitely threatening, making me hug myself. There's no sense that this could be an inside joke any more, or a Halloween prank. Instead it is a sick game of hide-and-seek, and one that is stacked against me. The only way I can think to even things up is by removing the key piece: Carrie. Then she'll be safe… but will I?

Fear and fury knot in my stomach, making me feel sick. Ugly, taunting, hurtful messages. How dare somebody send them? I scrunch the photos and envelopes up but it isn't enough. With a satisfying rip, they tear. *That's better.* Even the box with the first message across the top gets torn apart. Soon there is nothing left of anything but tiny pieces of paper and cardboard, which I throw into the sink and set fire to.

Only when there is nothing left do I feel satisfied, as if by wiping out the photographs and taunts, I've wiped out the malice behind them.

Confidence buoys me, a lightness I haven't felt in days. Yes, I'm scared but I'm not going to abandon Carrie. Nothing and nobody can make me do that. In which case, it's on to the next problem. I grab my tablet, open the Internet and type in the names of Carrie's parents and her home town of Plymouth. Spend a good hour trawling through results trying different spellings and permutations. I get nothing.

Huh? I must have got it wrong. We were talking about them the other day and I could have sworn she said Plymouth, because before that I'd wrongly thought it was somewhere in Derbyshire. Another search, another couple of hours scrolling through newspaper cuttings, electoral registers, social media pages, you name it. My eyes are starting to hurt; it's the small hours and I'm getting really tired. That's probably what's stopping me from finding them. Too done in to think straight, I'm making silly mistakes.

The exhaustion and the fact that it's a Friday night make me think of Owen, too. How we always seemed to argue at weekends, staying up all night. He had a weekday, nine-to-five job that meant he could stay in bed during the day on Saturday and Sunday, catching up on sleep, but they were my busiest days, so I'd be left bone-weary.

Generally, I only let myself think of our good times. Shame at thinking ill of the dead is the final straw that makes me abandon my current task. I'm not concentrating properly any more, my mind wandering.

I trudge up to bed knowing that I'm so tired dreams won't come. Exhaustion has its bonuses.

But as my eyes close, just as I'm tipping over the edge into sleep, I can't help wondering if the mystery sender knows something I don't. Perhaps Carrie is hiding something after all.

When I wake, still groggy, the sun is high, and the first thought in my head is this new mystery. Why is there no sign of Carrie's parents, either on the Internet or on her phone, when she talks to them so often? The thought this mini-mystery could be related to the messages from the watcher won't recede.

It makes me overly suspicious. Thinking about it, her parents have never called when I've been around, and we've spent nearly all our time together since we became friends six months ago. But why would someone lie about something like that? It makes no sense.

My vivid imagination is running away with me. I think again of Rosie's warning that I'm replacing an obsession with food with one for Carrie. Perhaps my counsellor has a point.

There's movement from the next room. Time for me to get up and make my guest breakfast.

Carrie looks bright-eyed, clearly well-rested, and looks delighted when I start making a full English for her. While turning the bacon under the grill, I toy with asking her what's going on but can't work out how without opening a can of worms. The whole truth would have to come out, including the fact that I've kept those notes hidden from her – and that would lead to questions about why, which would lead to the Simon revelation, and…

Too complicated to contemplate, I try to think of a way round it instead. My stomach churns as I speak.

'Are you looking forward to moving?'

She nods and takes a couple more mouthfuls of fried egg. Finishes it off before replying.

'It'll be so lovely to be back with my parents. They're really excited about having me home – they keep asking how I want my bedroom decorated, which is so cool of them.'

Sometimes, like now, she seems incredibly young. But she is – she's only twenty-four. I think of myself at that age and it feels like a lifetime ago. Hard to believe hers is coming to a close. It's not fair; she's still so vital. Another person I've loved, only to lose. I force my words to sound bright.

'That's lovely! What do you think you'll go for?'

'You know *The Greatest Showman*? It would be amazing to have a room inspired by that. It's so vibrant, all those bright circus colours, flames, you name it!'

Her eyes shine. I think of the nursery Owen and I painted for the twins, a fairyland above the clouds.

'They've got their work cut out recreating that, but it will look incredible. Hey, is there anything I can do to help with the move? Maybe I could get in touch with your parents, so I can organise things this end for them, which frees you up to relax.'

'Oh, that's not necessary.'

I push a little harder, but she won't have it. So I try another angle.

'When you move back in with your parents, I'll have to come and visit you. Where is it they live again?'

'Cromer.'

My eyes narrow infinitesimally. That's new.

She laughs. 'Where did that come from? I mean Plymouth. It's so early my brain hasn't started functioning yet.'

Normally I'd laugh it off, too. I'm not a morning person either, so I understand that thick-headed feeling that can take a while to shake off first thing. Today I'm faking, though, as my suspicion grows.

Everyone lies. I do it more than most. Maybe Carrie does, too.

What is wrong with me? How could I even think such a terrible thing about Carrie? I'm worried about myself. Of course my friend isn't a liar. She's dying, and the last thing she needs is a Spanish Inquisition from me. I'm being as bad as that weird stalker person I'm supposed to be shielding her from, acting crazy.

Still, I do need to find her parents.

There has to be some other way of getting their contact details. She isn't on any social media, and it seems her parents aren't either. There's no mention of them on any Plymouth electoral register, or on those of the surrounding districts, which is odd.

There is one person I could ask. I haven't seen Simon since the night we split up, and I told him I never wanted to clap eyes on him again. To his credit, he's avoided me. Now it's time for me to track him down, and see what he knows about Carrie's family.

# CHAPTER TWENTY-SIX

The afternoon is sharp and bright, the kind of day that takes your breath away when you first step outdoors, but that is glorious once you get used to it as you walk. There's a wind strong enough to blow away anyone's cobwebs. I pull my woollen hat down snug over my ears, adjusting it so my sunglasses don't dig into them, and pop up my coat's hood.

There's a bubble of nerves in my stomach as I head towards Longsands, where I'm guessing Simon will be at the Surf School as it's a Saturday. I'm furious with him for what he did, and not tempted to let him into my life again, but also can't help remembering the incredible sex we had. Thinking of him, his hands on my body, his lips on my skin, makes me smile and warms my blood.

As I head down the ramp to the beach, a man catches my eye and gives me the same kind of smile, as if he can tell what I'm thinking. Even from this distance I can see how brilliantly blue his eyes are. Blushing, I half turn away as I pass, toying with a piece of hair that's escaped from under my hat and is blowing in the light breeze. I glance back. He's still looking. He's younger than me, I'd guess around thirty-five, but that doesn't bother me. I'm tempted to continue the flirtation, as thinking of Simon has brought my libido back to life again. But I've more important things to think about.

There, on the beach in front of the long, low Surf School building, is a group of children who look to be mainly around eleven. They're in their wetsuits and raring to go, judging by the excited yells and laughter, the boisterous pushing and jeering of a handful of boys showing off in front of the girls. One or two look familiar, like the boys on their bikes who hang around Carrie's place. Simon isn't there, though.

I look around but can't spot him. It's slower going walking on the sand, but I wander over to one of the teachers I vaguely recognise as someone I've said hello to before. He recognises me, too. We nod greetings, and I have to sweep those stray hairs from across my face as I talk, turning to face the wind.

'Is Simon about?'

'Nah, he hasn't been here for months. Thought you might be bringing news of him, actually.'

'News? What do you mean?'

He stares out at the white-topped waves roaring in. 'He just upped and left, must be about six months ago now.' Cocks his head, thinking. 'Yeah, must have been end of April, start of May, 'cos I went on holiday a couple of weeks after. No one's heard of him since. He didn't even serve notice – it was a right hassle having to get someone at short notice to fill in for him.'

I'd finished with him at the end of April, and he'd dumped Carrie at the same time. He must have upped sticks straight after realising he and I were never going to be a proper couple. I wonder where he went, though, knowing how much he'd loved his home town and his teaching job?

I feel a bit guilty. Perhaps I'd been too harsh on him. He'd been left under no illusion about our future, during our confrontation.

'You're like one of those sleazy love rats you read about in magazines. If you'd sleep around when someone's at their absolute lowest, fighting against breast cancer, how the hell could anyone ever trust you? You're not the person I thought you were, Simon. You disgust me,' I'd shouted.

Of course, he'd come out with excuses and platitudes. Told me he'd never loved anyone the way he loved me. Nothing could justify what he'd done, though. He'd led a naive young woman to think the two of them had a future together – only to abandon her when the going got tough. And he hadn't even let me know what he was doing. He'd led me up the garden path the whole time, telling me he was single. Every time I thought of it I felt angry, skin crawling at my part in hurting Carrie.

Now, like the coward he'd proved himself to be, Simon had run off with his tail between his legs. I really needed to talk to him, though.

'Didn't he leave a forwarding address for his wages?'

'No, he took them when he left.'

'What about friends? He must have been in touch with somebody.'

The surfer pushed his sunglasses back over his hair, so that his eyes, though squinting in the bright light, met mine full on. 'Alex, pet, I was his best pal. We've been inseparable since primary school, and I've not heard from him. Oh, I know what he did, to you, to Carrie, so I get why he's done his disappearing act, but I'm still pretty damn raging with him. He's never been the most reliable type, doesn't deal well with pressure, but even I'm surprised by this. He hasn't contacted anyone here since leaving.'

Simon was upset, but it's hard to believe he'd leave the job he adored and completely cut everyone off. Confused, I say thanks and turn away. There are two of me as I walk across the wet sand, one real, one a reflection. Neither of us can get our head around what we've heard.

A headache is starting. The pounding in my head is in time with the rhythm of the waves, and no matter how far I walk I can't leave it behind. There are things going on that I can't comprehend, and the more I discover, the less things make sense. While I am left stumbling in the dark, feeling for clues, the watcher knows everything.

For the rest of the day I've got fittings, people nipping in to collect their finished dresses and meetings with potential customers to discuss design possibilities, prices and so on. Saturdays are always my busiest day, as most people are only available at weekends or evenings after work.

My mind's only half on the task at hand as I gather tear sheets from magazines and sketch out preliminary drawings to show possible clients what can be done with their ideas.

'I've got too many thoughts whizzing round my head, I don't know how to choose,' says a woman searching for the ultimate bridesmaid dresses, which could be green, blue, cream, yellow or soft purple, depending on which breath she's taking. She's brought armfuls of magazines. I nod my understanding, say soothing words that come automatically after years of dealing with stressed-out brides. Soon, she's less skittish. By the end of the session, she's opted for my suggestion of including all of those colours by layering chiffon and letting each one peep through in turn. 'They're the colours of the sea,' I explain. 'So the chiffon fabric will float like ocean spray hitting sunshine. We'll give it a handkerchief hemline to really accentuate that.'

She adores the design, and it decides the theme of the whole wedding. 'We can have seashells on the tables. Somewhere in one of these articles is a gorgeous driftwood centrepiece on the head table. There, look!'

'That's lovely,' I smile, glad I've helped.

She's the last customer of the day, but when Carrie sends me a text, I pretend I've got a couple more to come. I need some time alone.

❁

There's no trace of Carrie's parents in Plymouth or Derbyshire, but I remember her mention of Cromer. I've no idea why she'd lie about where they are, but between the messages and this little mystery, it's worth checking out.

Once again I type in their names, and this time add Cromer. There's a list of results, but none is an exact match. I'm desperate enough to look anyway, clicking on one after another.

A sportsman who shares the same name as her father; a founder and CEO of a business; a woman who's lost her dog and been reunited with it. I click on them, skim-read, close the page, growing more frustrated and bored with each link. Next is an old local newspaper report on a retiring head teacher with the same name as Carrie's mum. I read it in desperation, even though I know her mum is a solicitor. No clues, no family resemblance. I'm about to leave it when something catches my eye on the sidebar, where other news stories are listed.

There's a photograph of a woman who looks familiar.

Could it be?

The tablet is inches from my nose as I pore over the tiny photograph. The angle is different, but that shy smile, the white-blonde hair with a blunt fringe, the sharp chin and heart-shaped face, everything looks familiar.

It's the mystery woman whose photograph Carrie had been sent.

FEARS GROW FOR MISSING WOMAN, reads the headline.

# CHAPTER TWENTY-SEVEN

I open up the story for a better look. The headline leers large at me across the width of my screen. Looking at the much bigger image makes me more convinced it is the same woman, but I need to fetch the photograph to be certain. I stand – and swear as the realisation hits.

All that's left of the picture is ashes sticking to my kitchen sink's stainless-steel plughole.

*Great idea burning it, Alex, you complete tool.*

Sitting down again, I try to compose myself before skimming the report that's dated eighteen months ago.

> Fears are tonight growing for a missing 31-year-old woman who has been described as 'high risk' by police after she was last seen 72 hours ago.
>
> Norfolk Police are urgently appealing for information to help locate Joanne Freeman, 31, who was last seen in Cromer town centre on Saturday afternoon.
>
> Mrs Freeman is described as white, of slim build, with shoulder-length blonde hair that she usually wears tied up.
>
> She was last seen wearing a red jumper with a silver bomber jacket, dark leggings with a red pattern and black loafer shoes with silver buckles. She usually carries a handbag.
>
> From the initial police enquiries, the missing persons investigation was treated as medium-risk as it was not unusual

for Mrs Freeman to stay away with friends and there were no apparent concerns for her safety. But police have now reclassified the case as high-risk 72 hours later after there has been no contact from Mrs Freeman and no sign of her. This includes her presence on social media and bank account activity. She does have a mobile phone, but she does not have a charger with her. It is also believed she had very little or no cash on her when she went missing.

Her husband, Heston, 34, is said to be 'distraught'. No statement has been given by the family yet, but it is understood that it is the second tragedy to befall the Freemans. Their daughter, Alice, 10, lost her battle with leukaemia seven months ago. It is feared Mrs Freeman's disappearance may be connected to the loss of her daughter.

'Understandably, Joanne was in a state after losing little Alice. She was a devoted mother, and Alice's death changed her from someone who was happy and chatty to utterly lost. We're all fearing the worst,' says a family friend who wishes to remain anonymous.

Police are urging people to come forward as a matter of urgency with any information that could help locate Mrs Freeman, including possible sightings over the past few days. They are particularly keen to speak with her friend, Natalie Sheringham, who is believed to be the last person with Mrs Freeman, and who also hasn't been seen since Saturday afternoon.

If you can help the missing persons investigation, please call Norfolk Police.

At the bottom of the report is a photograph of Natalie Sheringham with Joanne Freeman. They're both grinning at the camera, faces side by side in the selfie. In this picture I'm even more convinced I recognise Joanne, because her face is slightly turned to a similar angle to the one

I'm used to seeing. Those lines and curves I spent so long studying slot into place now, and even though I don't have an image to make a direct comparison with, the one blazing in my mind is identical.

It's not Joanne I'm staring at, though. It's the other woman.

The hair is long and black, the face so chubby that the features are distorted slightly from those I've become familiar with. That might be enough to fool some people, but not me; I'm good with visuals, thanks to my work.

It's Carrie. There's no doubt in my mind.

I sit back, staring blankly ahead. Carrie is wanted in connection with a missing person. Carrie isn't Carrie at all, in fact, I remind myself, she's – I check the report again – Natalie Sheringham. That would certainly explain why I can't find her parents; but instead of solving a problem, all I've done is uncover a deeper mystery.

Who the hell is Natalie Sheringham? And why is she hiding in Tynemouth, using a fake name, when her friend has gone missing?

My new best friend, Google, steps in. I type in Natalie's name. Nothing besides that local newspaper article comes up for Cromer. Time to forget local and go nationwide instead.

After spending most of the night trawling through results, I can't find anyone of that name who is the right age on any of the council registers, Facebook, LinkedIn, Twitter, you name it.

Next, I do the same with Carrie Goodwin, looking across the whole of the UK. Nothing.

With each keystroke made a fear grows in my heart. Carrie Goodwin doesn't exist. Natalie Sheringham doesn't exist.

'Who the hell is my best friend?' I whisper. As always in times of trouble, I talk aloud, finding it helps me. This is when I usually imagine the twins. Elise pacing up and down, angry at someone making a fool of her mother. Edward is the peacemaker, though.

'There's got to be a reasonable explanation. Perhaps you're mistaken about this woman's face – after all, you're only remembering her, you don't have the photograph to compare with any more.'

'But what about Carrie? There's no mistaking her.'

I pull the tablet over again and stare at the image I've bookmarked. Doubt and conviction ebb and flow, creating a whirlpool of confusion.

Maybe I am mistaken. This Natalie is wearing all black, and the jacket is formal, structured, with shoulder pads, not at all like the multicoloured, flowing clothes my friend favours. No fashion Prozac here. She's also wearing heavy make-up to sculpt cheekbones and nose, like the Kardashians, but even with that it's not enough to show Carrie's distinctive cheekbones – if it is Carrie. Instead, her bone structure is hidden under a thick layer of fat, and her jawline has little jowls that melt into a double chin.

Natalie's eyeshadow and dark kohl liner is glamorous, her eyebrows are thick and high-arched and her lipstick is a deep berry red. Carrie only wears minimal make-up, and then only infrequently.

I squint, lean closer. Despite all that, I'd swear it's my friend. I've spent most of my spare time with her for the last six months. It's her. I know it.

So what next? Confront her with the truth? There isn't actually any proof of anything. If only I'd been able to speak with Simon, he might have shed some light on Carrie's past. But Simon has gone. Disappeared. Hasn't been seen since I finished with him. Since Carrie discovered he was cheating on her.

I go cold. That's two people who've disappeared, both connected with this woman.

The woman I know as Carrie has a hell of a lot of secrets she's hiding – and suddenly I'm no longer afraid for her. I'm afraid of her.

# CHAPTER TWENTY-EIGHT

There's a panic rising in me. I tell myself to calm down, but I'm shaking. There's no one I can turn to and share these fears with, and for the rest of the evening no amount of distraction seems to work. My food sits untouched on the plate until the salad leaves have gone limp, the dressing looks congealed, the chicken dried to unappetising jerky. It gets pushed into the grateful jaws of the bin, which swallows it up.

Most of the night is spent tossing and turning. I could swear I hear the handle of the front door moving, being tested. Everything's fine, still locked when I check, but it takes a while for my heart to return to normal pace. When fatigue finally pulls me under, weird dreams plague me.

By Sunday exhaustion and lack of food has me gripped so tightly that I feel wired rather than ready to drop. It's like the bad old days of my anorexia, but try as I might, I can't force down so much as a bowl of cereal. Once more, the bin gets fed the soggy leftovers, and after I've washed up I start to pace back and forth, thinking, thinking, thinking. There's no making sense of the maelstrom of information. Nothing fits together, and I feel like I'm trying to solve a Rubik's Cube with jigsaw pieces.

There has to be a solution, though. Time ticks by. My phone beeps with messages I ignore. Adrenaline rushes through my veins, making me jangle.

*Come on, come on. Think.* I keep walking, as if on a treadmill that will drive my brain.

Then I stop. Slap my forehead. Of course! There's one last option for finding Carrie's parents that I haven't tried yet.

I grab my phone ready to dial, but common sense screams at me to stop. If I'm going to do this, I need to at least try to be a little clever about it, rather than simply blundering ahead like a bull in a china shop. So I tap settings, choose phone, scroll down to 'show my caller id', click on it and toggle it to off. Now my number won't show up for the call I'm about to make.

Crossing my fingers that someone will answer despite it being the weekend, I tap out the number memorised from Carrie's phone…

It rings and rings, then finally clicks on to answerphone. Damn, I'll have to wait until tomorrow.

The rest of the day and night is spent in a déjà vu of repetition. Pacing, worrying, trying and failing to sleep, ignoring the growl of my stomach.

❖

Day dawns, but it's still too early to try dialling again. Finally, at 8 a.m., I give in to the urge.

'Sparkles Cleaning.'

'Oh, hi, it's Carrie here.'

'All right? You sound a bit funny.'

'I'm getting a cold. The joy of a poor immune system. Anyway, I won't chat for long, or I might lose my voice, I just wanted to check something with you.'

'Okay. You're not on shift again until Wednesday morning, if that's what you wanted to know.'

'No, it's, well, I suddenly had a panic just now that I've not put down the right details for my parents, you know, on the emergency contact form.'

It's a gamble, but most workplaces these days seem to ask for someone to inform in case of accidents and the like. I've got my fingers crossed Carrie's workplace is the same.

'I've been getting a bit muddled lately because of the cancer, and I'm worried I've given you their old address and phone number, not their new one,' I add.

My eyes screw up, trying to hide myself from that terrible lie. Using Carrie's cancer as an excuse is pretty damn low, if she's innocent. *If.* The need to find out about her family has gone way beyond wanting to simply help her, though.

'Hang on a sec, let me have a look.' A sigh. The sound of a drawer opening and closing. Some rustling. 'You still there? Yeah, the name we've got is Alex Appleby.'

My own number is reeled back at me.

I am Carrie's 'In Case of Emergency', and not the parents she claims to be so close to. I've hit another dead end.

The paranoid conviction grows that something is going on with this person, this Carrie or Natalie or whatever her name is.

I open up the saved tab on my tablet and look again at the news story. That Joanne is definitely the same woman whose photograph was sent to Carrie. I'd stake my life on it. What had been written on the back? The words come as soon as they are summoned because I've read them so often they are ingrained: *Losing patience. Give me what I want, or me telling everyone what you've done will be the least of your worries.*

Realisation unfolds to reveal the meaning. The person behind the messages is threatening to expose Carrie – or whatever her name is – for whatever she's done to Joanne. 'Give me what I want' must be a blackmail demand. If she doesn't do as she's told, the police will be informed of Carrie's real identity, I assume. Everyone discovering her shady secret will be the least of her worries, because if she's involved in Joanne's disappearance she'll spend what little is left of her life in prison. She'll be dead before a trial can happen.

What exactly is in it for the watcher, though? If all they wanted was to expose truth from lie they'd have gone to the authorities. There's only one thing I can think of that would motivate someone to send cryptic messages in this way: money. There's no mention of payment, but no other solution springs to mind. They're after Carrie's bucket list fund.

*Good luck with that, pal, because you'll need my signature to get hold of it*, I think, and can't help smiling with grim satisfaction.

To be sure, I go online and check the bank balance. It's just shy of nineteen thousand pounds, as it should be, boosted by extra money trickling in as a result of the newspaper article.

My stomach grumbles. Once again my routine has been completely ignored, and my breakfast and mid-morning snack forgotten because I'm so preoccupied. Must eat. As I reach across the kitchen counter to open a cupboard, the salt cellar clatters over. The spilled salt is automatically scraped together and flung over my left shoulder.

I hadn't always been superstitious; it crept up on me. Now it is a new way of feigning mastery over my life, sublimating one form of control, the anorexia, with another. *Knock on wood. Don't walk under a ladder. Never open an umbrella indoors.* But they are far healthier than my old ways. My entire world revolved around my desire. The irony? I thought I was in charge, but in reality, my condition enslaved me. It's taken a lot to back anorexia nervosa into a cage and slam the door shut. Every single day the door of its prison rattles as it tries to break free again. It's rattling now, but questions are drowning it out.

I stare at a grain of salt I've missed. Trying to come to terms with everything. Each thought thuds and echoes in my mind.

Carrie isn't all she seems to be.

Her name isn't Carrie.

Her last best friend disappeared without trace. So has her ex-boyfriend. What has she done with them?

As I ponder, another question hits me.

Has Carrie actually got cancer?

# CHAPTER TWENTY-NINE

I'm worried about myself. I'm starting to see fabrications that aren't there and monsters that are only shadows. I've seen Carrie's radiotherapy burns myself, rubbed cream on her arms and neck to soothe them. Seen the dots inked on her skin in permanent pen by doctors to mark where to line up the radiation machine every time she has treatment. Her hair fell out – it's still pixie-crop short. I've seen how weak she gets and heard her vomiting.

*She must have cancer.*

When she had her chemo port put in and was distraught about going out and about with the ugly bandage showing, I'd gone out and bought her a turtleneck jumper. She'd been so touched.

*She must have cancer.*

I went with her to chemo on more than one occasion. I saw her sign in and walk to the treatment room, while I waited in the hospital's café for her to be done.

*She must have cancer.*

I don't know what she's capable of lying about, though. There are already so many riddles stacking up, from her name, to her parents, to her best friend's disappearance. Then there's Simon – where the hell is he? Each conundrum tinkles through my consciousness like broken glass, slashing at my peace of mind.

Maybe I should confront her with my suspicions. There's no actual proof, though, so I'm loath to. My mum always used to tell me off for not having more confidence in myself, saying I should trust my instincts. She blamed the fact that I was adopted, thinking I felt rejected by my biological parents and so unworthy of the love she and my dad gave me. She was convinced it filtered into every aspect of my life, making me doubt myself. Perhaps she was right. I've always felt a freak, separated from the rest of the world. Always been a perfectionist, setting the bar impossibly high for myself yet incredibly low for those people I've surrounded myself with. Perhaps this is an example of me falling back into old habits – perhaps I should have enough faith in myself about my suspicions of Carrie to challenge her.

But...

To confront a dying woman and accuse her of lying, and then be proved wrong myself, would be awful. I'd look like a crazy person, a total bitch. She has enough on her plate fighting for her life without me sullying her reputation and starting unfounded rumours – because the fact is there's no proof of anything. Not really.

My phone pings. Talk of the devil. The text is from Carrie, asking if I'm okay and what I'm up to. We don't normally go this long without contact, and I've never ignored her before, but I've had a couple of missed calls from her from yesterday and this morning.

I stare at my phone for a long time, not sure what to do. Sometimes my thumb moves across as though to reply and then seems to change its mind and flick back. Finally, I type out a response.

*Morning! Sorry, still had a bad stomach so didn't feel like talking. Better now. Have you got chemo this morning? If you have, I'll take you.*

Unable to sit down, unable to settle to anything, I wait for a reply. When the phone lights up I pounce on it.

*You sure you're okay now? If you are, a lift would be great. But don't worry if you're still feeling dodgy. You take care of yourself! <3*

I reassure her I'm fit and well and arrange to pick her up in half an hour. That gives me just enough time to have a shower, get changed and make myself feel human.

By the time she climbs into my car, I'm calm.

Carrie seems in a great mood during the twenty-five-minute journey to the hospital. 'I've decided to quit my jobs and enjoy what little time I have left,' she announces. 'Money will be tight, but I don't really want to spend my final days scrubbing other people's toilets.'

My heart stutters. Finally, I scrabble together a reply. 'You're right, there's more important things in life. It's not even worth the time the call will take – let me quit for you.'

'Ha, like you're my personal secretary,' she laughs.

I'm not joking. If she calls her boss to quit, they might wonder why she didn't mention it when 'she' phoned yesterday. Questions might be asked.

'That's what I'm here for: to make life easier for you, Carrie.'

She rolls her eyes but agrees. 'If that's what you want, then fill your boots. Who am I to stand in the way of your fun?' A tilt of the head, amusement twinkling while studying me. 'You really need to loosen up and be more dog.'

My nose wrinkles. 'I have absolutely no idea what you mean, but it sounds vaguely insulting.'

'It's my philosophy for life: be more dog. Right, I don't worry about the past or the future, just live in the moment, like pooches do. Even if a dog loses its leg, it just runs on three legs rather than crying about what it's lost. What's the point of worrying about things you can't control?'

I can't help grinning. But then a traitorous voice whispers in my ear, and I have to ask…

'You seem very perky for somebody who is about to have a load of poison fed into their arm.'

Carrie shrugs. 'I'm just being more dog. Got to practise what I preach, haven't I?'

At the hospital, we walk arm in arm along the corridors, following the signs for Oncology. At the door Carrie extricates herself from me with a disarming smile.

'I really appreciate you coming with me, it means so much to me.'

'It's nothing, honestly.'

'Not to me.'

We stand looking at each other. Awkward, out of place, not knowing what to say, where previously we've flowed naturally. I'm starting to feel bad. Doubting someone is seriously ill while standing in a hospital with them seems ridiculous.

'Well, I'll see you when the treatment is over. Should only be an hour, so I'll meet you at the café, right?' says Carrie.

I've been thinking about this a lot. She always seems to have an excuse about why she should be alone during the treatment. Today I won't allow it, even if I am having doubts about my doubts.

'Listen, I said I'd come with you, and I meant it. I'm not leaving your side.'

'Oh, you are lovely! But do you mind not coming in today? It's only because another friend of mine, Wendy, has heard the news that she's not going to make it. I'd like the chance to talk to her – just me and her. I'm really sorry… is that okay?

'If you really want to come in, you can. It's just a bit awkward. I'm worried that Wendy might not feel that she can be as honest in front of me if someone she doesn't know is there. She might feel like she has to put on a brave face, you know?'

I hesitate. Her whole body language is so relaxed. No tension in her shoulders, no tightness around her mouth; her eyes look straight into mine. Everything about her screams honesty. Yet I don't believe her. I can't, because every time my suspicions slip I remember Joanne, who is missing, and Simon, who hasn't been seen since he split up with Carrie. I think of the messages, and the mystery of her parents.

*Liar.*

I'm about to insist when someone calls out a greeting. It's a woman with a bright scarf wrapped around her head. Her clothes are baggy over what is clearly a skeletal frame. Skin looks stretched paper-thin. Her movements are slow and careful, as though each one takes a lot of strength.

'Wendy!' Carrie rushes forward towards her, arms outstretched. Wraps her in a hug. They stand there for several moments, eyes closed, rocking gently in comfort. When they finally let go there are tears in Carrie's eyes.

'I'm so, so sorry. Oh, hon, it's so unfair.'

'Well, what can you do? At least I've got time to say my goodbyes to everybody, sort out my funeral so my parents don't have to think about it. I've, umm,' she licks her lips, 'I'm going to write letters to both of the kids, for when I'm gone. I thought I'd label them for key ages, like when they become teenagers, turn eighteen, their wedding day—'

Her voice breaks. She turns her back to me, clearly embarrassed as she wipes at her face. I feel mortified, putting a dying woman in this position. While Wendy's back is still turned, I put my hand on Carrie's shoulder to get her attention and motion that I'm leaving.

'See you at the café,' I mouth.

As I walk away I can't stop myself from looking over my shoulder. Carrie and Wendy walk through the doors to the treatment room, Wendy leaning on Carrie for support. My heart breaks for the pair of them. But there is something else, too, something I'm ashamed to acknowledge: part of me is disappointed I've been proved so spectacularly wrong. It's hateful of me.

Where does this leave Carrie and me? I love this woman like she's my daughter, but can we really salvage a relationship when there are so many suspicions in my heart? I always thought I was the keeper of secrets between us, and to discover I'm not alone has been a shock I'm not sure I'll recover from.

# CHAPTER THIRTY

I sit in the café, fingers wrapped around a cardboard cup of lukewarm coffee, wondering what on earth I'm becoming. I'm so used to deceiving others that I now see betrayal and treachery even when they don't exist. Lies have leached into my bones and poisoned everything I've come into contact with.

My phone rings. It's Jackie, from the support group, which is unusual because we don't chat apart from on Monday nights.

'I'm not disturbing you, am I?' she checks, voice slightly breathless.

Around me, people chat, eat, drink, try not to look worried. I push my coffee away from me and sink back into the chair. 'Not at all. What can I do for you?'

'This is going to sound a little odd, but I've been thinking and thinking about it and I just have to speak to someone about it.' A barrage of words, then an awkward pause.

'Okay… '

'I'm not sure about Carrie. She does have cancer, doesn't she? Only, I was talking to Lainey, and her experience seemed to be so different from Carrie's. Whenever I ask, she changes the subject. How come she's got her hair still, when she says she's having chemo? It makes no sense.'

'Jackie, I'm at hospital with her right now. She's getting treatment even as we speak.' Hearing her voice, my own worries makes me realise how crazy they are. 'What kind of person would make something like this up? I certainly wouldn't – it's almost like wishing something bad on yourself. You'd have to be mad.'

'Well, I had to ask. If she can afford that perfume she was wearing the other night, then it makes me wonder why we're raising money for her.'

I roll my eyes. 'What perfume? The one you mentioned the other night? She got it from a sample in a magazine, didn't she?'

'My sister says—'

'What's perfume got to do with Carrie having cancer? I'm surprised at you, Jackie. Making up gossip against a dying woman could get you vilified, and justifiably so. You run a support group. Where's your compassion gone?'

'I'm – I – you won't say anything to anyone, will you?'

'Of course not.'

The call ends. I drum my fingers on the table, thanking my lucky stars I didn't say anything when having my own doubts, because Jackie sounded completely paranoid. My coffee has gone cold. I need a fresh one. As I stand, a thought occurs to me. Carrie had mentioned that Jackie's been a bit off with her lately. She also said our group leader had made comments about my friendship with Carrie. What if *she*'s the one behind the messages?

Why? Disapproval at my brief liaison with Simon? Jealousy that Carrie's so popular? It doesn't seem likely. Nothing in this mess does. Although Jackie and I used to be closer than we now are, but I pulled back a little because she started asking awkward questions about my past. Digging in a way she couldn't during the support group.

Once again it's my phone that pulls me from my thoughts. Carrie has sent a selfie. Despite the tubes up her nose and the chemo port attached, she is grinning in the picture, thumbs up.

*Running a bit late, but should be done soon x*

Even now she's thinking of others. How can anyone, least of all me, believe that she's involved in anything dodgy?

Something bizarre is going on, though.

When Carrie appears, she looks drained.

'That was emotionally tough, as well as physically,' she admits. 'The nurse was making us all smile, though, saying we should imagine we were sucking on delicious sweeties rather than ice cubes, to help with the nausea.'

Despite that, she is determined to do something about Smudge, who still hasn't made an appearance. I try to tell her to slow down, that she needs to look after herself, but she refuses to listen. So we spend the afternoon together at my place again, making a poster on my computer:

*HAVE YOU SEEN THIS CAT?*

As she takes off her hat and ruffles her fingers through her soft blonde hair, I can't help looking. Jackie's awful accusation rises to the surface of my mind like pond scum, refusing to drown no matter how many times I push it under.

Carrie pats at her crop. 'What? Have I got a bald patch coming?'

'No, not at all. Actually, I was thinking it looks good. It's growing back well, isn't it?'

'Thank goodness. I'd hate to be a bald corpse. Don't wince, it's true!' Machine-gun laughter fires. 'I'm so glad this chemo mix I'm on hasn't had the same effect as the last lot.'

'Why hasn't it? Just out of curiosity,' I quickly add, trying to sound idle. 'I thought it always did.'

'No, not every chemo drug causes hair loss. Sometimes it's just thinner or has no change at all. I had a different treatment before, and it left me bald as a coot, even down below. Think Simon quite liked that, actually.'

The mention of our ex makes my eyebrows rocket skywards. It also doubles my guilt. What a cow I am for doubting, even for a second. I've seen the photos of Carrie with a bald head and no eyebrows – and after all, seeing is believing. I shouldn't have let Jackie get to me.

A quicksilver frown flashes across Carrie's face. Has she realised what's behind my questions?

'What is a coot, anyway?'

The change of subject throws me. 'Um, dunno. Type of bird, I think.'

'Is it bald?'

My head tilts, somehow loosening the information. 'No, but it's black with a white patch on the top of its head, so I suppose that's where the saying comes from.'

'Cor, you know everything.'

She's such an innocent abroad. Like Little Red Riding Hood to my wolf. What big teeth I have, all the better to tear chunks out of our friendship and eviscerate my peace of mind to such an extent that when Carrie nips to the loo to vomit, I do a quick Internet search. Cancer Research's website proves that what she told me is correct.

Of course. Did I seriously expect any different? There are enough real mysteries, thanks to those messages and the vandalised Golf. I should concentrate on them, not make up even more. I've got to get a handle on this growing suspicion and paranoia that's making me see danger everywhere and suspect friends.

# CHAPTER THIRTY-ONE

When she returns, Carrie chooses a lovely photograph of Smudge for the 'lost' posters. He's curled up on her sofa, and you can see the distinctive black marks around his eyes and the little red collar with a bell on that he always wears. She's only had him for about six months, but she loves that tomcat with all her heart.

I print off loads of posters, then insist that Carrie goes home while I trudge round the streets and put them up on trees and lamp posts. Anything to make me feel better about the silly suspicions of her that have been playing on my mind.

While walking, I think about the children. They'd have wanted a pet. Probably a dog. I can definitely see Edward with one, and they'd be inseparable. Elise is more independent, so she might be more of a cat person. Imagining them strolling by my side, putting up posters, too, lifts my spirits above the haunting loneliness.

Although, if Elise were here right now, she'd tell me to back off and get the hell away from Carrie, I'm sure. I can see her now, hands on hips, jaw tense. But Edward would understand.

Who am I kidding? If my children were alive today, I wouldn't be doing any of this. There'd be no need to go to a support group and tell lies or look after waifs and strays.

Perhaps it's time to stop rushing around and do as Rosie suggests by taking a long, hard look at my own life. I've been poking my nose in where it has no place. Yes, those messages Carrie's receiving are odd, but they'll stop once she's moved away. Time to stop worrying about her parents, too. Simon is big enough, old enough and ugly enough to look after himself. As for that missing random woman from Cromer, if anyone looks at a picture long enough they can persuade themselves that there is something familiar about a face. It's like making images from a Rorschach inkblot. That's all I've done.

It's time to start looking after myself.

❖

The light is fading fast as I pin the final poster to a tree at around 5 p.m. It's easy to forget how short the days are, this time of year. It doesn't help that there's a sea mist rolling in from the east, smothering street lights and choking off the moon and stars. Time to go home. Turning my collar up around my neck, and shoving both hands into my coat pockets, I hurry along, keen to get in now. Food, bath and bed for me. It's been a tough few days spent working myself into a frenzy, but now I'm feeling more like myself again.

I turn away from the seafront and am only a few streets from my house. Thank goodness. Behind me is someone who seems in just as big a hurry to get home, but I can't see anybody in the rapidly thickening mist. Turning the next corner, I can still hear them shadowing me. They must be close, because the fog is deadening all other sounds and it feels like I'm walking in a white bubble. A shiver of irrational fear runs through me as I hunch down in my coat and walk a bit faster.

The footsteps go faster, too.

Is someone following me? I whirl around. The footsteps stop.

There's someone out there. Watching me. Fog swirls. Opaque, translucent, transparent, dense, ever-shifting. I almost make out a figure. Peer, trying to recognise them, trying to work out if it's male or female, but everything is too indistinct, as if sketched in chalk. Even their size is hard to judge.

But the prickling of my skin tells me they're staring right back.

A clumsy pirouette, and I'm hurrying on. Telling myself I'm overreacting. Urging myself to go faster. I'm being silly, hysterical. My pulse stamps. I'm almost running. My muscles are still weak, my heart struggling from the anorexia. Behind me comes the echo of the person's footsteps. Their breath ghosts my own. They're getting closer. I can almost feel them reaching out for me.

The final corner appears, then I'm in my street. I sprint now, not caring what the person behind me thinks. Almost home and safe. Stumble but don't fall. I have to get distance between me and my stalker before reaching the front door. Gloved fingers fumble in my pockets as I push my weak body forward. Fling the gate open, thud up the garden path. The sound of my ragged breathing closes in on me, the fog stifling me. The key skates around the keyhole as my hands tremble. It skitters across the paintwork.

*Come on!*

A terrified glance thrown over my shoulder. The fog roils. Reveals a figure. Walking slow, calm. Getting closer. Another churn, and they disappear.

The key slides into place. I fall through the door and slam it shut. Lean against it for a second, gasping, then throw the chain and bolt across. Back away, then run upstairs. Edge to the bedroom window, trying not to disturb the curtains and give the game away.

All I see below is a white haze and the occasional halo of orange from the street lights, trying and failing to break through.

I'm safe. For now.

Half an hour or more must have passed, but I'm still curled up on the floor below the bedroom window, shivering, despite the fact that I'm still wearing my coat and hat and the central heating is on full blast. My arms are wrapped around my drawn-up knees, trying to stop myself from shaking apart.

Someone followed me. Despite my best intentions of forgetting about those stupid messages, and my suspicions of Carrie, I now know for sure that someone is after me. They followed me home, chasing me when I ran. This was no coincidence.

There's only one time I've felt more afraid. My mind flies back to it, no matter how hard I fight it, and the trembling grows worse…

❖

There had been so much blood that night. I remembered how I'd stared at my scarlet hand in horror, trying not to panic.

In the space of just a few minutes my fragile peace had been shattered. It was 2 a.m. and I'd been watching *Cheaper by the Dozen* on DVD because I'd felt a bit restless – but I'd put that down to the massive bottle of Lucozade I'd downed. It had had the same effect on the babies, because they'd been kicking like a good 'un all night…

… until I'd suddenly noticed they'd stopped moving. I'd had the funniest feeling, too, like my waters had broken, and a pain was building. Worried, but fighting to stay calm, I'd nipped to the loo and found blood streaming from me.

No, no, no, this couldn't be happening. I blinked, shook my head to try and shake the image in front of me.

But the blood didn't disappear.

I could feel it coursing down my legs. So much – too much to survive. And finally, finally I remembered how to breathe, inhaled a massive lungful and yelled with all my might.

'Owen! Help! I'm losing the babies!'

But Owen couldn't come, of course. He'd been killed four and a half months before that terrible night. I was alone, pregnant and terrified. I'd got another month to go, was only thirty-six weeks gone.

I called an ambulance.

'Help is on its way. You've got to stay as still as possible until then, okay,' urged the person on the end of the phone.

I wanted to panic. I wanted to scream. I wanted my husband with me, soothing me and holding my hand, cracking worried jokes. We'd been together for ten years, spent five trying for a baby. We'd been so excited when I fell pregnant, and we'd already chosen the names Elise and Edward for our twins.

*I'm going to lose them*, I thought. *But I'm going to do everything I can to stop it – and that includes not getting stressed.*

So I called the people I hoped would be rock solid: Owen's parents. Minutes later, Michelle and Colin turned up. Instantly I felt better, knowing I wasn't alone.

The ambulance arrived. I was still bleeding like crazy and contractions had started. At the hospital I was whisked straight in for a scan, Michelle gripping my hand, neither of us breathing until...

'I've got two heartbeats,' said the midwife.

'Thank God!' Michelle and I breathed at once.

'But you've developed placenta praevia, which means your placenta has separated from inside you. Your babies aren't moving because they're being starved of oxygen.

'We're taking you to surgery right now for an emergency caesarean,' the midwife added.

'Surgery?' I yelped. 'No! What if I don't wake up? What if I wake up and my babies haven't made it?'

A horrible panicky feeling clawed at my throat. Something terrible was going to happen during surgery, I just knew it.

'It's okay, love, we're with you,' said Michelle. Beside her, Colin nodded. This time their presence made no difference.

'I can't have an operation,' I insisted, the bad feeling growing.

'Hey, it's okay,' hushed the nurse, taking my hand. 'I've had three caesareans and I'm still here to tell the tale.'

My head was spinning. The room darkening.

'Alex? Alex! Can you hear me? You're losing a lot of blood. We're putting you under right now.'

Time had slowed and stretched, voices distorting.

Then there was nothing.

# CHAPTER THIRTY-TWO

Gritty eyes had blinked slowly open. I'd lifted my heavy head from the pillow and looked around. Panic thudded through me.

'Where are my babies?' I gasped.

'You've got a beautiful daughter. She's in a special ward so she can be well looked after,' replied Michelle, who was sitting beside me.

'Is Elise okay?' I demanded.

'Don't worry. She's little – weighs four pounds – but she's strong.'

I lay back, relieved. 'And how's my boy doing?'

Something wasn't right. Why couldn't Michelle meet my eye properly?

'What is it? Where's Edward? Please tell me.'

'I – I don't know how to find the words.' Her voice cracked; she hid her face. Colin took over.

'You've got to be strong, Alex. Your son, he didn't make it. He's with Owen.'

I shook my head. No screaming, no tears, only denial. 'What happened?'

'The twins were both born dead, first Elise, then Edward. Doctors fought for three long minutes, trying to resuscitate them. You'd died, too – you'd lost so much blood your heart had stopped beating. For two minutes doctors were transfusing pint after pint of blood into you, in a desperate bid to get your heart pumping again.'

Michelle squeezed my hand, her own face slick with tears. 'I – I felt so helpless watching the surgeons deliver the twins. They were so tiny – and silent,' she sobbed. 'The doctors needed to move fast. We were told to the leave the room while they worked on you, but I couldn't leave you. They pumped so much blood into you! I didn't know someone could hold so much blood… Then you and Elise took a breath, at exactly the same time.'

Elise had been whisked away to the Special Care Baby Unit.

'I want to see my baby,' I demanded. Tried to move but felt so weak, utterly exhausted. Panic rose, but not for me – I needed to see my girl, to see she was okay for myself. My hollow body ached for my children.

Just then a doctor walked in. She was holding a photograph of a tiny baby in an incubator. My daughter. I gazed down at it in wonder and cuddled it to my chest.

'When can I see her properly?'

'It's still touch-and-go for her. Once you're strong enough to sit in a wheelchair, you can see her, though.'

'What about Edward?' Despite the circumstances, it didn't feel hard saying his name aloud; it was the most natural thing in the world. As if he was meant to be out there.

'I'm so sorry for your loss. We did everything we could, but the umbilical cord was wrapped around his neck, which caused an extra complication that he was too weak to survive. We can bring him to you now, if you'd like to hold him.'

He was brought in. Beautiful. Perfect. His hair glinted auburn, his mouth a tiny rosebud. I held my son for the first and last time. Gently cradled him, stroked his petal-soft skin, crooned words of love and showered him with light kisses.

'Mummy loves you so much. Your sister and I will miss you more than words can say. But Daddy will look after you now, my angel. I'm sure he will,' I whispered, trying to banish all doubts.

For hours I sat with Edward. Until a nurse finally took him away, gentle but firm, bribing me with the news that I was strong enough to see Elise.

There she was, tiny but beautiful, in her incubator.

'She looks so fragile,' I whispered, my heart breaking.

'She's strong,' replied a nurse. 'In no time she'll have put on enough weight to be cuddled by you, then come home with you. We just have to build her up a bit.'

'And that's all that's wrong?' I checked.

'A tiny heart murmur, but that's all,' she qualified. 'Everything looks positive, even though she's got a long road ahead of her.'

Being able to see her cloaked me in calm for the first time since I'd gone into labour. Leaning forward in my wheelchair, I pushed a hand through the hole in the incubator's side and gently stroked her cheek.

'Stay strong, Elise. Your brother is by your side, lending you his strength.'

My fingers brushed along her arm to her hands. Fingers curled, grasping mine. So brief, so weak, but my heart soared.

That night, though, nurses noticed her stomach seemed distended. There was blood in her stool.

'We think it's a condition called necrotising enterocolitis, an infection and inflammation of the intestine.'

'What's the cure?'

'We'll administer antibiotics, but you need to prepare yourself for the worst. This condition is the leading cause of death in premature infants.'

I'd felt cursed that night, holding my daughter's hand and begging her to stay strong. Her struggle to live was clear to see – but she died that night.

Instead of my twins, I took home a memory box of photographs, Elise's tiny wrist and ankle tags and prints of my children's feet and hands. There'd be no nursery full of cries and laughter, no first steps, no birthdays. I wouldn't get to see my babies grow into fine young adults with their own ambitions. All my hopes and dreams lay shattered at my feet, lacerating every step I took.

It was all my fault.

Owen had died rushing to get presents for me and the twins. Then my body had betrayed my children, killing them with my inability to hold them inside me. Doctors said I'd miscarried because I'd developed pre-eclampsia and said it could have been 'just one of those things'. I knew it was because of my wallowing in grief, though.

My fault.

Too soon, I'd pushed my babies into the world instead of protecting them. I'd wasted precious seconds arguing about having life-saving surgery because of weakness and fear.

My fault.

The memories hurt too much, the empty nursery an open wound that would never close. Little wonder I punished myself with starvation.

Six months later, I moved to Tynemouth. Owen and I had spent a couple of idyllic holidays there, and often said we'd come back with the children. Despite claims of wanting a fresh start, I'd chosen a place that was still full of memories, because leaving them behind hurt as much as embracing them. There's no outrunning grief.

The one thing that's easier in Tynemouth is that no one knows me. I tell people Owen left me because I don't then have to live with the misty-eyed sympathy of people knowing I'm a widow whose children died. I lie to escape the well-intentioned questions, pitying looks, and sighs of sorrow. Because I don't deserve them.

❖

My stomach growls, bringing me back to the present. I'm still sitting below the window, arms curled around my legs, like I imagine my daughter would if she were frightened. My breathing has slowed to normal pace, but I'm shaking with exhaustion and my body, weakened by so much abuse and so little nutrition, is still suffering. Another rumble across my belly. When was the last time I ate? I think back. Two days ago. It can't be. I work it out again, retracing every step in my mind, convinced I've simply forgotten that I had breakfast, or lunch, or a snack, or—

No. It's been two days. I'm falling down the rabbit hole again. So, did I really see what I thought I saw? Or was it another hallucination?

It had to be real. It felt real.

The others did at the time, though. The crazy circus tent. The alternative me in the mirror. Everything.

I've got to get a grip and somehow sort out reality from fiction. That involves keeping my strength up, so I make my way slowly downstairs. Open the fridge. There is nothing appetising inside. But I must eat. I must. A sandwich will do. It looks huge, so I pull the top off it. Just one slice of bread. That's manageable. Right? It's forced down, along with a glass of milk.

It would be so easy not to eat. Don't get me wrong, I actually love eating, but half of me is controlled by anorexia. Like a parasite that has taken over much of me, it urges me to give in to the gnawing emptiness. It whispers that there is peace to be found in the control of not eating and the numbness of starvation. I'm tired of fighting.

But I'm trying hard to make up for my past mistakes. To show my kids I can be strong for them and beat this – even if they aren't around to see it first-hand. I owe it to them not to give up on the life they never had. I need to make amends.

That is the very urge that got me into this mess in the first place, though. I thought I was making things right for my affair with Carrie's boyfriend, and now my life is in danger. Past experience has taught me that no one will believe me if I share my suspicions, though. Who believes a liar, even when they're telling the truth?

# CHAPTER THIRTY-THREE

THEN

There should have been a thunderstorm. At the very least I'd imagined rain as the sky wept along with me. Instead there was nothing so melodramatic, and the day of Mum's funeral was a glorious summer day. The sun beat down on the back of my neck as I stood awkwardly outside the crematorium, sweating in my black jeans and cheap black blouse; the closest approximation to a suit that I could manage.

There was only me, my Aunt Alison, and Mum's best friend from school – who she hadn't talked to for years, to my knowledge. Mum had lost touch with all her friends and family thanks to Dad's manipulation. He'd cut her off like a predator picking on the weakest in the herd.

Dad himself hadn't bothered turning up. He was almost certainly raising a brown paper bag wrapped around cheap vodka in her memory instead, or possibly some extra-strong beer if it was on special offer. Like he did every single day of his life.

As if I had shaped the world with my lies, Mum had got cancer and died. For as long as I could remember I'd imagined Mum dying. Beaten, kicked, strangled, stabbed, pushed from a moving car even. Thanks to my vivid imagination I'd thought I was prepared for anything, but I'd never even considered it would be her body mutinying, rather than her husband kicking the crap out of her. By the time she'd realised what was wrong with her, there'd been nothing doctors could do but try to make her comfortable.

Aged seventeen, I considered myself an orphan, particularly as I spent quite a lot of time wishing Dad would drop off his perch.

The funeral ceremony was swift. A few words said by a vicar who clearly didn't know anything about the woman in question, a mouthed rendition of 'All Things Bright and Beautiful', chosen despite being so at odds with her life, and her coffin sliding silently away behind discreet curtains.

Outside, I gulped down lungfuls of welcome fresh air to blast away the claustrophobia of grief, and saw the bunch of carnations I'd spent the last of my money on tossed on the floor beside blooms from other services. My stomach growled, protesting the waste that would keep it empty tonight. It was the cheapest service I could get, and even then, I'd had to launch a crowdfunding page to afford it. Luckily, plenty of people were moved to dive into their pockets at the word 'cancer', so I hadn't even needed to be creative. Those who had abandoned Mum over the years salved their consciences with donations, which also absolved them of the guilt of not attending the funeral.

Back at Mum's, cards lined the mantelpiece and shelves. Many were sending condolences, but there were others, too.

*Keep fighting!*
*You're an inspiration.*
*To the bravest woman I know.*

My lip curled. They were from people who had barely spoken to Mum in years. Where had they been when she was fighting Dad?

Outside, I heard a scuffling noise. No doubt it was the man himself, coming home drunk. A voice lifted in song. 'Sweet Caroline'. The hypocritical, pickled old bastard was singing Mum's namesake. Moving swiftly to the front door, I shot the bolt across, then did the same at the back door. After forty-five minutes of hammering and yelling, he fell asleep on the doorstep.

The sun had barely risen when I finally opened the door. The ammonia tang of urine stabbed my senses. Eyes watering, I stepped over the prone form of my dad and the puddle he lay in and didn't look back.

As I strode down the garden path, I told myself I'd rather die than go back to that house. Kicking a tin off the path, it landed with a soft thud in the overgrown grass. Maybe Dad's dream would finally come true, and that would be the one to take root and grow into a beer tree.

No keepsakes from the home I'd grown up in weighed me down. I didn't want any. My mementoes lurked inside me. Dad's predilection for lies and cruelty, or Mum's cancer gene, I couldn't help wondering what my inheritance was.

# CHAPTER THIRTY-FOUR

## NOW

The sound of the sea always soothes me, even today, against all odds. It's freezing cold, with glowering clouds billowing across the sky thanks to a strong wind that pushes me from behind, too. I stride along, lost in thought, trying to work out what on earth to do next.

I didn't go to the support group last night, didn't dare to set foot outside in the fog, for fear of who might be waiting for me. The fog still seemed to be swirling in my mind, too, stopping me from seeing properly, obscuring the best path to take to dodge this nightmare. When morning arrived I had to escape outside to try to blow it away, ignoring the voicemail from Carrie.

'Hope you don't mind me checking up on you, but you don't seem like yourself lately. I'm worried,' she'd said. I don't feel like myself. I might be going mad.

Jackie's left a similar one, checking up on me. For now, it's better to avoid everyone, because I've no idea who to trust – including myself.

A large pile of seaweed has been washed ashore by the huge rollers. The kelp is as wide as my forearm and for a moment I feel claustrophobic, imagining it binding my wrists in prayer, tethering me to the waves. The cathedral of the ocean closing over me until I'm encased for ever in deep blue. I shake my head and walk on, the sense of doom keeping pace.

If there's one thing my counselling has taught me, it's that I can't always tackle problems on my own. No more telling myself I can solve this mystery single-handed, playing detective when I'm just a seamstress using up all my strength to stay healthy. It's time to report what's happening.

The nearest police station is North Shields, so on returning from my walk, I drive to my neighbouring town. The station's car park is full. I abandon the car on a street in a pleasant-looking residential area that seems at odds with my tingling nerves. As soon as I enter the long, low, two-storey modern building, a man behind reception gives me a friendly nod.

'I'd like to speak to someone about a crime – possible crime – please.' My clammy hands clasp, unclasp and repeat the movement.

Ten minutes later, a uniformed officer introduces himself as Constable Gadin. He has a kind face that invites confession, even if he does look young. It gives me confidence to speak once we're settled in a side room.

Haltingly, with much backtracking to explain bits I've forgotten to mention then realise they're important, the story comes out.

'So you want to report the anonymous messages and the car being vandalised on behalf of Ms Goodwin?' he checks.

'No. Well, yes, I suppose so. But it doesn't just involve her, don't you see? I'm involved too. I must be. By my reckoning, this person smashed Carrie's Volkwagen up by mistake when they actually wanted to destroy my car.'

PC Gadin isn't reacting to the tumble of words.

'The vandalism was to send me some kind of message. Then there's the photographs sent to Carrie – they also involve me. It can't be a coincidence that there is a picture of the two of us, or that the next picture was of Simon—'

'He's the one you were both dating?'

'Exactly, and now I think him going missing might have something to do with Carrie.'

How she's managed to make a grown man disappear is another matter, but the whole point of coming to the police is so that they can find the answers, not me. I'm only glad to be dumping all the problems on someone else. That probably explains my verbal diarrhoea.

PC Gadin refers to his notes. 'Right, you mentioned this. And you believe she's involved in the disappearance of somebody else as well? That she is someone my colleagues in Norfolk are keen to speak to?'

Again I nod, leaning forward eagerly. 'That's right.'

The officer himself leans back in his chair. Taps his fingers on the table. 'I'm a bit confused. The messages you mentioned, do you think Carrie Goodwin sent them to you?'

'No, they weren't sent to me. They were sent to her.'

'Okay. But you think she's done something wrong. She's made people disappear.'

'I'm not sure. Possibly.'

'Do you know how?'

I chew my lip, thinking. Shake my head. My leg starts to jiggle.

He rubs his temples. 'You say that the woman in the photograph, is – now where is it… ?' Another quick reference to his notes so he can quote me, 'Ah, here it is: "Looks like my friend, but doesn't".'

'She's changed her appearance, you see. She's lost weight, got a new hairstyle, wears completely different types of clothes. But it has been two years almost since this Joanne went missing, so there's been plenty of time for those changes.'

'We can definitely look into this for you and contact Norfolk. Do you have the photographs and messages?'

'Ah, well, the thing is, I destroyed them. I panicked. It was stupid of me, but I'm afraid I burnt them.'

'You're the only person that's ever seen these messages?' The doubt in his eyes infuriates me.

'Why does that change anything? I'm telling you, this missing woman and my friend are both being looked for by the police. It really isn't that hard to comprehend. All you have to do to check out my story is contact Norfolk police. Why don't you do your job, instead of sitting there looking at me over steepled fingers as though I'm insane? Look at that frown on your face!'

'You need to calm down, ma'am.'

'Don't call me "ma'am" in passive-aggressive fashion. Just listen to me. I know the story sounds mad and convoluted, and I'm doing an atrocious job of explaining, but somebody has been sending threatening messages to my friend. They involve me, I'm scared, and now I think that my friend is somehow involved in a woman going missing. Someone followed me last night. My life may be in danger. I also strongly believe that Carrie is linked somehow with Simon disappearing. You need to look into this and stop treating me like I'm mad.'

'I am listening to you, ma'am, but you really need to calm down.'

The officer doesn't believe me. He's trying his best to hide it, but he's placating me, using a soothing voice as though I'm hysterical. If only I hadn't burnt those photographs; they were the only evidence I had. Instead of calming down, my voice rises in volume.

'You've got to believe me. I'm in danger, someone is after me. Carrie Goodwin isn't who she says she is, that isn't her name. Her last best friend disappeared – and I'm next!'

'Why do you think you're in danger?'

'Because someone followed me last night.'

'And you believe it was Ms Goodwin?'

'No! Why would Carrie follow me? She knows where I live.'

My head is thumping. I push my chair back. Stand up, stumble, holding my head in my hands. The room is spinning like a gyroscope, but I cling to consciousness because PC Gadin has to be made to understand. One last go, shouting over the blood pounding in my ears.

'You've got – you've got to listen to me. Someone followed me last night. They want to make me disappear like they made Joanne and Simon disappear. I don't understand how I got involved in this. You've got to help me, you've got to save me.'

The room seems to somersault, the floor rising up to meet me. The last thing I hear is a shout of alarm.

# CHAPTER THIRTY-FIVE

After a brief check over when I came round, the police doctor has given me the all-clear. Once again, I'm in the interview room, but this time with someone else, a Dr Sharma. She's about 50, but doesn't have a single grey hair in her glossy black bob. She doesn't sit on the opposite side of the table, instead she perches beside me, her chair turned to the side so that it's facing me. It's so she seems friendlier. She clearly doesn't want to scare me and make me freak out again.

'Alex, do you understand that you're being temporarily detained for your own welfare under Section 136 of the Mental Health Act? We can keep you here for up to seventy-two hours until we reach a decision on your mental state.'

Movements are careful and considered, words are carefully pitched to be professional but non-threatening. An expectant silence waits for me to reply, so I nod my compliance.

'Are you on any medication or taking any form of drugs?'

A flicker of surprise when I say I'm not. My hands are getting clammy again, but I push on anyway, mimicking Dr Sharma's tone.

'Look, I know I got a bit hysterical earlier, and I apologise sincerely. It was completely unnecessary. But it doesn't change what I'm saying, and I'd be incredibly grateful if someone would listen to me and take me seriously.'

'We're taking your claims very seriously, Ms Appleby, I can assure you.'

'Thank you.' My smile is hesitant because she opens up a cardboard file. Studies some paperwork inside it.

'The thing is, Alex, when you passed out we had a look in your mobile phone for an emergency contact and we found the details of the eating disorder clinic you've been attending. I've spoken with your therapist, Rosie Knight.'

'I don't see what she's got to do with this.'

'Okay, I need you to stay calm.'

'I am being calm.' I'm literally biting my lip. Surely everyone gets annoyed when they're told repeatedly to calm down when they already are.

Dr Sharma glances at the paperwork again.

'Ms Knight has made us aware of your medical background, Alex, which is why we are now going to be looking into assessing you.'

'So you're not actually investigating what I've reported to you. You're checking to see if I'm mad or not.' Deep inside I'm fighting not to give in to the desire to shout in order to be taken seriously, but on the surface I'm controlled. A switch has flicked inside me now that my liberty is in danger. I must sell self-assurance. This is simply another lie people need to believe about me – I've done it before; can do it again.

'You have suffered states of delirium previously, as a result of undernutrition,' observes Dr Sharma.

'There's no point denying it. One morning I even woke up with another me screaming at me to get up. That was the incident that got me sectioned and kept in the clinic for my own good until I started putting weight on. As you've stated yourself, it was the result of undernutrition.'

*Straighten your back, maintain eye contact, keep the voice low and steady. Minuscule alterations to make me believable.*

'This is different. Everything I've said today is real. Please help me persuade the police to look into this.'

'While you've been here, Alex, officers have looked into part of your claims. You are concerned about your friend, Simon, correct? He's been tracked down in Cornwall. Family members have confirmed that he decided to move there to, and I quote, "ride the waves". Our colleagues in Cornwall have spoken with him and can confirm that he is safe and well.'

The images that have been running through my head of him lying dead somewhere, his tanned body blue and lifeless, disappear. Muscles unknot at the knowledge I don't have to feel responsible for his death any more.

'Thank you for finding him! I can't believe it! So, what about this Joanne Freeman, will you be talking to Carrie about her?'

'Norfolk police aren't looking to speak to anyone named Carrie Goodwin in relation to the case—'

'Yes, but that's not her real name, she's… crap, I've forgotten her real name, but anyway, Carrie is a pseudonym. Oh, Natalie Sheringham, that's it. Look her up.'

'Alex, there is absolutely no proof Ms Goodwin is the person that the police want to speak to. You said yourself she doesn't look like the woman in the photograph—'

'She does, it's only that she's changed her appearance.'

The radiator in the room makes a strange gurgle and clunk. It's the only sound to be heard for several minutes. Finally the doctor speaks.

'You do realise this story doesn't make sense, don't you? The police have investigated your claims as far as they can, and we can confirm that Simon is fine. They really don't have time to waste on wild goose chases. There's no evidence of any threatening messages existing, because you destroyed them. As for the vandalism, Ms Goodwin needs to report that herself.'

I almost argue. Almost. But there's a little nagging doubt in my head. Elise, ever the voice of reason, seems to be whispering in my ear.

'You sound insane. You thought Simon had been hurt, or worse – but he's fine. You're banging on about threatening messages, but you're the only one who's seen them. You doubted Carrie had cancer, against all evidence to the contrary. You've been forgetting to eat. Face it, Mum, you're losing the plot.'

Elise isn't the only one who thinks I'm losing the plot and sliding back into old, bad ways. I've only been allowed out of police custody so that I can transfer into the clinic. Now they plan on assessing me themselves, to see whether or not they should keep me in. My whole team sits in front of me, looking dour. Rosie's even brushed her hair. Things must be serious.

'I feel terrible for wasting the police's time,' I offer apologetically.

'Our main concern isn't the police, Alex, it's what's going on with your health,' says Rosie.

My medical doctor, Sandra, chips in. 'Your blood pressure is low again. It's not dangerous yet, but it's enough to be ringing alarm bells with us. How much walking are you doing?'

'Nothing excessive,' I say. Although I suppose actually the miles have been racking up lately, what with going back and forth to Carrie's, then wandering along the beach. Is that too much, in my weakened state?

'Regardless, if your blood pressure falls much lower we're going to have to think about you using a wheelchair again.'

*No way.*

'We also have some concerns about your weight.'

'But my weight is fine! I know I haven't put any on lately, but you always say that maintaining is good, too.'

'Let me show you something.' Rosie pulls out a large piece of paper. On it is a graph with three lines climbing slowly across. 'Anywhere between these two lines represents an acceptable weight gain on your part. This third line represents your actual weight measurements at every weigh-in you've had since leaving the clinic as an inpatient. See how it hugs the line that illustrates the lowest acceptable weight gain?'

Rosie runs a finger along it to underline her point.

My medical doctor, Sandra, chips in. 'We're uneasy that you're deliberately doing the minimum to get better so that you can be discharged from outpatients – and go straight back to your old ways.'

'Rubbish,' I splutter.

'Anorexics can be very manipulative,' says Rosie. 'Is that what you're doing? We need to know the truth.'

I stare hard at the bottom line. They've got a point about it clinging to that third green line. It wobbles a little bit, sometimes falling slightly below, sometimes slipping slightly above, but overall I really am only gaining the least amount of weight it's possible to get away with.

Worse, the last two weigh-ins show a slight drop in weight.

*Why? Why am I lying to myself about wanting to get better?*

I'm a perfectionist. I've always tried so hard to get things right for everyone, and I've failed them all. Owen, Elise, Edward, and now even Carrie. That's why I need to be punished – but my own punishment is also why I'm now letting down my best friend.

'I can see why you're concerned. I've been letting myself get distracted by things. Things that, maybe, shouldn't really concern me.'

Sandra clears her throat, and as she stands so does everybody else in the team apart from Rosie. 'We're going to leave you two to it.'

'Oh, okay, thank you for everything,' I reply.

Only when the door closes does Rosie pipe up.

'You mentioned letting yourself get distracted by things that shouldn't really concern you. We need to explore this. Do you think it's possible that you're making things up in order to have something to distract yourself with?'

I frown and give a helpless shrug, honestly at a loss.

'Think hard about everything that's been happening in the last couple of weeks, Alex. Since your friend told you that she's dying, your eating habits have been badly affected, and by coincidence a series of strange events appears to have been triggered.'

I look at her. She looks at me.

'By coincidence,' she repeats.

'You're suggesting that subliminally I've been making up problems that aren't really there?' I almost laugh. 'The footsteps last night weren't just a figment of an overwrought imagination.' *Were they?* 'And what about those messages? They were real, they were sent to Carrie.'

I know what she is going to say before she's even said it.

'Did you show them to Carrie?'

'You know I didn't. You don't think they existed, do you? Why would I make it up? I'm not a fantasist.'

'I'm more interested in exploring what you believe has really happened here. Fantasist isn't a label I like to use.'

She may not like to use the label, but it certainly feels like it's dangling off me right now. I *was* followed last night. I heard the footsteps; I saw a figure.

Although it could have been somebody as keen as me to get home from the fog. Maybe I felt them staring at me because they could tell I was scared, or because they knew that I was staring at them, or because they got lost, or...

Doubts are creeping in. Perhaps this whole elaborate web has been spun by a grief-stricken, food-deprived brain in danger of shutting down.

'Look up the news article on the Internet,' I ask.

# CHAPTER THIRTY-SIX

Sensing victory isn't far away, Rosie does as I request immediately and turns her computer screen to allow me a better view.

Looking at the woman again, I can't be absolutely certain that it's the same person who was in the photograph that was sent to me. *If the photograph was sent to you*, I can almost hear Elise add. Instead I study the image of the friend, Natalie Sheringham.

Digging out my phone, I open up the selfie Carrie sent me in hospital. She beams out at me, thumbs up, nasal tube in place. I hold it up beside the one of Natalie and Joanne.

Where Carrie's features are fine and delicate, Natalie's are hidden beneath a layer of fat. Even so…

'See? They've got the same eyes and lips. Oh, and what about her nose? It's the same woman. It's Carrie!'

My therapist's head tilts. 'I don't know, to me her eyes seem far more almond-shaped than Carrie's, and her lips much fuller. Is that a bump on Natalie's nose, or a shadow? The women are similar, yes, but I'm not convinced they're the same person.'

'That's just the way her make-up's done,' I argue. There is defeat in my voice.

'You've always said Carrie is quite outgoing. Look at her eye contact with the camera, the bright, clashing colours she wears – she screams openness and confidence. This is a woman at ease with herself. Then there's Natalie, masked behind heavy make-up, chin down as if trying to hide from the camera even as she poses, the black clothes. Nothing like your friend, would you say?'

Put like that, it was true. Look at each part individually and they don't add up to Carrie.

Everything is getting muddled in my head, and even I can no longer make sense of the conspiracy theories I've woven and tangled. Maybe I didn't burn the box and the photographs, because maybe they never existed. Maybe I wasn't followed. Maybe this isn't Carrie. After all, Simon is fine and my friend has cancer – two things I started this week being convinced were the opposite.

'What about the smashed windscreen?' I clench my fists, frustrated with myself at not being able to stop arguing even when it's in my best interests.

Rosie sighs. I'm on thin ice. If she doesn't like what she sees during this assessment, she has the power to detain me here, whether I like it or not, for my own good. I have to convince her I'm recognising the error of my ways. In other words, I have to say whatever it takes to get out of here – because I am not going to let myself be sectioned again.

'I'm willing to admit that you've got a point about everything else,' I say. 'But the windscreen, that's not a figment of my imagination. Carrie saw it. Her car is still parked on the street outside my house, with slashed tyres and taped-on cardboard for a windscreen. Someone did that.'

Brushed hair gets messed up as Rosie runs her hand through it from back to front, as she often does when working.

'Sometimes when people develop obsessive behaviour, it's possible to transfer that behaviour from one thing to another, Alex. For example, it's possible for someone to exchange an obsession with food for an excessive interest in a person.'

My eyes narrow. Then widen.

'That's what I've done, isn't it? This all started when Carrie told me she was terminally ill. I've tried so hard to look after her and protect her, but I've felt a failure. It's like losing the children all over again. Since those feelings began to develop, that's when everything started to fall apart,' I gasp. 'I – I think maybe because I can't control her cancer I've been making up something that I can control, weaving a mystery where Carrie is in danger and only I can solve it and save her.'

Hands cover my head in embarrassment. 'Maybe I even smashed Carrie's windscreen myself then blocked it out – I don't know, I just don't know. Or maybe it was just vandals, and I've taken the coincidence and added it to my fabrication. Oh, Rosie, is it all really about control? About finding an excuse not to eat?'

I look up and meet my therapist's eyes. Shake my head in determination. 'I'm not going to let that happen. I'm beating this eating disorder once and for all.'

Truth burns through my words, making them blaze as I continue.

'I've been trying to control everything since my children died. But it can't be done; the world is full of chaos and I have to accept that. To acknowledge it, I have to acknowledge what is happening to Carrie – and what happened to my family, and—' my voice catches, the room blurring from my tears, 'and I have to mourn. It's time I started being honest with myself and everybody around me.'

Rosie lays down her pen, leans back and gives me an appraising look.

'How do you feel about facing your grief for your family?'

'Liberated – and terrified. The pain of loss is gut-wrenching, and I'll never stop wondering whether, by choosing to tell the truth instead of a lie, my life could have been totally different. Who can say? I may not have chosen the fabric of my life, but I cut it out and sewed it together, and now I have to figure out why it doesn't fit me and fix it.

'The only way to stop the cycle of anorexia and punishment – and delusion – is to face facts. My husband and children are dead. Carrie is dying.'

A tear trickles down my face at saying it out loud.

'I can't tell you how pleased I am with this breakthrough,' Rosie says.

The cold air outside greets me in a celebratory embrace. I'm free! Of course, the clinic will still be keeping a close eye on me, and I still have to go there for twice-weekly weigh-ins and counselling sessions, but at least I'm still an outpatient. Rosie is really pleased with the progress that I've made today, and the significant breakthrough. As long as I continue to do well, be honest and put on weight, I won't be permanently admitted, she says.

Edward, normally so calm, is agitated in my imaginings right now. As usual, I'm humanising the internal arguments that rage inside me. It helps me to think. I put my hands in my pockets and head towards the beachfront to walk home via the longer but prettier route beside the sea.

'None of this makes any sense, Mum. If it walks like a duck and quacks like a duck, it's a duck.'

'So you're saying… ?'

'I'm saying that your explanations don't compute – but neither do anybody else's. This whole situation is walking and talking like it's a mystery, like something stinks here, so trust your instincts, keep digging and get to the bottom of it.'

'I couldn't have said it better myself.' In my mind, Elise claps her brother on the back and grins. 'Sorry for doubting you. Don't listen to anyone else, do what you think is right.'

'Oh, don't worry, I had no intention of doing anything but keeping on digging. Come on, you know how stubborn I can be. But I had to convince Rosie to let me go.'

'What's the next move then?' asks Elise.

'At the centre of everything is Carrie. That's not an obsession, that's a fact. So—'

Before I can continue my phone bleeps with a Google alert I set up a few days ago, when I first discovered that news article. What I read makes me feel weak.

Bones on Beach are Joanne's screams the headline.

Sinking down onto a bench overlooking the sea, and glowered at by the ancient priory ruins, I make myself read on. There's the now-familiar photo of Joanne and Natalie, below a much larger picture of the man and his big, shaggy bear of a dog, on the beach.

> Bones washed ashore at Cromer during Saturday's storm have been confirmed as those of missing woman Joanne Freeman, police say.
>
> The horrifying discovery was made by Mike McFarlane early on Sunday morning when he was walking his dog.
>
> 'My German shepherd, Rex, ran over to me with something in his mouth. He was ever so pleased with himself. I got him to drop it so that I could throw it, because I thought it was a piece of driftwood,' says Mr McFarlane, 28. 'When I realised it was a bone, I went nuts. You don't expect to see that sort of thing, not in a quiet town like this. When the police arrived they cordoned off the whole beach. I later heard they'd found more bones – human bones by the look of it.
>
> 'Straight away I thought about that poor woman that's missing. My heart goes out to her family.'
>
> Forensic officers have reportedly run a number of tests on the remains and have now confirmed that they do belong to Mrs Freeman.
>
> A police spokesperson exclusively told The Inquirer: 'A number of bones were found by a member of the public several days ago. As a result we have broken the news of her death to Mrs Freeman's family. Although the case will remain open, there is insufficient evidence to show whether what happened to her was suicide, a tragic accident or foul play.'

> A source close to the police informed The Inquirer that only a few bones had been washed ashore, and that much of the remains are still missing. As such, it has been impossible to tell how Mrs Freeman died, or even when.
>
> 'What little was left of her had been picked clean by crabs and other scavengers in the water, so we'll probably never know the full story,' the source says.

I race over the background of how she was last seen eighteen months ago. Police are still eager to speak with Natalie Sheringham, or anyone else who may know Mrs Freeman's last movements. The article ends with contact details.

They're still looking for the mysterious Natalie, then. It's so frustrating that the police won't take seriously my assertion that she and Carrie are one and the same. A quick analysis of fingerprints or DNA or something would surely show they are; a background check would prove Carrie Goodwin doesn't actually exist. I do understand it, though. I've read too many news reports in the past of leads not followed up, missed opportunities, where people have ended up being hurt or even killed as a result. It's not a criticism of the police that they don't have the time or resources to follow up everything reported to them; more a reflection of the limited funding and increasing demands stretching a thin blue line to breaking point. And let's face it, I sound like a crazy person even to myself, so why on earth would they listen to me?

I'm not crazy, though – and somehow I'll prove it.

# CHAPTER THIRTY-SEVEN

Carrie's voice washes over me as I drive her to hospital the next day. While she chit-chats about what she did yesterday, I nod, smile, laugh and play the part of clueless friend, chipping in when needed but never mentioning that I spent all day having my sanity questioned.

'I had a relaxing day sewing,' is my reply when asked.

My hand gives a little twitch as I change gear.

Knowing that she'd be attending hospital again for treatment, I sent Carrie a text last night offering her a lift.

As I drop her off I apologise that I won't be able to wait for her.

'I've got to get back for the clinic. Let me know when you're done, though, and I'll give you a lift back. How long do you think you'll be?'

'Not sure. But it's no problem if you can't give me a lift back. Honestly.'

'Will Wendy be there?'

'Umm, maybe. Anyway, see you later – and thanks again for doing all this running around for me.'

She doesn't watch me drive away, instead she heads straight into the hospital. But I'm watching her in my rear-view mirror, checking she doesn't see me turn in to the multistorey car park. She's got no idea that my weigh-in and counselling have been cancelled because it was all done yesterday, and I'm not due back until my Friday appointment – which frees me up unexpectedly today. Perfect.

❁

I park as quickly as I can and then hurry into the hospital, doing something between a walk and a jog in my desperation to reach Oncology quickly. Every time I've come to hospital with Carrie there's been a reason why I can't come into the treatment room with her. *She's felt embarrassed about how sick she'll get; she doesn't want to bore me; someone else getting treatment that day has a really low immune system, so no one else is allowed in other than patients.* They've always been plausible, so I've never question them. Today, though, I'm determined not to let anything stop me getting inside that room.

I open the door with such resolve that it bounces off the wall and starts to swing back towards me. I have to put my hands out to stop it smacking me in the face. A handful of women sitting in a line all look up at me, surprised. They are in comfy chairs with padded armrests, many in a reclined position, feet up, like a sun lounger. This is no holiday camp, though, as beside each woman is a drip feeding into their arm and a machine that is regulating the medication.

'Chemotherapy: must be handled with caution', blaze yellow stickers over the bags of clear liquid.

Two nurses behind a semicircular desk greet me with a chorus of: 'Can I help you?'

'I'm looking for one of your patients, Carrie Goodwin.'

'We can't give out information on patients, I'm afraid,' says the shortest nurse, with auburn hair. Her colleague continues typing into the computer.

'Of course, sorry.' I glance around, and Carrie isn't anywhere to be seen. 'I just thought she was having treatment today, and wanted to surprise her, show my support, you know, in her time of need. But I must have my days muddled up. She's about yay tall, very slender, short blonde hair. Really pretty. I know she was here on Monday at the same time as her friend, Wendy.' My voice goes up a little at the end, even though I'm not asking a question.

'Oh, Wendy's friend! She isn't sick. She's a hospital visitor, sits with patients while they have treatment. Tall, tiny build, cute pixie crop, right?'

'That's her.'

The other nurse interrupts. 'Can't be her, her name isn't Carrie, it's Louise.'

'Louise, of course. I'm sorry, what's her last name again?' But neither nurse will say, something to do with privacy and data protection, or something. When I show them a photo of 'Louise' they give me the nod, though it's reluctant. They're starting to frown, wondering what the hell is going on, I bet, so I say thanks and leave.

It doesn't matter, because I've got her. The woman I know as Carrie has at least three names and is lying about having treatment, which means she's lying about the fact that she's got cancer.

So where the hell is she now? When I find her I'll confront her, tear a strip off her. First I have to hunt her down, though.

I start wandering slowly back towards the exit, trying to work out the answer. If I had to kill time in the hospital, I'd go to the café. But I know she doesn't go there because I've sat there so many times waiting for her. I try anyway. Then check the stairwells, but there's no sign of her. I'm at a loss, walking aimlessly. Until a sign catches my eye.

PATIENTS' LIBRARY

A thrill of anticipation runs through me upon reaching the room. I've got a good feeling about this: Carrie and I both love reading, and it is one of the things that bonds us, yet she's never mentioned this patients' library to me.

Gently, I push open the door, not making a sound. The distinctive smell of old books fills the air, enticing me. There are three people inside and not one of them looks up, too engrossed in what they're reading. One of them is Carrie.

No, no, no, that couldn't possibly be true. Confronted with the truth, I realise how much I'd been hoping to be proved wrong. Who would lie about having cancer? And why?

*Financial gain. All that money that's been raised for her bucket list.*

Something stops me from surging forward and shouting at her, as planned. There are still so many unanswered questions, but gut instinct tells me that if I confront her she won't give honest answers. Right now, it's enough to know that I was right, that this hasn't all been in my imagination. Finally, I'm starting to make headway and get the upper hand.

I step back before anyone can spot me, holding onto the door until it eases into place. Turn to go back to the car – and bump headlong into a man.

'Sorry!' He holds onto my shoulders as if to steady me. 'Nearly sent you flying.'

He's not much taller than me, but is really strong, judging from his grip. His eyes are bright blue, and they turn down slightly, just like Owen's. But it's his smile that I notice. It seems familiar, and he's looking at me as if he recognises me, too.

Searching my memory, I suddenly realise I have seen him before – outside Crusoe's. He's the man who smiled at me when I was remembering my night of passion with Simon, and blushing.

'Do we know each other?' he checks.

I shake my head, make my excuses. With only the briefest glances back over my shoulder, I leave him behind. He's still watching me, a curious expression on his face that makes me want to turn and speak to him again. Now is not the time to be flirting, though.

❖

After forty-five minutes of sitting in my car thinking about everything I've learned, I drop Carrie a text.

*Clinic was super-fast today, so am already back at hospital. Let me know when you're ready.*

The reply doesn't take long to arrive – her treatment is over and she's all set for her lift with me, apparently.

When she gets into the car I force my sneer into a smile.

'How are you feeling? Did chemo go okay?'

'Same old, same old.' Her smile is weak and weary. There are grey smudges under her eyes, and I can't help wondering how she manages that. Maybe there really is something wrong with her, but if there is, then why not tell the truth about that rather than pretend to have cancer? It's just one more question about the conundrum of Carrie.

Pulling up outside her house, I watch her ease herself from her seat. Ginger movements, slow and painful. She's one hell of an actress. Me, too.

'I'll pop back later and bring you a lasagne that I'm making. Got to keep your strength up,' I smile. It only slips into a glower after I've waved and driven off.

I actually really resent making her meal now, but if I don't it will look suspicious because, sucker that I am, I almost always do cook for her. On her birthday I'd even baked her a rainbow cake to celebrate because she loves rainbows. It had been a big step in my recovery, making it. Now I feel a total idiot.

Worse, other people have been made a fool of by Carrie, thanks to my encouragement. She must be doing it for the money – it's the only logical explanation – but surely if she planned to steal the bucket list fund she'd know that I'd report it the minute it went missing. Then, like clouds parting to reveal the sun, I see what would happen. She's waiting for the cash to be handed over when she 'moves to be with her parents', then she'll skip off into the sunset with it, free to squander it away from prying eyes.

❖

Back at home, instead of seeing a client, as I've told Carrie, I spend some time on the Internet again. First I check my account's balance. Everything looks in order, but I change all of the security passwords, just in case.

There are some legalities I want to check out, and I'm not going to risk asking the police after yesterday's debacle.

By the end of another long day of research on the Internet, I'm exhausted, and once again unsure of what to do next. The fact is, as vile as Carrie's lies are, she hasn't broken any laws by pretending to have cancer. To my knowledge she hasn't submitted any insurance claims for her fake illness. I remember a while back asking Carrie if she had any kind of critical injury cover, and her joking that cleaners don't have the money for that type of thing. Also, when I was looking for her address book, I didn't come across any paperwork of that kind.

She hasn't claimed any benefits she shouldn't, either, always insisting she's too proud – she even turned me down when I offered to look into whether she was eligible for anything and to fill in the paperwork for her. I can only assume it's because anything official like that would ring instant alarm bells that she's using a fake name. So no crime there.

And here's the big one: she hasn't defrauded anyone. Carrie hasn't raised any money under false pretences – it's me that's asked people to donate to her fund, and the money is currently sitting safely in my account. All I have to do is give it back to those who've given it.

I can't help thinking I should wait, though. She deserves to be punished for these horrible lies, and money must be at the root of it, so I'll hold onto the cash for a tiny bit longer and see if I can trap her into making a mistake. Then moral and legal justice can be done.

If it doesn't happen soon, though, I'll let everyone know the truth anyway. Let Carrie face the wrath of the community.

Besides, there are still things I don't understand. Who followed me? Who is sending the messages, and what do they mean? Does someone else know about Carrie's lies, and is trying to blackmail her? Perhaps it's Jackie, support group founder and former friend, who is perfectly placed to know so many people's secrets. Until the whole story is revealed, I'm going to keep all fears and theories to myself. I have to, because the authorities already think I'm mad, Rosie believes I'm obsessed and no one is on my side. This has to be played carefully.

There's something else troubling me, too. Several times now I've offered to give Carrie money from her bucket list. She could easily have got me to hand it all over. But every time I've offered her the money, she's refused.

So what on earth is going on?

# CHAPTER THIRTY-EIGHT

With a new day comes a new determination to end this nonsense. I've spent all night thinking about it, and I can't see any other way of getting to the truth besides confronting Carrie. All this running around trying to play detective like a character in a film is going to lead to unnecessary complications. Instead, I'll go straight to the source, tell her I know she's lying about the cancer and find out the full story from her own lips. I need the closure of looking her in the eye and hearing the truth.

After making myself eat a full breakfast to give me strength for the confrontation, I walk round to Carrie's house. The wind is whistling, blowing a fine, powdered snow into my eyes that billows around like a bitter sandstorm. On my right, below my pavement vantage point, the sea boils and churns a cauldron of death. The clouds, laden with snow and icy rain, seem to mirror it.

Despite the freezing conditions, that group of boys is racing around Carrie's cul-de-sac on their bicycles. Children don't seem to feel the cold like adults, and for a moment I indulge myself, imagining Elise and Edward on their bikes, eight years old, their cheeks glowing as they race each other, and me and Owen calling them from the warmth of our home. I can almost see them. Sometimes my imaginings feel so real I feel like I'm being given a peek through to another life, where everything worked out perfectly. Owen and me and our two beautiful children are all happy together. But not in this universe. Deep down, I know the idyllic images would not have been anything like the reality.

These are the thoughts running through my head as I nod an acknowledgement to the boys that makes them scatter like billiard balls across a table. Then I press on, steeling myself for a horrible confrontation with the person I've come to think of as a second daughter.

A swift rap on the door. When Carrie answers and invites me in, she seems so normal. Although if I look closely there does seem to be a little tightness in her jaw, her shoulders set slightly higher than normal. She's clutching a jumper.

'Everything okay?' I can't help but ask. I've been worrying about her too long now for it not to come automatically, despite myself.

'I'm fine, as well as can be expected that's for sure. But I've been talking to my parents, and we've agreed it's time for me to move back in with them. They're coming to get me tonight.'

'Tonight? Why the big hurry, all of a sudden?'

'What's the point in wasting time I don't have? I was going to call you later, but I'll be honest… I wasn't sure if I could really face saying goodbye to you.'

There are tears in her eyes as she glances at me, then looks quickly away and starts folding the jumper in her hands. Perhaps she's realised her charade has been discovered. Either that, or she's about to ask me for the money.

'Carrie, are you really leaving with your parents, or is there something else going on?'

The folded jumper goes onto a pile of clothes. She picks up a pair of jeans, fingers fumbling.

'Of course I'm leaving with my parents. What are you trying to get at?'

'If this is the way that you want to play it… I know, Carrie. I know you don't have cancer.'

Carrie's hands are on her hips, and her eyes are wild with indignation, but I'm sure I can see a seed of panic there, too. She barges past me, out of the room, me following closely. Vitriol cascades behind her.

'I can't believe you'd say such a vile thing. What's wrong with you, are you sick in the head or something? You been having weird hallucinations again because you're not eating properly?'

The words are like a slap. I step back, gasp in shock that she would deliver such a low blow. Instantly she turns round again, and I brace myself for more accusations. But Carrie doesn't attack, instead she wipes at her wet face.

'I'm so sorry, I didn't mean that. It was an awful thing to say.'

'That's okay,' I reply. 'Attack is the best form of defence, after all. I get it, you've been caught out and you're trying to put me on the back foot. It doesn't change what I'm saying to you, though. I. Know. That you. Don't. Have. Cancer.' I hold up my hand. 'Don't try to deny it. Yesterday when you said you were having treatment, I followed you, and you were nowhere to be seen in the chemotherapy room. I spoke to the nurses, and they confirmed that you're not sick. In fact, you're just a hospital visitor, aren't you – who isn't even called Carrie. That's how you know Wendy.

'I have to admit, that was either incredibly lucky or incredibly clever of you, bumping into her the other day, because I was already suspicious of you. Seeing you two together made me doubt myself – I thought I was a terrible person for thinking you could lie about something as hideous as having cancer.'

'I've... You're mad. I just got muddled about the time of my treatment yesterday, and got embarrassed about you putting yourself out giving me a lift – that's why I pretended to have chemo when I hadn't. No, you've had your say, let me finish. I don't know which nurses you spoke to, but they don't know what they're talking about, clearly, because I *have* got cancer. Terminal cancer.'

She starts to glance around, searching for something. 'I can, erm, I can, hang on, I can give you my doctor's number if you want. No, actually, she's really busy, so if she doesn't know you then she might not speak to you. But if I call her then I'm sure she'll find time to speak to us.'

'You're babbling.'

'I'm not! I'm just, just shocked by what you're saying. It's horrible. Horrible! Look, I'm phoning my doctor now.'

Her hands are trembling as she pulls out her phone and pretends to scroll through a contacts list that I know only contains my number and the pub where she does cleaning and bar shifts. It feels tragic, watching her pacing up and down, talking to a make-believe person, lying through her teeth. Like I'm watching the death of the person I thought I knew.

'Dr Patten? Yes, hi, it's Carrie Goodwin. I just wondered if you had a moment speak to a friend of mine, Alex Appleby. I know it sounds crazy, but she wants to hear the details of my condition, and I'm giving you permission to speak to her about it freely. What's that? Oh, you're busy right now. Any chance of speaking to her later today? That sounds perfect, I really appreciate it.'

She rattles off my mobile number before saying goodbye, looking at me triumphantly as she ends the call. 'She is hoping to be free in the next ten minutes to half an hour. She'll call you then and explain everything.'

My hands rub over my face, eyes, cover my mouth, because I don't know where to look or what to say. It's mortifying, seeing her like this. I thought I'd be furious with her; instead, I'm embarrassed by her desperation to dig herself into a deeper and deeper hole. She can feel it, too.

'Would you mind leaving? I know we still have things to sort out,' she says, gently taking hold of my elbow and leading me towards the front door, 'but I'm feeling a bit queasy, to be honest. This is all too much for me, and I really need to sit down and rest. There's still so much to do.' She gestures around at the few goods she has to pack. It's only a couple of bags of clothes, to be honest. She owns so little.

Pity is the last thing I should feel after what she's done, yet for the sake of the friendship we once had, I'm tempted to leave her with what tiny shred of dignity she has left. She doesn't deserve it, but all I ever wanted was the truth, and now I've proved my point I'm not the type to pursue vengeance. There are still things to be cleared up between us, though.

She takes advantage of my hesitation and chivvies me out the door.

'Hang on! Carrie!' I protest.

That little body of hers is stronger than it looks. Before I know it I've been shoved onto the step. She closes the door on me with the good grace to look embarrassed. I'm left on the doorstep doing a goldfish impression, mouth opening and closing.

# CHAPTER THIRTY-NINE

The red door glares back at me, implacable. I don't know what to do. Part of me wants to rap on it and give her what for; the other part never wants to clap eyes on her again. There were so many other things that needed to be tackled between us, but what's the point?

Staring at her door isn't doing any good, that's for sure. I head for home, pondering. Do I just let her go without any punishment for her lies? She's taken people in, fabricated and fawned, but I suppose she hasn't actually hurt anyone – and she hasn't even benefited. Thoughts swirl like the fine snow that's freezing my face.

I'm a few streets away when my phone rings, making me jump I was so lost in my thoughts. The number is withheld but I answer anyway.

'Hello? Is that Alex Appleby? This is Dr Patten. A patient of mine requested I call. What would you like to know?'

A huff of impatience clouds the cold air in front of me. I plough through the wisps. 'Carrie, stop putting on that phoney Scottish accent.'

'What on earth are you talking about? I've never been so insulted. Now, what exactly do you want to know about Carrie Goodwin? She has inflammatory breast cancer, which is rare but aggressive – it starts with a rash, you know, not a lump, so don't forget to check yourself for that. The tumours have now spread to other parts of her body: her lungs, spine, brain and in her bones. It's terminal.'

The accent wavers in and out. I'm not convinced one bit – in fact, I'm furious at the obvious lie. All thoughts of letting her off the hook disappear. She's treating me like I'm an idiot! Turning round, I march back towards Carrie's house.

'Okay, Dr Patten, I'd really love to come in and speak with you about Carrie's condition. Is that possible?'

'Well, I'm happy to answer any questions that you have on the phone. I don't really have time for face-to-face meetings at the moment.'

'I bet you don't.'

'I really don't understand your attitude, Ms Appleby. I'm speaking to you now to try and help you, and help a patient, but all I'm getting back is attitude.'

'That's because I know you're lying, Carrie.'

'I'm trying to be helpful, but I don't know what else to say to convince you. Your friend has cancer. She's been getting treatment here for several months now and is receiving palliative care as her condition is now terminal. You really do need to come to terms with this. I understand that you're in denial, but—'

The wind catches my laugh and tosses it into the North Sea.

'You're so right,' I reply. 'That's why I'm actually heading back to my friend's house right now, because it would be very helpful for me to speak to both of you at the same time. No doubt that will help me come to terms with everything that's happening.'

'I'm afraid I can't stay on the phone any longer, another appointment's due here any moment—'

'Just a second longer. I'd like you to help me understand how much longer Carrie has left to live. You see, I'm struggling with the reality of the situation, and would so appreciate your help. Oh, and I'm almost at your door, I mean, Carrie's door.'

The 'doctor' is making spluttering excuses. Putting on a fake voice is the action of a child; I can't believe she thought it would fool me. I'm feet away from her home now. There's a parcel or something on her doorstep, but it barely registers as I stomp on, ready for a right royal row.

'Stop playing games. Open up, Carrie.'

The phone goes dead, the door opens up… and at the same time we both look down at what's on the step.

A box with raging red writing across it.

*YOU'RE NEXT*

Carrie lurches sideways, grabbing onto the door frame to keep herself upright. Mouth hangs open as she stares at the box. Mine too. The mystery messenger who kick-started all of this has returned. Carrie barely seems to notice I'm there as she reaches with shaking hands down to the box and picks it up gingerly, almost as if she's afraid it will explode.

Finally, she looks up, terrified eyes huge in her tiny features. I search her face for signs of lying and see none.

We're both still holding onto our phones, but all thoughts about our conversation have flown away.

'Carrie?' I ask gently. 'Do you know who sent this?'

Her gaze seems to find focus, as if realising I'm there for the first time. The nod she gives is slow and unsteady. The box is held at arm's length and is bobbing up and down because she is shaking so much. Any second now she might fall to the ground. With an arm around her waist, another at her elbow, I guide her inside, pushing the door shut behind us with my foot. My voice is soothing and low.

Eventually we reach the living room and I let her sink onto the sofa. The box rests on her lap, then she seems to realise what she's done and quickly puts it on the coffee table in front of her as if it burns. I break the silence.

'Tell me who's behind these messages.'

Her eyes sharpen. 'What do you mean, messages? This is the only one, isn't it? What do you know about them? How are you involved with him?'

Despite the barrage of questions, I only say one word.

'Him?'

It seems to rest between us as solid as a brick wall.

'Don't tell me Andy has worked his charm on you.'

I've never heard her talk about an Andy, have no idea who she is talking about. She doesn't seem to hear my protestations, though. Her gaze slides from my face, drawn inexorably towards the box. For several minutes neither of us speaks or moves to open the box. Our fear has become chains that bind us in place.

My throat is swollen with questions. Lips dry and cracked. I lick them, swallow hard.

'Carrie, who is Andy? And what's inside the box? Answer me! Why are you so afraid?'

My heart is thudding so hard I can hear it in my ears. There's still no answer from Carrie. She's freaking me out. Snatching up the box, I rip it open even as she screams, 'No!'

Too late. The contents have been revealed.

A 'lost' poster with Smudge's picture on, and a red cat collar identical to his, smeared with dried blood.

Low moans of panic and horror. From her. From me. They twine together in terror. We're both scrabbling to get distance from the hideous contents.

No, no, no, Smudge can't have been hurt. My mouth's gone dry, legs weak.

Through Carrie's hysteria, I manage to make out some words.

'He's going to kill me. Oh God, he's found me at last.'

# CHAPTER FORTY

## THEN

The hot-pink PVC and lace peephole bra I was holding didn't look very comfortable. As for the funny, egg-shaped device that vibrated when I pressed the button on it…

'What on earth do you do with that?' gasped one of the women.

I was trying to earn a bit of cash as an Ann Summers party organiser. It was a laugh, and really built up my confidence in myself. Aged eighteen, and finally free from Dad's shadow, and the guilt of leaving Mum before her death, I was starting to learn to like myself a bit. I'd even got some friends. One of their mums had suggested party planning to me. Turned out I was a bit of a natural at thinking on my feet and coming out with sales patter. Within moments of meeting someone it was possible to intuitively know what approach would work best to make them buy: discreet, boisterous, technical, teasing, or even giving some women a shoulder to cry on because they were trying to solve very real problems in their relationship.

That night, the wine was flowing and the front room was packed with giggling women holding up basques and saying things like, 'I reckon my Dave would have a heart attack if I wore this,' and 'Oh no, I wouldn't wear that, it looks like it might chafe!'

Someone else had got hold of the egg thing now, and was looking at it like it was an alien life-form.

'No, this is great,' I insisted to her. 'What you do with it is—'

The doorbell rang, interrupting me. Briony, whose house it was, left me mid-explanation to answer it. I opened my mouth to continue speaking, when Briony called me into the hallway.

'I know it's meant to be girls only, but my son Mark and his mate Andy have just arrived.'

What was I supposed to do with a couple of blokes at a saucy party? Not wanting to seem rude, I invited them in… And shut them in the kitchen with a can of lager each.

'Sorry guys, but the girls might be a bit shy about buying stuff from me if you're in the room with them,' I told them, before disappearing back into the front room. Still, I felt guilty, so popped in to check on them regularly.

In fact, I spent more time chatting to Mark and Andy than I did convincing my mates to buy undies and sex toys. Not that they minded – from the shrieks of laughter, it sounded like they were having a whale of a time. So was I. Andy was lovely. It turned out he'd gone to school with my new pal Kelly, who was letting me sleep on her sofa until I got myself sorted out. He'd move to Birmingham as a kid but still had a lilting Welsh accent. Kelly had just got me hooked on gaming, especially Call of Duty – and Andy was a huge fan, too.

When I heard his online name I couldn't believe it.

'Mad Wolf? No way! I killed you the other day!' I laughed.

'Yeah, well, maybe next time I'll kill you,' he winked.

We kept talking over each other because there was so much to say. By the end of the night, I'd made some money and got the phone number of a really cute guy. Life was definitely looking up.

It wasn't long until we were inseparable. He'd walk me to work, hang around outside, then walk me home afterwards, just so he could spend as much time as possible with me.

All my cynicism about love melted away and suddenly I saw that the one thing in the world everyone was looking for was to be truly known. Because it was only when we were truly known that we could be truly loved. I'd found that with Andy. When he looked at me, it was like he'd found my lost soul.

That's why I forgave him the first time he hit me. I made excuses about his own injured spirit, thanks to some of the horrors he'd seen during his time in the Army. We'd heal one another and become stronger for it.

The second time was somehow easier to forgive because he'd already crossed that line once, so it was less shocking.

The stillness I'd learned in my childhood, the appeasing words all came back to me. Second nature. Everything was twisted to be my fault and I accepted. Watching television together was a nightmare because he'd accuse me of fancying actors. Yeah, like one of them was going to come round for tea and I'd run off with him.

It wasn't all beatings, though. Andy could be controlling and cruel without ever lifting a finger. If I needed to go food shopping he'd give me a time I had to return by – and heaven help me if I were late. If I got caught up in traffic I was a nervous wreck, bursting into tears and crying over the steering wheel.

He never said I couldn't have friends, but the atmosphere was always so bad that people didn't want to come over, and if I went out he'd give me the Spanish Inquisition – often including the torture. Eventually, I got cut off from my freshly-minted friends.

One day I caught sight of myself in the mirror. Shoulders sagged in defeat, scared eyes. Andy had changed me inside and out.

I'd turned into my mum.

# CHAPTER FORTY-ONE

## NOW

Carrie is running around the house, shoving clothes into a bag. Panic pours from her.

'Wait a minute. Just… explain what the hell is going on,' I beg. 'Who's Andy? Why is he going to kill you?'

'I've got to leave. Now.' Muttered words thrown over her shoulder. She doesn't pause in her manic movements.

'Where? Not to your parents – I know you've been lying about that, just like you've lied about the cancer.' I grab her shoulders, force her to face me. 'Talk to me!'

Eyeball to eyeball. She gives first, sagging visibly.

'I suppose it's the least you deserve.' An anxious glance tossed out the window, this way and that. Neither of us can see anyone suspicious. She grabs my hand, leads me back to the sofa. Side by side we sit, and still she holds my hand. I can feel her tremble.

'I don't know where to start.'

'I'm not surprised. I want to know why you've been lying to everybody about dying. But let's start with these messages first.'

Carrie wipes at her face, sniffing, and sits up a bit straighter. 'You're right, I'm not dying. I don't have cancer, and never have. It's all been a huge, horrible lie. I'm so sorry – and I'm sorry that "sorry" is such an insignificant word. I can't undo my betrayal. The way I've taken advantage of the kindness of good people kills me, and the worst of all of it is that our friendship's been destroyed.'

A shattering sigh, then she continues. 'Believe it or not, it was never my intention to hurt anyone. Never. I'm not that kind of person, Alex, you have to believe me.'

The vacuum of my silence sucks more words from her.

'Don't worry, I won't insult you by trying to wriggle out of it any more. God, pretending to be a doctor was pathetic! Everything I did was wrong, and I'm more than willing to stand up and admit that. But… but I can't tell you any more than that or I might be putting your life in danger, too.

'You don't have to believe me, or trust me, but you do need to let me pack up and leave right now – and get the hell out of here as quickly as you can.'

Letting go of my hands, she makes a gesture as if pushing me away. I hadn't expected her to make such a full and frank confession and apology – not so quickly, anyway. She seems to think that's enough, though, but it isn't. I need to understand why, otherwise I'll never get my head around how someone I thought I'd got to know so well, even in such a short space of time, could do what she's done. Nothing can ever justify making up such a twisted story, of course, but still I need to hear what drove her to it.

Instead of explaining further, she stands up. Conversation over.

'Hang on a second, that's it? That's all I'm getting? A half-baked apology and a "sorry, I've got to run"? Then more lies – pretending my life is in danger is a new low, Carrie.'

'I don't expect you to understand—'

'Good job.'

'Whether you listen to me or not, I've got to go. Time has run out.' Her voice wobbles and breaks again. 'You deserved to know the truth before I left. Now you've got it.'

She's off, running upstairs while I'm frozen in place. When she reappears, she has a bag hanging off either shoulder and a suitcase bumping down each step behind her. She seems shocked that I'm still sitting where she left me.

'Alex, go. If you ever cared for me as a friend at all, trust me now: you have to go, or you'll get caught up in this mess.'

'It's too late, I already am.' I point at the box containing a tragically delicate collar encrusted with blood. 'Who killed Smudge? It's sick!'

She wobbles, has to steady herself. But her voice sounds unshaken.

'I'm ordering a taxi now—'

'I might not know everything, but neither do you.' I shout the words in desperation. Confusion clouds Carrie's face. 'This box isn't the first message you've received like this.'

'I don't understand. When… ?'

'Sit down and I'll tell you.'

'No, I—'

'Have to go, I know. But you're clearly running from someone and you've only got half the information. Don't you want to know the full story before you scarper? That's right, sit down – and cancel that taxi, this may take a while.'

Carrie looks like she's been poleaxed since I explained I'd found other messages at her house. Her already tiny frame has collapsed in on itself; she's scrunched up in a ball on the sofa.

'Three notes,' she murmurs. I can barely hear her. Curled up as she is, she is speaking into her knees and arms.

'That's right. And I'll only tell you their contents if you tell me your secrets first.' Paying out a little information at a time is the only way I can think of playing this game.

Her face comes out of hiding. 'Let me guess, they're all threatening, right?'

As I nod she runs her hands through her hair. 'Then it's definitely Andy. If you really want to hear the full story, then sit down because it's a long one.

'Andrew Baker is my husband – and my real name is Sarah Baker, but I hate it, so please keep calling me Carrie. Anyway, Andy and I first got talking at a party five years ago. I was living on a friend's sofa in Edgbaston – which is where I'm from – at the time, and feeling down about having no prospects, scraping a living selling Ann Summers stuff. Then suddenly there's this handsome older guy chatting me up – he felt heaven-sent.

'He was a friend of a friend, so I felt safe letting him into my life. We had a laugh, I kept joking about the awful hat he wore, one of those pork-pie hats, you know? He looked like a pretentious muso, and it became a running joke between the two of us. We liked loads of similar stuff.

'The banter was great, so meeting up again for a date the next day was natural. I did check up on him before I went. I googled him, and even looked him up at his address on the electoral register. He had also sent me videos of him playing five-a-side on a pub football team, so I was fairly certain that he was who he said he was.

'I was shaking with nerves the whole way on the bus to Birmingham city centre. Already I felt so much for him that it was scary. I got off the bus, and as soon as I saw him waiting by the bull statue for me all my nerves were gone. It was like being covered in a big, comforting duvet. Best of all, he felt the same – we walked around the Bullring Shopping Centre hand in hand, both stupidly smiling.'

She's smiling now, at the recollection. Then shivers. Hugs herself tighter against her before continuing.

'From that moment, we were inseparable. I stayed over at his that night and moved in the next day – and not because I wanted to be free of sofa-surfing, but because it felt wrong being away from him. It sounds cheesy, but we had this instant connection, like nothing I'd felt with anyone else. The age gap didn't matter – if anything, he made me feel safe because he was so worldly, especially because he'd been in the army, seeing all sorts, while I was quite naive.

'Looking back, though, the signs of manipulation were there from the start. He was the one who insisted I stay with him, so that I was reliant on him. We were in such a whirlwind of love that it was easy for me to ignore friends and family, dropping them so that I could spend more time with him.

'After just two months together he proposed. I loved him to bits, but it felt a little too rushed, and he took it as a total rejection, said I didn't love him. He was crying, I was begging forgiveness and reassuring him that of course I adored him. "If you really loved me you'd have said yes," he insisted. "The fact you didn't proves you don't, so it's best if we split up. I'd sooner my heart was broken now than later."

'Daft cow that I was, I threw my arms around him and told him I'd been an idiot and that I'd love to marry him. Meant it, too – couldn't think of anything better than spending the rest of my life with this fantastic man who had turned my life around. I'd finally got the happy ending I'd always dreamed of as a kid. But we agreed to have a long engagement.

'That afternoon we went into town on the pretext of him buying me a lip gloss. The next thing I knew we were in a jewellery shop buying a ring. The following day, he booked a register office as a surprise for me, and I didn't object for fear of upsetting him again, especially when it felt like he was doing all of this to make me happy.

'We married three weeks later. I was only just nineteen, and Andy was thirty-eight. It wasn't a big deal, neither of us had a lot of family or friends to invite, and besides, we both viewed the wedding as a natural next step in life rather than an excuse for a big party. The whole thing cost us about a thousand pounds – Andy got his suit from Oxfam, I got my dress on eBay. I bought all the decorations online, and we held the reception in our house.'

She comes up for air from her memories, shaking her head sadly. For several moments there is only silence as she seems to be gathering strength for the next part of her tale. I barely breathe as I wait.

'The violence started that night. We'd both had too much to drink, celebrating. By the time everybody had left we were off our faces, to be honest. I went over to him to give him a kiss. I remember wrapping my arms around his waist and looking at him, giggling, because I was so happy. But he pushed me away from him. I'd have fallen backwards but he grabbed my face in his hand, like a vice – the next day I had bruises from his fingertips and thumb along my jawline.

'"I saw you flirting with that redhead friend of yours," he slurred. "Should have known you'd be a tart, look what you do for a living, selling sex."

'I told him I didn't even have a redhead friend. "Lying slut." That's what he called me. Then he let go of me and slapped me, backhanded, across my face. His wedding ring split my lip.'

She points to a faint scar. There's the proof.

Even so, I have to ask.

'What's this got to do with these messages, you lying to me, everything you've done here?' I demand.

# CHAPTER FORTY-TWO

A thread has been pulled, and at last tall tales are unravelling. Suspicion and relief knot together as Carrie continues to tell her story. She sits on the edge of the sofa, hands tucked between her legs. I'm utterly motionless, afraid to break the spell.

'I should have got out straight away, of course I should have. Common sense screams it, and we all kid ourselves that it's a case of one strike and he's out. But I was a young girl under the spell of a much older man, and I made excuses: we'd both been drunk, he hadn't been himself. He'd never been violent before and wouldn't do anything like it again. When he saw my face the next morning he cried, holding me in his arms as if I was something delicate and precious. He was inconsolable over what he'd done.'

She shrugs. 'I couldn't walk out on my marriage before it had even begun. Besides, I loved this man and certainly wasn't going to prove right all the people who'd warned me that things were moving too quickly.

'I don't know, maybe it was because my own childhood hadn't been great. My whole life I'd craved attention and love in a family of my own, but never had it – and now I thought I'd found it, I wasn't going to give it up because of one mistake.'

'Inevitably it wasn't just one mistake, though,' I say at last.

'How can I best explain to you why I stayed?' She gazes up at the ceiling, biting her lip. 'Have you heard that thing about frogs? If you put them in a pan of boiling water they'll jump straight out, but if you put them in a pan of cold water and slowly turn up the heat they'll stay in the water until they boil alive. That was me. I was the frog and Andy increased the heat underneath me so slowly that I barely realised it was happening. He undermined my confidence until he was telling me what to wear and what to eat. If I argued back, he'd hit me.

'I was in fear of my life every single day, and had no idea how I'd got myself into that situation. Instead of the longed-for safety, all I found was cruelty and control. After twelve months of marriage there was no love left inside me – I stayed purely because he made it clear that if I ever left he would track me down and kill me.'

My heart broke listening to her, remembering, making sense.

'One night he beat me so badly I thought I'd die. That's when I knew I had to get out – because whether it happened in our house or while I was on the run, I was going to be killed by my husband.'

Fingers scrabble through cropped hair, then return to their prayer position between her thighs. 'One day while he was at work I took a bag of clothes and never looked back. I was penniless, but free.'

'Penniless?'

'I'd no money of my own because we shared a bank account, and Andy didn't trust me with anything more than was necessary to buy our shopping every week. He always checked the receipts to make sure I hadn't kept any change for myself. So when I left I literally didn't have two pennies to rub together.

'That day I walked as far as I could and slept under a bush in a park at night. I've never been so scared in my life.'

'Couldn't you have gone to a refuge?'

She shook her head. 'The first thing Andy would have done is check local refuges.'

'Their addresses are normally hidden, aren't they? How would he have found them?'

'Oh, he'd have found a way somehow. Don't forget, he used to be in the army. He knows all kinds of ways of tracking somebody down. He used to love terrifying me with tales of how he'd go about it if I ever escaped.

'For two years I was on the run, moving from town to town, always changing my name. As a foster kid I'd learned how to survive, becoming a bit of a magpie and stealing people's lives by pretending to be them. It had been a comfort blanket from reality, back then, and I'd often introduced myself with their last name to fit in with my new 'family', but it never lasted. As a result, I've never felt particularly attached to my real name. I slipped back into those old ways, and they helped me get by.

'Finally I found a place to settle because a lovely woman called Joanne befriended me.'

I freeze. Cromer, the missing woman Joanne Freeman and her friend Natalie Sheringham – I'd been right. Honesty is glittering through the slag heap of duplicity at last.

'Letting my guard down was a big mistake. Instead of moving on, I got myself a flat and allowed myself to build a life. I got sloppy about covering my tracks, convinced that after all this time Andy would surely have given up on me. Underestimating his obsession proved fatal.'

A storm of tears roll down her face. 'He – he killed Joanne because she stood up to him for me. She confronted him on the beach because she thought that she'd be safe in a public place, but it was winter and nobody was there to see him strangle her. I tried to help her, I really did, but he was too strong. He just let the sea take her body away… '

For several minutes there is nothing but the sound of sniffling. I nip to the loo and come back with a roll of toilet paper for us both to wipe our faces. Carrie blows her nose before speaking again.

'It doesn't matter what happens to me, but if something happened to you because of me I couldn't live with myself. I'd rather let Andy do what he wants with me. After he killed Joanne I was in such a state of shock I let him take me back home with him.

He kept me prisoner for six months, until I managed to escape again. Living on the streets once more, being on the run, it was a horrible déjà vu, but far worse was knowing that I was responsible for the death of my best friend.'

'You aren't, he is,' I say.

'It's because of me. Now I've been stupid and selfish again, by staying in Tynemouth and getting close to you. I knew I had to keep on the move, but I liked it here, liked you.'

A hollow laugh escapes her lips. 'I had lost a lot of weight with worry. I make myself vomit, it's useful for pretending to have chemo and it makes me feel better—'

'That's called bulimia,' I point out, realising that's also why Carrie often looks grey and weak.

'Well, I thought it might make Andy less likely to recognise me, too, but a fat lot of good it did me. I'm so tired of running, having no friends or home. But I've got to leave this town, not just for my sake but yours, too.'

Sifting through the mountain of information thrown at me is mentally exhausting. There's one thing this tragic tale doesn't explain, though.

'Why did you lie about having cancer? It's despicable.'

'There's no excuse, it's unforgivable, so I'm not even going to try to explain.'

'Well, I want you to. I need to understand what on earth drove you to it, because nothing I've heard so far justifies it.'

'It can't!' She throws both hands up in the air, but when she realises I'm not going to stop asking, she finally starts to talk again. Her comments are firmly aimed at the floor; she can't meet my eyes.

'It's pathetic, okay, but I pretended to have cancer because I felt so lonely. It's hard making friends when moving from town to town, always on the run, and when I reached Tynemouth something about the place made me want to stay here. I don't know, I just felt comfortable and wanted to fit in,' she says. 'I knew I couldn't stay here for long, but wanted to make friends and feel loved and safe, protected and cared for, no longer alone.

'Pretending to have cancer meant that happened quickly. I know, I totally get why you're pulling that face – it's dreadful, isn't it? I'm stealing those emotions from people. But it meant that for a little while I slept easier, despite the guilt, because I didn't feel alone any more. People gave a damn about me and called me every day to check on me – you did that.'

Another blow into her hanky, before continuing.

'Why did I pretend to be terminal? It would force me to move on and not get too comfortable here.' Her face crumples. 'Because I love it here. Everyone's been so kind to me. And…and I love you like the mother I never had.'

Hearing those words tears me to pieces, because I love her like the family I lost.

'In the end I hated all the sympathy people gave me,' she adds. 'Everyone being so kind, telling me I'm brave and inspirational when actually I'm just a coward. My mum died of breast cancer, so I've seen first-hand what it's like to suffer from it, and that makes me even more ashamed of what I've done.'

There is desperate sadness in her eyes when she finally makes herself look up at me. 'I don't expect you to believe me, but I never wanted anyone's money. If you think back, I kept telling you I didn't want the bucket list donations.'

'I remember. I tried to get you to spend it several times, and you always turned it down.'

'Exactly! This was only ever a pathetic attempt to get attention. Most of the time I feel like no one would notice or care if I disappeared off the face of the earth, but everyone's reaction to my "diagnosis" was incredible. I felt part of the human race again. Crazy, isn't it, that only by pretending to be dying did I truly feel alive again.

'And now… now Andy is here, and he's going to murder me if I don't go back with him. Then he'll probably kill me anyway, at his leisure.'

Putting my arm around her, I give a sigh. 'I'll find a way of stopping this. I promise.'

'That's what Joanne said. You can't put your life on the line for me.'

'Let's go to the police, tell them he's a murderer.'

She shakes my arm free and looks at me like I'm mad. 'There's nothing tying him to what happened to Joanne. And no proof of what he did to me, either. Plus, I've got a juvenile record as long as your arm and a reputation as a liar, thanks to a misspent youth. No one would ever believe me – especially as Andy comes across as charm personified.'

I think of the newspaper report from the other day. All that's left of Joanne are bones washed clean of all DNA and other evidence. Police aren't even sure how she died. Proving someone killed her, let alone who did it, would be impossible. If I go to the authorities with this, given my own reputation with them, they'll lock me up.

# CHAPTER FORTY-THREE

Outside Carrie's house, normal life continues. Children shout and play, on half-term. Car doors slam shut, engines turn over. People are enjoying day-to-day life, while inside I wrestle with everything I've been told.

Carrie reaches out and gives my knee a friendly squeeze.

'Now you know everything. So, tell me what you know about Andy.'

Ah, yes, the bluff that started this confession.

'Honestly? I don't know anything about Andy. But I do know that someone has been sending you messages. I'm so sorry I didn't tell you – if I'd had any idea what was actually going on I'd never have hidden them away. I thought I was protecting you from worry. Instead, I've made things worse.'

'Hey, you were looking out for me, and it's been a long time since anyone did that. I love what you did.'

Encouraged, I reel off the whole story. As I talk, mysteries are solved.

'Andy's first picture was of you and me?' Carrie checks. 'That makes sense. He knows the best way to scare me into doing what he wants is to threaten those I care about most. Killing Joanne got me to go back with him last time. I bet he was furious when I didn't respond this time around.'

I frown, doubt flickering like a faulty lightbulb. It takes a moment for me to know what to say. 'But how would you have got in touch with him? There were no contact details or instructions on how to do that.'

'In all these years, Andy has always kept the same mobile phone number. He wouldn't change it now. It's etched into my brain, and he knows it. If I had seen that picture, along with the jumper he must've stolen off my washing line to let me know how he could get close to me any time he wants, I'd have dialled that telephone number immediately.'

'Instead poor Smudge paid the price.' Carrie's beautiful tomcat had gone missing immediately after that first message. I dreaded to think what had happened to him. 'Why the picture of Simon?' I add.

'Andy must have thought I was still with Simon, and of course the third photograph was of Joanne, to remind me of exactly what he was capable of. Typical of him that in all those messages, he never once spelled out a blatant threat that could be taken to the police. He's so bloody clever.'

It's all incredibly cunning, no doubt about it. 'He must have followed you to my house and smashed up your car, too.'

'He's the reason I don't have insurance. I'd have to use my own name and, call me paranoid, but I'm sure he'd find out somehow. He always finds me, no matter what.'

'He's been following our every step.' I shiver. 'A killer has been dogging me. Following me in the fog. I'd no idea how close to death I've been.'

More random pieces of the puzzle fall into place as I think. Hearing how Carrie has an answer for everything that's happened leaves me reeling. A thought needs testing out.

'Hey, there's a random guy I've bumped into a couple of times, on the beach and at the hospital. He always stares at me. Bit taller than me, blue eyes, blond, bit of a charmer – does that sound like Andy?' I ask.

'Oh my God, yes! I can't believe you've seen him. He must be after you, too!' says Carrie. 'The first message happened after the bucket list got loads of publicity. That must have been how Andy found me.'

'Yes, well, I'd also put something on Facebook and Twitter a few days before,' I confess. 'Now I understand why you were so angry with me about the press taking photos.'

I close my eyes to shut out the betrayal. When I look at her again, she's gazing at me.

'Don't beat yourself up about this. It isn't your fault, Alex. Andy would have found me eventually, anyway. He's never going to give up on me, so realistically I don't think I've got any choice but to give him what he wants.'

'You can't mean… ?'

She picks up her mobile. I snatch it away. Stand, so it's out of her reach.

'There's nothing else to be done, Alex! I don't want to do this, goodness knows, but we're all out of options. No one else is getting hurt for my sake.'

'Over my dead body – literally, if that's what it takes. Carrie, I've got to know you over the last few months. You're a lovely person who deserves better than this. Yes, you did a bad thing by lying, but it's still possible to get past it. I'm guessing you've been through so much that you're not thinking straight.'

Time for my own confession. I sink down beside her again. 'I understand better than you can imagine the need to hide inside a fabricated world because the truth of your reality is too awful to handle.'

A deep breath, then another. No more delaying.

'I've been lying to you, too: my husband and children are dead.'

Carrie looks like I've punched her in the gut, and I'm guessing my expression is similar.

After I've explained everything to her, she seems shell-shocked.

'I can't get over everything you've been through,' she says.

'No more than you,' I shrug. 'Maybe we bonded so quickly because unconsciously we recognised our mutual pain. You're desperate for love, and I'm desperate for a family to give it to now that I'm finally ready to open my heart again. As for the lies that you've told, yes, they were awful, but I do understand the place they came from, even if I don't agree with what you did. Who am I to judge you, after my deceit? There's got to be another way.'

'Oh, Alex, I was getting ready to go on the run again, but telling you about it has made me relive it and, as pathetic as it sounds, I've no strength left. I give up. I'll welcome the peace of death when Andy finally kills me.'

A cheer from outside, boys whooping. Their joy so at odds with the tension in the room.

'In all of the time I've known you I've never heard you be defeatist before,' I say. 'What happened to "be more dog", or the glass being half-full, and all that about rainbows and happy endings that you're always spouting? Together we can work out a way of you being free once and for all.'

'You really think so?'

'I know so.'

The nod Carrie gives is determined.

'That's the spirit!' Hugs and grins punctuate our speech. Buoyed up, we start brainstorming ideas.

A plan is beginning to form. It's risky, but if it pays off it will be totally worth it.

# CHAPTER FORTY-FOUR

'You're nuts!' It's the only thing Carrie seems to be able to say after I've laid out my plan to her. She just keeps staring at me and shaking her head.

'I know it's a huge gamble, but we can totally pull this off.'

'Nope, no way. I'm out of here – and you should be, too. If we try this, we'll both end up like Smudge.'

Inexorably, our gaze is pulled over to the scarlet-caked poster and collar. The sight makes me all the more determined to see this through.

'Put your bag down and listen. If we're successful you'll never have to worry about Andy again.'

'And if we don't we'll both be sleeping with the fishes. If I go now I'll have a head start on him, hopefully, even if it does mean sleeping rough again. Argh, why didn't I save more money while I was here?'

My idea is simple. Carrie will text Andy, letting him know that he has won and she's willing to come back home with him. She'll arrange to meet him at my house. But she won't be there; it will be me waiting for him. Carrie will be staking out the place and will call the police anonymously the second he arrives, claiming that she can hear screaming.

'I'll keep him talking,' I insist. 'If that doesn't work, I can run to the loo and lock myself in there until the cavalry arrives.'

'It's stupid, amateur, risky – you name it! Just let me run away again.'

'Not going to happen.'

'At least let me be the one in the house.'

I hold up my hand to stop her talking. 'We've been over this. It has to be me in the house with Andy because you can't be involved in reporting him to the police, owing to your record. You said yourself you can't go to the police as it might be held against you, or Andy might find a way to wriggle out of it by using it against you. I have no connection with him, past or present, and therefore no reason to lie to the police about what happened. They'll believe me and arrest him, and he'll go down for burglary.'

Honestly, I've no idea if this will work, but at least my voice isn't giving away any hint of doubt. Carrie needs me to be strong. At long last, whether she appreciates it or not, I'm stepping up for those I love. I feel lighter and freer than I have in years – it seems Rosie has been right all this time.

I'm not sure how supportive she'd be of me trying to trap a murderer, though.

With that in mind, I try again to persuade Carrie.

'You've told me the only thing in the world Andy wants is you, Carrie. Let's make him believe he's going to get what he wants. This *will* work.'

Shoulders hunched, head down and shaking, finally she gives an exaggerated shrug. 'Okay, okay! I give in. We'll try it your way. But if anything happens to you, I will never forgive myself.'

'Best send that text now before you have a chance to change your mind again.'

Together we work on the wording until we feel we've struck the right balance of anger and despair.

'He mustn't be able to sense any hope in my message or he'll know something is being planned,' says Carrie.

My nod is emphatic. 'The only way this scheme can work is if we catch him unawares.'

❖

We wait and wait for a reply. Nothing comes.

'Are you sure there's service?' For the thousandth time, I pick up Carrie's mobile and check how many bars it's showing. Full service.

'It's not going to work – he should've been in touch by now. I expected him to reply immediately. Maybe he's changed his number,' Carrie panics.

She's been pacing for the last hour. Generally that's what I'd be doing, too, but in this moment of utmost stress my normal coping mechanisms are obsolete. There's no haunting compunction to burn calories. Instead, I nibble on a cheese and salad sandwich. I don't know why I feel so mentally strong, and can only assume it's because I've found somebody to be strong for. Whatever the reason, it's welcome. After all these years I'm finding myself again – exactly when it's most needed.

With so much happening out of the ordinary, it feels surreal to glance at the clock and realise I've got an appointment.

'Damn! Someone's coming over to pick up their dress. I've got to run,' I gasp. 'Are you going to be okay on your own? Maybe you should come with me.'

'You go. I'll let you know the second I hear anything.'

A hurried hug, and I'm on my way.

I reach home in the nick of time, as the client is knocking on my door and checking her watch. There's an almost dreamlike feel to having a conversation about darts, hemlines and pleating, as my mind drifts to blackmail, murder and violence.

My client doesn't seem to notice. She's really pleased with the gown, and doesn't want a single thing changed. I thank my lucky stars for that. The smile on her face couldn't be bigger as she finally gets to take her wedding dress home, the future shining bright in her eyes.

❖

I've barely closed the door when frantic knocking makes me jump up again. It's Carrie. She's breathless. Shoves her phone towards me.

There's a message from a number I don't recognise.

*I'm coming to get you at 9 p.m. tonight. Don't keep me waiting.*

# CHAPTER FORTY-FIVE

*Check the time, peer out of the window, check under the pillow for the hammer, feel in my pocket for the travel-sized hairspray can, wonder if I have time to go to the loo again because my stomach is churning…* I'm on a seemingly unbreakable loop of activity. Any minute now I could be facing a killer as they realise a trap has been sprung.

I jiggle in place, psyched up for anything, trying not to think of the million ways that this could all go horribly wrong for me. I've made Carrie promise to stay outside, no matter what happens.

*I could end up in hospital. I could end up dead. Carrie could get dragged back to a life of terror and servitude.*

Or it could work, I remind myself. Stranger things have happened.

It's 8.30 p.m., and I've been living on my nerves ever since Carrie hammered on my door. Both of us have been paranoid that Andy will turn up early. I swear time has slowed. Each time I check the clock, only a few seconds have gone by. It doesn't seem possible.

That sandwich from earlier was a mistake. I feel sick.

*8.55 p.m.*

Any minute now. My heart feels like it's going to explode.

*8.58 p.m.*

Cold-sweat hands. Clenching and unclenching.

*9.01 p.m.*

He's late; why would he be late? Has he realised it's a trap and taken Carrie, while I stand like an idiot in my bedroom, waiting? Trying not to disturb the curtain, I look out of the window again. There, hidden behind a tree, I can just make out Carrie peeking round the trunk.

She's safe.

*10.15 p.m.*

I'm exhausted from being constantly keyed up. Any second I could be attacked. I just want it over and done with.

*11.20 p.m.*

The click of the front door; the shush of it opening over carpet. My fingers clench round the can of hairspray, ready to blast it into my attacker's eyes. I step out of the bedroom, brace myself at the top of the stairs. And gasp.

'What the hell are you doing here?'

'I'm going crazy standing out there,' replies Carrie. 'I don't think he's coming. If he were he'd be here by now – he's never late.'

'Perhaps he's just trying to catch you off guard. You know, lull you into a false sense of security, then come and get you.'

'That doesn't make sense. He thinks I've given in to him, so why would he delay the opportunity to gloat in person?'

Sitting down on the top step of the stairs, I send a shrug to my friend. 'Sounds to me like he enjoys cat and mouse games.'

'No, he likes to win. And he knows he's won this.'

'Unless… Okay, what if he's watched us together and sensed something is going on? What if he's actually realised that he's not going to win this game, because you're not alone any more? This is it, Carrie. You're free!'

I jump up and run down the stairs and hug her. Her whole body is tense.

'Alex, you've no idea what you're up against,' she says at last. 'You're talking about a man who has spent the last five years making it his single aim in life to hurt me. Think of all the time he's spent hunting me.

'Last time he found me he strangled my best friend right in front of me, just to prove what would happen if I didn't do as I was told. That's not someone who quits because two women have come up with a half-cocked plot to get him arrested.'

She looks over her shoulder.

'He's out there somewhere, waiting for me. He's just proving that when he does finally get me it will be on his terms, not mine.'

I can guess what's coming next. Grab her hand, scared to let go, a symphony of sorrow making my body thrum.

'Unless we keep facing whatever's coming together! I'm here for you, no matter what.'

Her only reply is a squeeze of my hand.

'Carrie, please, don't leave.' My other hand wipes furiously across my cheeks, trying to keep up with the flow of tears.

'You've been so brave, Alex. You are amazing, and I'll never forget what you've tried to do for me. I'd rather die than let anything happen to you. Waiting under that tree, imagining what the hell was going on in here, that was worse than the worst beating Andy has ever given me, and harder than all the sickest mind games he's ever played. All I could think of was Joanne's face as her life ebbed away – and then imagining you in her place.'

She shook her hand free of mine. Stepped away.

'I'm leaving, Alex. There's nothing you can say to change my mind.'

The world has narrowed to just Carrie and me. I am a liar, an aberration, an unfit mother who must do whatever is necessary. There's only one option left to me. I have to let go of this woman

I have loved like a daughter. I mustn't waste any further time arguing, like I did when the twins were born.

Calm enfolds me.

'Andy clearly has some kind of twisted game in mind that he wants to play with you, and we're helpless to end it because we don't know the rules. So, do you have all your clothes packed, and did you bring them here with you?' I ask.

'Everything I own is in those two bags and that suitcase, back at mine. I've got about forty pounds in my purse, which is enough for a night at a homeless shelter.'

'Then you're ready to go. But you've only got around forty pounds?'

'Maybe I can pick up some more cash by begging. I've slept rough before. I'll be fine.'

'You know I can't let you go without money. All the donated funds for your bucket list are sitting in an account in my name. First thing tomorrow I'll empty that account and give you the cash.'

Carrie raises her eyebrows. 'That's, erm, that's a really sweet idea, but I couldn't possibly take it. People gave that money for someone who is genuinely in need.'

Once again, I'm struck by how good she is.

'*You* are genuinely in need. Your lies were committed in extremis. All you ever wanted was to feel the love and support of friendship, right?' I point out. 'Everyone who donated money is a good person. If I were to get in touch with them right now and tell them everything you've told me, there's no doubt in my heart that they would still want you to have the money.

'Like me, they might not approve of what you did, but they'd understand why you did it. At the end of the day, Carrie, they gave money to a woman whose life is about to end – and if you don't take this money, that's exactly what will happen.'

Fingers wrenching short, cropped hair. She's in an agony of indecision. 'I don't know. It just doesn't seem right.' A pause. A sigh. 'You know what? I know this is going to sound strange, but if there were more money, then I'd say yes. As it is, though, I think the donations should be refunded to everybody after I'm gone, because it just isn't enough to make it worth taking.

'It's not that I'm being ungrateful – I really, really am blown away by everyone's generosity – but although twenty thousand is a lot, it's not enough to start a whole new life away from Andy. I don't know how much would be, but tons more, that's for sure. I'd have to go abroad, probably, to be sure of escaping him for ever.'

Her logic tries to tear a hole in my swelling conviction. She's right: £20,000 is a lot, but it's not life-changing. I've already got the answer to all her problems, though.

'Take my money, too.'

She laughs. 'Take all the millions you've made from dressmaking?'

'Kind of, yeah. You know everything I told you about Owen? How he was killed while crossing train lines at an unmanned pedestrian crossing? It took years for Network Rail to be held accountable for what happened. Eventually I received compensation, as well as Owen's life insurance. So I'm comfortable financially, and don't need to make dresses, apart from to keep me occupied. I'd give back every single penny and then some if I could get my family back. You're like family now, so you have it.'

Her mouth moves but no sound comes out, so I speak for her.

'How far do you think you could go on one million?'

# CHAPTER FORTY-SIX

Carrie is choking. A strangled noise crowbars its way out through tight-closed lips. One, two, three, I slap her on her back, but she shakes me loose and steps back. The noise comes again, and this time I recognise it as a cross between a cough and a laugh.

'Now probably isn't the best time to joke,' she manages.

'I can log on to my bank account right now and show you the balance. With interest, it's over a million now. The compensation was generous—'

'You're not kidding… ?'

'Three years before Owen was killed, a safety report had been undertaken about that crossing. The findings raised serious concerns about having an unlocked wicket gate for pedestrians beside a lockable crossing for vehicles.' If she asked, I could quote the damn thing almost word for word. 'The report strongly recommended that a locking mechanism be fitted, in addition to creating a footbridge.

'Those recommendations weren't acted on. If they had been, Owen would be alive today. So, possibly, would Elise and Edward, because I might never have miscarried. That's why I received such a large compensation payment.'

She's almost hyperventilating. Leading her into the kitchen, I make a cup of strong, sweet tea. I blow across my own mug to cool the steaming liquid, then pick up the tale.

'I didn't want all that cash, but I got it anyway. Spending it feels wrong – I can't enjoy it, it's blood money. It's just sitting in the bank, forgotten. It would be great if it could do some good. Real good. Don't you agree?'

The ticking of the clock is the only sound. Darkness outside has shrouded the streets in silence. While neighbours slumber peacefully, Carrie struggles with the shock that has robbed her of words.

'A new identity, a new life. Andy would never find me. I'd be free.' A breath of words. Her expression coalesces into something different. 'Come with me.'

A fresh start, with all our troubles left behind. What could possibly go wrong?

A Pandora's box of possibilities has opened up. I can almost feel them swirling around me, sweeping me along. First, though, we've got to get through tonight.

We lock and bolt all the doors and windows against the possibility of Andy coming, double- and triple-checking them. I log on to my online banking account and message them to let my branch know I'll be going in tomorrow. Then Carrie and I agree to sleep in shifts.

Of course, neither of us can. Trepidation and excitement has adrenaline jangling through us, despite our exhaustion. We talk all through the night.

'Do you really think we should do this?' I check, suddenly doubting and needing to be certain.

'Life rarely comes knocking on someone's door. You have to step outside and grab it by the collar as it whizzes by. Where do you think we should live?'

'Well, we've got the whole world to choose from,' I say, pulling my duvet closer under my chin. 'We could live in the middle of nowhere. A really remote place, where Andy could never find us.'

'Better to be in a city – it's easier to be anonymous when you're surrounded by lots of people. When you live in a small community everybody knows everyone else.'

Hail rattles against the windows, inspiring me. 'How about Spain? Nice to be somewhere hot.'

'Wherever we go we need to be surrounded by CCTV. We'll want to feel safe.'

'Ooh, Australia! That way we don't even need to learn a new language.'

'Even better, America. No new language to learn, we can still choose a warm part of the country, say California, and we could live in a gated community—'

'Sometimes they have their own private security guards over there, driving around, I've seen them on programmes—'

'Exactly! And we can have guns.'

'I'm not sure I'd feel comfortable carrying a gun.'

'Then I'd learn to shoot for the both of us.'

Wow, Carrie is hardcore when given the chance. The happy-go-lucky woman I know has disappeared momentarily, cloaked by a veneer of steel that's unexpected.

'You don't go up against a nutter like Andy for years without hardening,' she says, seeming to catch my expression.

I turn over, on a Mission Impossible to find a soft spot on the floor. Give up and turn back again. Carrie gives me a gentle shove with her foot. 'Sure you don't want the sofa?'

'No, you have it. I'm supposed to be staying awake anyway, remember.'

'I don't mind taking this shift.'

But I won't hear of it. There's no way sleep can be risked.

Outside, a fox barks. Carrie and I sit up, on high alert. A heart-beat, then we ease back again. I'll be glad when tonight is over.

'What will you do with your new-found freedom?' I ask, keen to keep the conversation going and stop my mind numbing with fear.

'Not sure. I'd love to study acting – did I ever tell you as a child I got a bit part in *Casualty*? Anyway, no matter where I am, I can't risk that, for obvious reasons. It's been years since I've allowed myself to dream of a life that consists of anything other than scraping by on crappy cash-in-hand, unskilled jobs – and that's when I'm lucky. So often I've had to rely on other people's charity… ' A sad chuckle. 'That's what I'm about to do again now, though, isn't it? Live on your charity.'

'It's totally different. I'm coming with you, for starters. Come on, Carrie, do you think I'd be making any of these plans if it weren't for you? Without you I'd still be starving myself to death, punishing myself for the loss of my family. My life has changed because of you.'

'Huh, well, I seem to have something in my eye now.'

Now it's my turn to give her a playful kick. 'Soppy bugger.'

❖

The achromatic hues of night slowly blush into dawn. We've lived to see another day.

'Right, let's go over today's plan one more time. First, I empty the bucket list account, so that we can use the cash—'

'I've been thinking,' Carrie interrupts, 'it's best if I leave Tynemouth today, alone, because if Andy is trailing me then it needs to be just me in his firing line.'

'That's not what we discussed. We stick together.'

'Alex, it's safer this way. I'm used to evading him. It's far easier for me to move alone. Then we meet up at Heathrow, as planned, buy our tickets there and then in cash, and board the plane together to start our brand spanking new life.'

Every part of me wants to scream an argument, but instead I agree. 'You've got a point. You're used to life on the run, I'm not. The last thing I want to do is give the game away, not when the stakes are so high. Still… Surely if Andy finds you, together we stand more of a chance?'

'Alex, there's more chance of him finding me if you're with me. I'll be safer without you.'

I know what she's doing: using reverse psychology on me. She knows damn well that if she argues about it being safer for me, I won't listen, but I'll never do anything to put her in jeopardy.

'Okay, I give up!'

That telltale line appears between her eyebrows. 'Ah, I've just thought, I might need some money, in case it's a while before I can shake him.'

'Makes sense. If you're going it alone then you need to have all the money. I'll make the transfer of compensation funds to you, and give you all the cash, too.'

'Don't be daft! I can't clean out all your money! What if something happens to me? If you could lend me just enough to get to Heathrow, I'd be grateful.'

'Take the lot. Isn't the whole point that you need it to start a new life?' I ask in a sing-song voice. 'Look, it's nothing more than I offered last night, anyway. I'm happy to give you all of my money to escape this monster. You're the one who's thrown the lifeline to me by inviting me along.'

'If you're absolutely certain. At least you know we're in this together now – I've shared all my secrets with you, and you could easily turn me in to the police if you wanted to.'

'Like I said last night, anyone hearing your story would happily hand over their money to give you a life away from torture and pain.'

There's a war being fought internally. Various muscles twitch as her expressions shift.

'I suppose you're right,' she admits.

'No more talk. We need to save our energy for Andy and whatever trick he may have up his sleeve next. He's been so clever, trailing our movements without us noticing, taking pictures of us. I'll see you back at your place between ten and ten thirty, okay?'

She hesitates. This is the riskiest part of her plan. I reach out and rub her arm, reassuring.

'Get into the house, grab your bags and sit tight. Make sure the place is locked up and that you're safe. I'll be there as soon as I can, promise.'

I stand on my step and wave her off. A cocktail of emotions churning my stomach as she leaves me. Everything that's been happening is all too much for me. I should be getting ready to go to the clinic for my usual weigh-in and counselling, and instead I'm dealing with all this. My brain is in knots tighter than a ligature. No sleep, emotionally exhausted, walking a tightrope that could kill me if I fall off. The ground wavers beneath me. Feeling dizzy with fatigue, I make my way to the living room, blink…

Darkness swallows me whole.

# CHAPTER FORTY-SEVEN

Eyes open slowly. Head floating and heavy all at once. Sleepless nights and lack of food have well and truly taken their toll. Fighting the inky world that wants to drag me back, I struggle into a sitting position against the coffee table I'd fainted beside. Wipe a mark from it absently, then shake my head, tell myself to get it together. There are places I need to be. Check the time.

Damn it! Muscles too weak to do what they're told are bullied into submission until I stand on jelly legs, holding the sofa for support. One step turns into several, until I've wobbled like a drunkard over to the mirror, rubbing at my eyes.

The state of me! For a second I can only stare at my dishevelled condition, then I'm pulling a hat over my crazy hair, yanking on my coat and scarf, grabbing paperwork I'll need for the bank and running out of the door. Almost send my neighbour, Mrs Bridges, flying.

'Sorry! Can't stop!' I shout.

'Someone's in a hurry,' she mutters.

Her grumpy comments are left far behind me as I race to the high street.

By the time I burst through the bank's doors, I'm so out of breath I can barely speak. Cashiers and customers throw curious looks my way, especially as I can hardly keep still while waiting in line. Finally, I reach the front. Lean over the counter, glance over my shoulder and then say in a quiet voice: 'I'd like to empty this account, please.'

'I'm sorry?' The cashier doesn't bend closer to catch my words, and I'm loath to talk any louder about such a large amount. I look around again, worried someone might overhear me. Pull my coat a little closer around me.

'I, er, said I want to empty this account. The paperwork's all here, it shouldn't be a problem – please don't tell me there's going to be a problem.' My voice becomes a low moan.

A sidelong glance, and then she is tapping away at her computer. Seconds later she is looking at me again, studying me intently. 'Are you certain you want to withdraw the whole balance of £19,450?'

'Yes! How many times must I say it!' My hands leave sweaty palm prints on the countertop.

'In cash?'

A nod. The heating in the bank is on full blast. Sweat trickles down my face. I push back my hood, pull off my hat and scarf. People are staring, nudging, whispering. The more I urge the cashier to hurry, the more glacial her movements become.

'Just one moment and I'll arrange for a personal banker to speak to you in private.'

'I don't want—'

Too late, she's already on the phone to somebody, a murmured conversation that I can't quite make out. Almost instantly someone appears by her side. Straight back, confident gaze, firm voice, clearly a woman in charge. She asks me to follow her, and my knees feel weak as water as we go into a side room and she closes the door behind me.

'I understand from my colleague that you wish to withdraw a large amount of funds in cash, and to close an account. Is that correct?'

'What's all the fuss about? It's my account, and the paperwork's here. I gave twenty-four hours' notice, like I'm supposed to.'

'You seem a little agitated, so I'm going to ask a question and need you to know that you're safe to give me an honest answer. Whatever you say will be treated in strictest confidence. Are you under some form of duress to hand over this money?'

'What? No, of course not! The money was raised for somebody else, and now I'm just giving it to that person. Everything is fine.'

There is an edge of hysteria to my voice that makes me shift uncomfortably, even though I'm telling the truth.

It takes another half an hour before the cash finally appears, and I don't sit still for a minute of it.

By the time I finally make it out of the bank with nearly twenty thousand pounds stuffed into my handbag, I'm running horribly late. At least the wind is behind me, pushing me along. I'm bundled up against the cold, hood up, its fur trim cocooning me, but still I've got a woollen hat on under it, pulled down to my eyebrows for further protection, scarf over my nose and mouth. Everyone is similarly attired – the few people around, that is. The sea rages beside me, a white, mercurial fury that urges me on ever faster.

*Am I doing the right thing? Is everything in place? Will I be safe?*

These are questions no one has the answers to. No knocking on wood, or tossing of salt over my shoulder, not even starvation will influence the outcome one way or another. Life can't be controlled or planned; if anyone understands that, it's me. It should make me feel insignificant, but embracing that knowledge fills me with power. At last, I'm strong enough.

I reach Carrie's cul-de-sac. Knock on the door, then bend down and call through the letterbox.

'Don't worry, it's only me!'

Footsteps. The door opens on Carrie's relieved face. 'I was starting to think something had happened.'

I push past her, closing the door quickly behind us. Shoot the bolt across.

Then all hell breaks loose.

# CHAPTER FORTY-EIGHT

## THEN

The bonds of fear refused to give, no matter how hard I strained. No one could hear my screams, because they echoed only in my head. The single most terrifying thing that Andy had done to me during our one-year marriage was turn me into a version of my helpless mother.

All those years I had colluded with her, feeling sorry for her but also slightly superior, and now here I was in exactly the same situation. I'd fallen for a man identical to my father. Years of terror stretched in front of me like a rope with which I would hang myself.

But there was another rope I could grab. A lifeline tossed my way the last time I went to hospital after Andy had broken my arm pushing me down the stairs. My grip on it became stronger than steel.

The doctor had been suspicious on that visit, but with my husband by my side I hadn't been able to tell the truth.

'I haven't been sleeping well lately, and took a tumble because I was being dozy,' I'd lied.

'She's always dozy,' Andy had laughed.

The doctor had written a prescription for a short course of sleeping tablets as well as painkillers.

Now I stood in the relative privacy of my kitchen and stared at the sleeping tablets. Was I really going to do this? Wrapping them in foil, I picked up the rolling pin and bashed them until there was nothing left but a fine powder. That should make them easier to swallow all at once.

Andy would be home soon, so it was now or never. I'd reached the point of no return, couldn't take another day of pain.

A nod to make me feel stronger.

This way it would be over for good.

❁

Andy gave me a kiss. Soft, tender, loving. He was in a good mood, teasing me with a glimpse of the man I fell in love with. It seemed particularly poignant as this would be our farewell meal. Peace enveloped me, lifted me up and let me float free.

'Good day at work, love?'

'Yeah, the boss is on about giving me a rise if this job comes off.'

'That's great news! You really deserve it. I've done your favourite tonight, sausage and mash with onion gravy. It can be your celebration meal.'

'Great, I'm starving.'

He flopped onto the sofa, turned on the telly and started channel-surfing for something to watch as we ate. Settled on *You've Been Framed*. I could hear him chuckling away as I disappeared into the kitchen, reappearing with his loaded plate on a tray.

He was already tucking in by the time I sat beside him with my own food. On-screen, someone somersaulted off their out-of-control motorbike and landed in a bush. Andy guffawed, sending a bit of mash flying from his mouth. He wiped his chin.

'Potatoes are a bit grainy,' he complained.

'I'm so sorry.'

'You can't get anything right, can you, you stupid cow.'

I held my breath. If he beat me now, he wouldn't finish his food. He reached across the table towards me.

'Pass the gravy, then,' he scowled. Poured more onto his potatoes, then kept shovelling, eyes glued to the television.

It wasn't long until the plate was clean.

He sat back with a satisfied groan, undoing the top button of his jeans, just as another episode started. By the time Harry Hill was telling viewers where to send their home videos if they wanted to appear in the programme, Andy's head had dropped back, mouth wide open and drool slithering, slug-like, from it.

So far my plan was working like a dream. Time to put the rest of it into action.

It was hard work stripping him off. The dead weight of him flopped around and was hard to control, but eventually I managed it.

Posing him was much easier. He snored peacefully as I took picture after picture of him with various sex toys. My particular favourite was a close-up of him with his mouth wrapped around a massive dildo covered in realistic-looking veins. To a macho man like Andy, people thinking he was gay would be a fate worse than death. He was well known at work and down the pub for his vile homophobic comments – he often said that it was the most disgusting thing in the world, and that given half a chance he'd like 'to kick the gay out of them'. If people saw these photographs, he'd be completely vilified by the nasty little friends who shared his views.

Moving quickly, unsure of how long Andy would be out for, I packed the few belongings I would be taking with me, then waited for him to stir. Played *Call of Duty* to pass the time. There was no fear. I wasn't Mum any more; I'd rediscovered my true self: the girl who could survive anything.

A small groan. The smacking of lips. Andy yawned, stretched. Eyes still out of focus finally found mine.

'Hello, sleepyhead. Do you see this photograph?'

He blinked slowly, still too sluggish to react properly. Finally, he seemed to focus on my phone's screen. Lethargic face wrinkled with dumb confusion, various expressions moving across it with the speed of plate tectonics.

'I'm leaving you now, Andy, and if you try to stop me, this photograph and all of these others,' I paused, scrolling through the private peepshow I had created, 'will be sent to your friends and family via email, social media and text message.'

Leaden realisation and horror were starting to make themselves known on his face. He tried to sit up, but fell back, too weak from the effects of the sleeping tablets still.

'If you come after me, the same thing will happen. If anything ever happens to me, a friend will make sure that these photographs are spread far and wide. You'll be a laughing stock. Do you hear me?'

He swiped at my phone, sluggish as a sloth. It was an easy blow to dodge. He floundered on the sofa, trying to stand, trying to sit, but falling back prostrate.

'Don't be stupid, Andy. Even if you destroyed this phone, all of the photographs are backed up.' I'd sent them to a second emergency pay-as-you-go phone I also had, that he didn't ever need to know about. Two phones made me feel safer, in case I ever got into trouble and was forced to hand one over.

'So, are you going to let me go and leave me alone?'

A slow nod.

'Oh, and if this little bit of blackmail isn't enough to keep you away from me, just remember: this time it was sleeping tablets that I put in your food, next time it could be poison. Let me walk out of this house and never follow me, and our lives will both be better for it. Make me stay, and I'll make your life as hellish as you've made mine.'

Sleep seemed to be taking him again. Just in case he was too out of it to remember this conversation properly, I sent him my favourite snap. That dildo really did look realistic – and Andy appeared to be deeply happy about it. That would give him something to remember me by when he woke properly.

Eyelids fluttering against slumber, he watched me helplessly while I slung my bag over my shoulder and started to walk out.

Suddenly I stopped. Went back, unplugged his PlayStation and stuffed it into my bag. Ideally, I'd be able to keep it myself and play it. It was the least I deserved. Failing that, I might be able to flog it; and if I couldn't do that, at least I'd have the satisfaction of knowing that Andy didn't have it any more.

# CHAPTER FORTY-NINE

## THEN

The house I'd grown up in looked like a ghost of itself. It had never been particularly well looked after, despite Mum's best efforts, but now it seemed to sag inward apologetically, the windows soulless as well as curtain-less. The living room window had chipboard nailed over it, and a local joker had graffiti-sprayed a generously proportioned penis on it.

My feet shifted from side to side, making up their mind whether to walk away or walk on in. My brain wasn't involved in the decision; if it had been I wouldn't be anywhere near my childhood home.

I was just about to turn away when the door opened. At least it didn't creak. Dad shuffled out. Clothes baggy on his spare frame, sunken cheeks, grey stubble on pasty skin, a double whammy of bags and dark circles under his eyes. He saw me on the pavement and stopped. Even from this distance I could hear the rasp of his nails scratching across his chin. As he did so, he opened his mouth, like a dog enjoying an ear scratch. Feral. He'd lost two front teeth in the two years since I'd last seen him.

What on earth had I been thinking, going there? Had I imagined he'd have changed for the better after losing Mum? Of course he hadn't; he was even worse, if anything. But despite everything, I'd gone back to that house rather than become homeless – just like Mum had been isolated from friends by Dad, one by one mates had dropped away as Andy's influence had grown over me.

For all my big talk in front of my husband, I had nowhere left to go and nobody to turn to.

Dad stepped closer.

'Come to see your old man, eh?' He rubbed his hands on his legs, anxious, distracted. Leaned closer, a smile conning its way on to his face and pulling his wrinkles. My dad was only forty-eight but looked two decades older. 'Don't, er, don't suppose you've got any money? Just a few quid for a drink?'

I could have got drunk on the fumes from his breath.

Anger barrelled through me. Why couldn't I have had a normal dad, like other people? Why couldn't he have been more like the dad of my imagination?

'Look at you. It's 11 a.m. and you're desperate for booze,' I snapped. 'Your hands are shaking! I used to be so scared of you, but you're pathetic. You've picked on people all your life, to make yourself feel big and brave and strong, because deep down inside you know you're none of those things. Because of you, I spent years hating Mum, blaming her for not protecting me, when all the time I should have been angry with you.'

I wished with all my heart that Mum was still alive, so that I could finally get her away from this man. So that I could finally talk to her properly and tell her that I understood what she'd been through, but that she was stronger than she believed. She must have been to have survived everything that he'd put her through, which meant she could have been tough enough to walk away and live a happy life without him, if only she'd had a little more support from me.

Too late for Mum. Not for me, though.

I dug into my purse. 'Here! Drink yourself to death for all I care.'

My last tenner floated to the floor. Dad launched himself forward like a starving man and snatched it up.

I'd no funds for a meal or anywhere to stay, but it was worth giving my money away if it meant putting Dad in an early grave.

❁

The people in my life had proved themselves to be worse than useless. It was time to rely on myself. I didn't let myself down. Living on the streets was hard. No one would give money to a beggar with decent, clean clothes and fresh breath. The weight of judgement in the gaze of strangers made me rage. I knew what they were thinking: that it must be a con, that I was a career beggar who climbed into my BMW at the end of a hard day's begging and drove to my luxury flat. It didn't seem to occur to them that everyone has to begin somewhere, and even rough sleepers don't start out filthy and dishevelled.

After just two nights I found an alternative. My clothes were still decent, my hair brushed, my face clean. I didn't yet look like somebody who was homeless. I went to Broad Street, where loads of pubs and clubs are in Birmingham, and stood just down from a busy pub where people were spilling onto the pavement. I was careful not to approach anybody. Instinct warned me that if I did, the person would be on their guard, waiting for me to ask them for the inevitable. So instead I hugged myself and started to cry, looking helplessly up and down the road as if not knowing what to do. A young woman about my age peeled away from her group of friends.

'Are you okay?'

'Yeah, no, um, not really. I just… I'll be fine, honestly, it's not your problem.' The tears came easily; all I had to do was think of how desperate I was and what the alternative might be if I didn't get some money. *Falling into prostitution. Perhaps being raped or murdered. Freezing to death one winter night, trying to sleep in a shop doorway in sub-zero temperatures.*

'You don't look fine. Come on, what is it?' She came closer, almost on my hook. The intuition that had always told me how best to approach someone to make an Ann Summers sale kicked in again. I knew what to say.

'It's so stupid of me. I was out with my friends and have lost them, they must have moved on to another pub without me. And my mate's got my purse and phone in her handbag. I don't know how I'm going to get home.'

A jagged whimper shook from me. She put her arm around me, comforting. Her head close to mine.

Hooked.

'Hey, we've all lost our pals at some point.' As if remembering, she turned and shouted to her own group. 'Oy, don't leave without me!'

A couple of them came over. 'What's going on?'

She explained everything. Perfect – it sounded even more believable coming from her.

'Here, use my phone to call someone to come and get you.' One of them started to pull out her mobile, but was stopped by my sob.

'I don't know anyone's number off by heart. Not even my boyfriend's. They're all stored in my phone. I'm such an idiot.'

'Yeah, I'm exactly the same,' they all chimed.

'Look, how much will it cost to get a cab back to yours?' said the first girl.

My sniffing slowed. 'Um, twenty quid.'

'We could cover that between us.' Her friends looked reluctant.

'No, I couldn't possibly accept,' I hurried. 'Not unless you give me your phone numbers so that I can get in touch tomorrow and arrange to pay you back.'

'You don't have to do that,' said the dark-haired girl, but she pulled out a pen all the same. I wrote all three of the numbers down on my forearm, careful to get them right. The three of them then gave a fiver each, then called another of their gang over and she pitched in the final £5.

'Thank you, thank you, thank you,' I gasped, hugging each of them in turn. 'Have a great night!'

As I turned towards the road, holding my arm up to hail a taxi, they waved goodbye and walked away. Disappeared into another pub. A black cab with its orange light glowing pulled up beside me, and I leaned in at the partially wound-down window.

'You're all right, I've changed my mind. Sorry,' I said.

Pocketing my £20, I sauntered on to another section of the street. Ran the same scam over again on men and women. The later it got, the more drunk people were and more generous, their instincts too soggy to warn them I might not be everything I seemed. That night I stayed in a nearby hotel and treated myself to a slap-up breakfast in bed in the morning.

Just like I had as a little girl, I'd found a way to survive through storytelling. The stolen sweets I'd said a kind stranger had paid for. The puppy I'd found wandering in the street, which Dad had eventually taken from me and sold to a man down the pub. The amazing coincidence of me doing brilliantly in that maths test for the first time ever, and scoring exactly the same as the school brainiac who just happened to be sitting next to me but whose paper I absolutely definitely had not stolen the answers from… I remembered all those times from when I was a kid, and how happy they had made me. Now, with a decent night's sleep for the first time since Andy had first hit me, and a belly full of food, I had that same sense of happiness.

I wasn't proud of how I'd solved my problems, but was proud of the fact I had. So many people had tried to break me – Dad, kids in innumerable schools, Andy. They had all thought I was weak and had tried to smash me to pieces emotionally. But I was stronger than stone. Stone could be cracked and demolished or worn down through attrition eventually. Instead, I'd discovered I was something else. I was water. No matter the obstacle, I would always find a way round it or through it. I couldn't, wouldn't be stopped.

I would make the happy ending to my story. Even if it meant stealing someone else's.

# CHAPTER FIFTY

## NOW

The police officer wraps a blanket over my shivering shoulders. Enveloping me in my own lies. Cloaked in them, I try to gather my tumbling thoughts. Soon questioning will start, but for now I have a brief moment to think, line up the memories and decide what to say, what to miss out. How many lies to tell.

A paramedic car pulls up, lights flashing, sirens blaring. It has barely come to a stop before its door is opening and a man in green gets out.

'Alex! Are you okay? What happened? I'd no idea… ' he gasps.

His expression has gone from businesslike to shocked in seconds.

'You're bleeding,' he adds before I can answer. Carrying a bag of medical tricks, he strides over to me, kneels down and studies the laceration to my eyebrow that is dripping blood all over my face and clothes.

'It looks worse than it is,' I promise.

I hadn't realised that Leon would be called out to this. We were only introduced two days ago. He'd held onto my shoulders so tightly after bumping into me in the hospital as I'd hurried away from the patient library. I'd been desperate to leave Carrie's betrayal behind; seeing her sitting reading books instead of getting chemotherapy treatment had hurt me so much. But the recognition of Leon's smile had stopped me in my tracks.

'Do we know each other?' he'd asked.

I'd started to walk away. At the last moment something had made me turn and answer.

'Crusoe's Café, in Tynemouth. I think I saw you there the other day.'

'Of course!' That smile again.

'Anyway, if you'll excuse me, I've got to go.'

'I'm going that way too, mind if I walk with you?'

He'd fallen into step with me before I could object. All I'd wanted to do was get away from Carrie.

'Erm, are you stalking me or something?'

'Sorry, sorry. It probably looks like that, doesn't it, the way we keep bumping into each other. But I work here, I'm a paramedic, so I do actually have a valid reason for being in the hospital. Are you visiting somebody?'

'Long story,' I said shortly, hurrying on. He kept pace with me.

'I'm Leon Cassera, by the way.' Him offering his hand threw me. The shock of my discovery about Carrie fought with this Leon bloke's disarming charm. I found myself shaking his hand and telling him my name, discombobulated by my own actions.

'Actually,' he hung his head and looked sheepish, 'this is going to sound, well, weird, definitely, but I've got a bit of a confession to make. I already knew your name.'

'So you are a stalker?'

'No, nothing like that,' he laughed. 'But a week ago a friend of yours kind of told me all about you.'

He was either some kind of busybody, or was possibly linked to the clinic in some way. Whatever it was, I wasn't interested, needed to get back to my car and get my head straight. My feet moved faster, patter, patter, patter along the lino-lined corridor.

'Phew, you walk quickly. Look, okay, I get that this sounds insane, but I'm just going to tell you anyway, so that it's out there. Then you can do what you want with the information.'

Annoyance and attraction warred inside me just enough to keep me quiet.

'Okay.' He was nervous, kept repeating the word. 'Your mate, she mentioned that you're single. And I'm single, so I wondered... I'm a paramedic, and friendly, fairly outgoing, respectable, I like surfing and a spot of drawing every now and again. Quite a mean chef. My wife left me recently, but try not to hold that against me—'

'You seem really sweet, but I'm not interested in dating right now. I don't know who you've been talking to about me.'

He bit his lip. 'Ah, right. Fair enough. She didn't sign you up to the dating app after all, then?'

'I truly have no idea what you're talking about. Anyway, must go.'

I'd turned my back on him, when his next sentence hit me.

'Your mate, Carrie, must have got the wrong end of the stick, sorry. We got talking in the pub one night. She kept telling me about her amazing friend, Alex. Explained that you were too shy to meet blokes but that you're really lovely and said she's going to sign you up to some dating sites without you knowing, to see if she could get you together with someone. Only problem was, she didn't have an up-to-date photograph of you, so she asked me to take a sneaky snap of you both because you'd be suspicious if she took one. Gave me a time and place where you'd both be, and bought me a pint for my trouble.'

He'd chuckled, not realising his words had trickled ice down my back.

'Got to admit, I thought it was a bit strange, but figured I shouldn't stand in the way of true love. So, I took the picture that night.' He looked at his feet, then smiled up at me through blond eyelashes. 'I have got say I, erm, I think you're really beautiful. Feels like fate that I've seen you twice since. What do you think? Fancy having a drink with me sometime?'

'You took a photo of Carrie and me? Together?'

'Here.' He pulled out his phone and showed me. 'Sorry it's not great. Bit blurry. Not sure it's usable, but Carrie seemed pleased enough when I texted it to her. Did she show it to you? I promise I don't normally take sneaky snaps of women I don't know.'

'Oh, that picture. Yes, I saw it. You texted it to her? You didn't print it off and leave it on her doorstep?'

He hadn't. In that moment I'd realised Carrie not only didn't have cancer, she'd also sent those messages to herself. Her tangle of lies grew knottier, and the more I had tugged to undo them, the tighter they seemed to become.

The sting of Leon cleaning up my bloody wound drags me from the past. All around me, police scurry backwards and forwards outside Carrie's house, setting up a cordon with blue and white tape. A man and woman in police uniform walk over to me and introduce themselves.

'We'd like to take a statement, please,' says the woman.

'Can you just give me a minute to finish cleaning her up?' Leon requests. He is all business while doing his job, giving no hint of the flirtation from two days earlier.

The officers do as they're asked and stand some distance away, while Leon continues to fuss. He gently presses my left cheekbone, and I gasp.

'Hmm, I'd like that X-rayed just in case it's a fracture. Even if it's not, it's going to be a hell of a bruise. There's a strong chance you're concussed. Can you follow the light for me?'

A tiny torch's rays blind me momentarily. Only after several rapid blinks am I able to do as requested. Left, right, left, right, its hypnotic beam sends me flying back into the past again…

To when I tried to confront Carrie about everything. I'd marched round to her house, told her I knew she'd lied about the cancer, starting there because that was the worst of her deceptions. That call from her, pretending to be a doctor, had been the last straw. But before I could mention the messages or Leon, Smudge's collar had arrived.

She'd looked so horrified. What an actress! Confused, I'd no choice but to go along with her to find out what the endgame was – especially as I'd just learned that confronting her with what I knew *wasn't* the way to uncover the truth. As one liar to another, I needed to understand.

Her story about Andy had resonated with me, but the more I looked at everything as a whole, the more it felt as though I was reading a book I'd dropped and sent pages scattering, and now I was reading them out of order.

Andy might not be behind the messages, but that didn't mean he hadn't existed in Carrie's life at some point, I decided. Perhaps she was emotionally disturbed. Maybe she even had Munchausen's syndrome or some such, or Andy was the product of a psychotic break brought on by terrible things that really had happened to her in the past. It was hard to accept that the woman I'd come to think of as a daughter was a compulsive liar. Mad or bad, until I knew which I'd reserved judgement.

I thought about talking it through with Rosie. Fear that it would only reinforce her suspicions that I was a woman on the edge stopped me. That's why I hadn't confided in Jackie, either, despite her having her own reservations about Carrie. Besides, her involvement wouldn't solve anything, only complicate matters.

There had been, of course, the possibility of going back to the police, but the fact was there was nothing to tell them. I'd no further proof to persuade them to look into Carrie's connection with Joanne's death than I'd had the last time I'd spoken with them. The story of how Joanne died may or may not have been true, but I didn't trust it because I wasn't convinced Andy even existed. To test the theory, I'd described Leon to Carrie and asked if he sounded like her evil ex, and she'd eagerly agreed.

Perhaps Carrie had killed Joanne. If so, I'd have to tread very carefully indeed, but somehow, despite everything, I couldn't bring myself to believe that of her.

The obvious conclusion could only be that Carrie had done all of this for money. The problem was, she'd repeatedly turned down my offers to take the bucket list donations. A con would have explained lying about the cancer, but not lying about being on the run from a murderous husband.

Suspicions were starting to form about her true target. Nausea spread through me alongside the realisation. Still I'd denied the truth. Instead I made a decision: if I wanted to get to the bottom of this, I had no choice but to play along and see how the cards fell.

That's how I ended up sitting on the front wall of Carrie's garden, having blood wiped from my face.

# CHAPTER FIFTY-ONE

Blood tickles my cheek, and I pull my sleeve over my hand to dab at it with the material. Leon gets there first.

'That's definitely going to need stitches,' he sighs.

I'm barely listening; instead I'm remembering watching Carrie cry over her cat's collar. In my mind's eye, I see again the dry flakes of blood cracking across the 'lost' poster. I remember the flash of inspiration that made me suggest texting Andy, because I hadn't expected her to get a reply. I'd gone back to my house thinking I'd trapped her, and she'd be forced to confess everything when he didn't come.

As I'd walked home, I'd spotted that knot of boys on bikes who I'd once accused of playing tricks on Carrie.

'Hey, remember that twenty quid I gave you?' I called. The leader had nodded, keeping his distance as he did nonchalant wheelies. 'Did you ever see anyone hanging round my friend's house?'

'Nah. Saw her putting a box out on her step yesterday, then you coming back and finding it. Was she playing a joke? She looked dead pleased with herself after.'

That answered the mad or bad question, then. Before I could answer, he was speaking again. 'Oy, is there any money for her cat?'

'What do you mean? Have you seen Smudge?'

'Seen him round the bins yesterday. Tried to catch him but couldn't. I told your mate, but she wasn't bothered – but if you're willing to pay, I could trap him for you.'

'You sure it was the same cat in the posters?'

The whole group had stopped, eager at the chance of cash. 'Yeah!' they chorused.

'Got cool eyes,' added the one with the skull balaclava.

'Leave him be tonight, but if you can try and get him for me tomorrow morning I'll give you all fifty pounds to split between you. That's a tenner each. No telling anyone, though, otherwise everyone will want in on it and you'll hardly get any money.'

They agreed eagerly. 'Tomorrow morning,' I repeated. 'I reckon he'll be by the bins round the back at about ten, so be there from then. Ten sharp, yeah?'

That night, waiting for Carrie to confess had been nerve-racking. Everything swirled round my head. *Carrie didn't have cancer. Carrie was somehow involved in her friend Joanne's death. Carrie was sending herself weird messages, and even pretended to kill her cat.*

My former friend didn't crack, though. Instead she used the fact that Andy hadn't shown up to her advantage. As she'd cast her net of lies over me and I'd let myself be pulled in, in a strange way I'd been impressed by her audacity. One liar to another, I had to hand it to her.

Still, hearing her say she was leaving, realising my worst suspicions were right, had hurt deeply. I'd loved and trusted that girl and had thought she loved me. So I held her hand, crying, begging her not to leave me. I wanted her to know what I was willing to do for her and hoped it might make her change her mind.

Carrie had proved she was going to forge ahead with her nasty plan, though. When I'd offered her the bucket list cash, she'd shown her true colours.

'If there were more money then I'd say yes,' she'd said. 'As it is, though, I think the donations should be refunded to everybody after I'm gone, because it just isn't enough to make it worth taking.

'It's not that I'm being ungrateful – I really, really am blown away by everyone's generosity – but although twenty thousand is a lot, it's not enough to start a whole new life away from Andy. I don't know how much would be, but tons more, that's for sure. I'd have to go abroad, probably, to be sure of escaping him for ever.'

It was a clever manipulation of a target by a con artist. Turn down the small prize in order to line yourself up for the big pay-off, which will be offered because you're clearly such an honest person. I knew that because I'd seen a con man first-hand, although admittedly one of the heart. My own heart sank at that moment, along with all hope for her, as I gave her what she'd wanted from the start. Her reaction to my revelation about compensation had been well acted, but I was looking out for the signs – and know them well because I'm a phoney, too.

Clearly she'd targeted me, somehow finding out about my money. The glaringly obvious thing to do, therefore, was offer it. The tangled web of Carrie's subterfuge unknotted, and I could see all the threads. How despicable. How clever.

I'd played my part until the end. Listening to fake plans for our future together, letting myself be manoeuvred and engineered by an expert, her arguing just enough to make me feel it was all my idea. If I hadn't known better I'd have fallen for it hook, line and sinker.

I knew I'd have to be careful – after all, I'd no idea what exactly Carrie had done to Joanne. Even if Carrie told me the truth, I wouldn't believe her. Not now. The skilful way she'd reeled me in to get me to hand over willingly everything I owned made me convinced I wasn't the first person she'd done this to. The cleverest part was that she'd done nothing legally wrong here. Morally, yes; legally, no.

Carrie's research may have revealed Owen's death and the large compensation payout, but there was something it wouldn't have shown, because I'd never told anyone apart from Rosie. Owen had been my real-life version of the fictional Andy, a chimera who swapped from charming to the devil in the blink of an eye. I'd got used to hiding my real feelings living with him, so slipping the mask on again hadn't been too hard in front of Carrie. I'd been working on my idea of how to get rid of Carrie once and for all since meeting Leon, hoping I wouldn't need to action it, but knowing I might. I'm a survivor. Even when I've tried to destroy myself, I've failed.

So, with all legal options for me to bring Carrie to justice stymied, it was obvious how this was going to end. The blood on my hands seems to stare back at me. I wipe them on my trousers, smearing the scarlet, while telling myself to stay strong. I did what had to be done: I'd no choice.

# CHAPTER FIFTY-TWO

## THEN

For the better part of a year I had been a pathological and compulsive liar. It was my job, my life, my saviour. I was brilliant at it.

My small-time cons were fine to get by on, but they meant that I was constantly living from hand to mouth still. I needed something with a bigger pay-off in order to get me more security. It occurred to me one day that the very best place to meet vulnerable marks was at self-help groups. There, I could sit back and learn all about their backstories, discover vulnerabilities, find ways to endear myself, and all with minimum effort, because they wanted to tell me.

Like water, I had found the path of least resistance.

After moving to affluent Buxton, Derbyshire, I found a support group and put the plan into action. Mum was my inspiration – when I spoke, her struggle against cancer became mine.

The shock of discovering that the red rash on her breast was a form of breast cancer was what hit first and foremost. 'I'd dismissed it for months because it wasn't a lump. Cancer's always a lump, right? I'd no idea a rash could kill me, that this form of breast cancer invades skin cells and lymph nodes and is so aggressive that survival rates are worse than usual,' I cried. Many of the women looked shocked, unaware themselves of inflammatory breast cancer. At least by pretending, I was spreading the word. Mum would like that.

How hard she'd cried when her hair started coming out in chunks in a matter of hours after treatment. 'Seeing the visible effects of cancer and knowing they were there on show to everybody hammered home how little control I had over my body,' I told the group.

The positivity she'd found against all odds through her diagnosis. 'I've learned to appreciate every single day I have. This is a beautiful world, if we allow it to be,' I parroted Mum's words into the room, and they were gobbled up by these strangers.

Even after Dad set fire to her wig one night in revenge for not making him dinner, when she'd been too weak after chemo, she still talked about the beauty of life. Pretending those words were my own made me feel closer to her. Then I was reliving her terminal diagnosis. People dabbed at their eyes as I spoke, moved by the truth of my words.

'Do you have a bucket list? You should make one,' said one of the women, who introduced herself as Anne Dempsey.

'Umm, I've never heard of the term, Anne,' I frowned.

She smiled at my innocence, explained it to me. Instinctively I saw an opportunity to profit.

'That sounds like a wonderful idea!' I gasped. A glance around at other members took in their nodding heads. Time for a spot of reverse psychology, to show what a lovely person I was. 'Instead of funding a bucket list, though, I'd love to raise money for Cancer Research. This is my chance to give something back for all the help I've been given during treatment. We need to wipe out cancer for good.'

Everybody was so enthusiastic and supportive. They came up with ideas for fundraising and made donations themselves. Soon I got a tidy little pot together. The problem was that people, particularly Anne, got suspicious about the fact that everything was in my name. In the end I actually had to hand the money over to charity. Clearly I needed to come up with a cleverer plan.

I moved to a new town, Reading, in Berkshire, and tried again. This time I put much more effort into it. I learned to draw convincing-looking radiation dots on my neck with a permanent marker, to mimic the tattoo doctors often give patients so they know where to line up the radiation machine every day. I rolled up a bath towel, stretching it between my hands and rubbing it back and forth against my neck as fast as I could to give myself 'radiation burns'.

From the Internet I bought oxygen tubes, bandages and a chemotherapy body port, so that I could send my new friends photographs of myself 'getting treatment'.

I shaved my head with a razor, plucked my eyebrows bald and made myself throw up from chemotherapy nausea when somebody was around to hear me.

I took about eight thousand pounds from that group, and thought my ship had come in. Unlike in Buxton, the Reading group believed me when I 'moved away to die at my parents' home'. I even put an 'in memoriam' notice in the local paper, giving details of my funeral, but ensuring that it was placed after the date of my 'burial' so that no one could attend. It was all organised from Thailand, where I blew the cash on a holiday of a lifetime.

As time went on, I got better at the big con, ironing out the crinkles. It financed so many dreams come true for me. I swam with wild dolphins in the warm waters of Bali; did a parachute jump over the Blue Mountains in Australia, as eucalyptus oil perfumed the air and gave it the blue haze the area's named after; partied all night long in Belgrade to the brilliantly kitsch turbo-folk music, where it got seriously boisterous. If I'd had a bucket list, it was growing shorter item by item.

The bulimia that I developed came in handy for my scams. Pretending to have chemotherapy gave me the perfect cover for my eating disorder, and my eating disorder really helped sell my story of having cancer. It certainly wasn't all good news, though.

Aside from the adverse health impacts that an eating disorder has, it also costs a small fortune. I'd sometimes spend £150 on shopping in a week, so that I could binge on 11,000 calories in one day – then vomit it back up. Then there was the cost of laxatives, diet teas and pills. I had to have clothes of different sizes as a result of weight fluctuations – but that, along with altering the style and colour of my hair, helped me maintain an ever-changing appearance, decreasing the chances of anybody I'd previously conned recognising me.

The love that was poured out to me was worth more in some ways than the cash. It was almost like being a celebrity. People would give me money, insisting that 'you can't take it with you. Enjoy it now, while you can'. They sent me messages of positivity.

*So young.*
*So brave.*
*So beautiful.*
*You're an inspiration.*

The adoration was addictive. When had I ever been an inspiration in my entire life? All right, so it was built on lies and fraud, but if they knew the real me they'd never like me. This way, though, I felt loved for the first time in years. Maybe ever.

People actually wanted to be with me.

They also wanted to hold my hand while I had treatment. That was always tricky, and sometimes making excuses for why they couldn't be with me was exhausting. I often let them come as far as the hospital and ask them to wait in the café, while I would sit in the stairwell for several hours, reading a book, before returning with tales of my latest cancer treatment.

People generally felt so sorry for me, too, buying me food and other bits and bobs, as well as donating to the fund. I had a good life.

The weakness in my fraud was that it was always touch-and-go whether or not people would believe I was moving back in with my parents to die, taking my bucket list money with me. Buxton had proved that. There was always the fear at the back of my mind that someone might get suspicious and start researching me.

That was when I came up with the really clever part of my fraud. The double bluff. Even I was impressed with it, because it set me head and shoulders above other rip-off merchants. By ensuring people discovered I didn't have cancer, I'd actually make even more money as a result.

The principle employed was identical to my first swindle on the streets of Birmingham, only on a bigger scale: don't approach the mark yourself, make them come to you. All the best con artists know that the most effective way to get someone to offer what you want is to pretend you don't want it. The skill is in knowing which buttons to push to manipulate them into it.

So I let my target get to know me, showed them what a decent, reliable, positive person I was, then started a breadcrumb trail for them to follow. It couldn't be too obvious; they had to feel they'd cleverly put the clues together themselves. Once they uncovered the fact that I didn't have cancer, I unleashed my full sob story.

*'Woe is me, I'm on the run from a violent ex who wants to kill me.'*

Being backed into a corner before telling them this story made them all the more convinced it was the truth. The first time I did it was in Salisbury. There was a church group I joined. I was nervous, but had found a whale of a target, a woman with no kids, dying herself, and conveniently finding God at the same time. She'd spent all her money on flash holidays and designer clothes, and now she wanted to buy her way into heaven. Handing over £50,000 in cash to me did the trick. It never occurred to her that I might lie twice. It never occurred to anyone.

The pure genius of the con was that people voluntarily handed over the bucket list money, knowing I would use it for my personal gain, and they were happy not to report me to the police. In fact, they were left with a warm, fuzzy feeling for helping someone in such dire need.

I almost felt like thanking Andy and Dad for giving me such great material to work with. Almost, but not quite.

# CHAPTER FIFTY-THREE

## THEN

When I spotted Alex at my new support group, there was something about her which drew me. There was a twitchy vulnerability about her, like a bird poised to take flight. As she spoke to the semicircle of members, spilling her story for us, I sat forward.

'I'm fighting to leave behind adult-onset anorexia, a condition that's controlled my life for four years,' she explained. 'It was triggered by empty nest syndrome – and because of it, I've told so many lies over the years that I've alienated my twins, Edward and Elise. All I want is to be a mother to them. It's – it's like I'm one of those Russian dolls and I've been left empty. Missing them is like a physical pain inside me.'

I liked her. Something about her desperate need for approval reminded me of my own mum. Her expression when she talked about her ex-husband, Owen, was like a step back in time. Mum's big-eyed gaze, mouth slack but fingers twisting, seemed to hover tantalisingly in front of me as Alex spoke.

There was something she was holding back, though. My instinct screamed it.

'You haven't been on any dates with anyone since Owen?' I asked, when the floor was opened up for us all to speak. She shook her head. 'Well, don't worry, you'll find someone. You need to move on.' *The way my mum had never managed to.*

As others from the group spoke, my eye kept being drawn to her, thinking of her backstory. Then it clicked. She was the one Simon had dumped me for. She fitted the description, the story my pathetic ex had spilled eagerly when he announced so melodramatically that he'd fallen for another woman. I ground my boot heel into the perfectly polished wooden floor, desperate for revenge, as I glared at her instead of listening to the other people's stories.

Simon was weak and pathetic and clearly led by his privates, so I'd never fallen for him – but he'd been convenient. He'd provided a free place to crash when I'd arrived in Tynemouth in March, while I'd sorted out a place to live for myself in this new town. He'd only been a hook-up, and he'd been quite generous, paying for food and nights out. After a month together, I was ready to move out and told him I'd been having treatment for cancer, to get rid of him. He went so pale! I'd thought my news would make him run for the hills, but instead he turned out to be one of those decent blokes who felt like he couldn't possibly dump me in my hour of need. It had been quite fun watching him struggle for days, when he clearly wanted out as much as I did – enjoying his turmoil was the reason why I hadn't been firmer kicking him into touch.

The fun had ended when, days later, he split with me by announcing he'd fallen in love with someone else. Love? Stupid man. We'd only been together a month, and for a fortnight of that he'd been screwing some other woman.

Just because I hadn't wanted him didn't mean I wasn't put out that someone else did. He'd been mine, and someone had taken him from me.

Now, there she was in front of me at a support group. What I couldn't figure out was why she hadn't mentioned her new boyfriend. It must mean they weren't together any more.

Suddenly I realised the hall had gone silent. Everyone was looking at me.

'Oh, it's my turn?' I checked. Thrown, I hesitated, unsure of whether to go for my usual story. Instinct kicked in, and I let it take the lead. It rarely steered me wrong.

I spun my story of cancer – and added in heartbreak at the hands of a love rat. It felt right to rub salt into Alex's wounds. She watched my every move, hung on my every word and almost cried. Guilt was clearly eating at her, making her susceptible to a tale of woe.

'We weren't together long, but I really thought he was the one, you know? I could see us getting married,' I sniffled. 'You know the old couples you see shuffling along side by side still holding hands? I was convinced that would be us. I'd just finished my treatment when suddenly it all got too much for him.

'I can't blame him. He probably only stayed with me out of pity, and as soon as he knew that I was well he did a runner. I suppose I should just be grateful he stuck with me during the chemo. When I lost my hair I felt so ugly, and he – he… ' I hiccuped through tears, 'he said I still looked beautiful to him.'

The last word was a heartbreaking wail. Alex almost wet herself with horror. At the end of the meeting she made a beeline for me.

'You've been through so much. Come over to mine sometime, I'll cook us something nice,' she offered. 'I miss having someone to look after. I could get some of the others to come, make a bit of a do of it.'

So eager to be my friend and get others to befriend me.

I agreed instantly. A free meal was the very least she owed me after stealing my bloke. I wanted to take every penny she had there and then – but I knew better than to choose a target purely on emotional grounds. Instead, I spent the rest of the night and next day researching the other members of the group, using the information gained at the meeting to help me. There were a couple of interesting possibilities, but no one who seemed to be jumping up and down shouting 'pick me, pick me!'.

The very next night we all went round to Alex's place for a meal. It was a useful opportunity to get to know the group a bit better. At her large three-bedroomed house, with en suite, family bathroom, massive dining room and kitchen, and garden with mature trees, I became even more convinced that Alex was the perfect mark. She couldn't be funding all that on her profits as a dressmaker; she must have received a decent settlement in her divorce, I reasoned.

When I spotted her sudoku and cryptic crossword books, I almost laughed. I'd give her a puzzle she wouldn't be able to resist solving, and the prize would be a wad of cash for me.

Back at home, I finally gave in to my desire to research Alex. After a couple of hours, I sat back and whistled.

Jackpot!

After that, it was easy, particularly as the guilt of her coincidentally sleeping with my fling blinded her to everything. Even without that, I'd have reeled her in once I put my mind to it, but it certainly helped. She was my new best friend. Still, I didn't want to rush things and ruin my chances. With a potential payout of over a million pounds, I was willing to stick around longer than usual, even getting a job as a cleaner and barmaid to make my cover story believable.

It meant I spent more time with her than I had with any other of my previous targets. I didn't understand why she was lying about Owen and the children, but felt sort of sorry for her, despite her nicking Simon. After all, I hadn't been in love with him. Alex was clearly struggling to come to terms with everything that had happened to her. We really did get on, and she genuinely seemed to want to look out for me. Around her, I found myself trying to be the kind of daughter that she wanted – not just acting the role, but actually trying to change. It was almost like being given a second chance with Mum, and getting a glimpse of who she could have been if it hadn't been for Dad. Being around Alex was making me soft.

Several times I was tempted to call the whole thing off, just simply disappear without a trace and without her cash. Or to put down roots and stay. Perhaps I could announce I'd been miraculously cured. I found myself fantasising about settling down, and even took in Smudge, the stray cat, because he was a survivor like me.

Going soft wasn't an option, though, I reminded myself often. Alex was lying to everyone as much as I was with her bullshit story about her husband and kids. Although I gave her opportunities, she didn't come clean about Simon, either. I reminded myself of all the times I'd trusted somebody in the past and they'd turned around and metaphorically kicked me in the teeth. Alex was clearly capable of doing the same. I wouldn't let myself be taken in by her.

# CHAPTER FIFTY-FOUR

## NOW

Leon still kneels by my side, trying to persuade me to go to the hospital.

'I'm fine,' I insist.

'Well, I can't make you, but I strongly recommend it.' His eyes are full of fear for me, and the guilt is hard to take.

'All right, I accept defeat – but only to shut you up. But first I think these officers want to speak with me.'

The two uniformed police have come closer at overhearing I might be leaving the scene of the crime.

'Are you ready to tell us what happened here today? Someone from CID will want to take a formal statement later, but if you could just talk us through it now it would be really helpful,' asks the officer. Beside him his colleague pulls out her notebook, her pen ready to pounce on my words.

I'm prepared now, ready as I'll ever be. I've been lying for years, and this won't be the first time I've done it to the authorities, either. Still, I battle nerves.

'I, um, went to the police recently with suspicions that my friend, Carrie, didn't have cancer. I don't blame anyone for not believing me, I didn't come across very well. And afterwards I was convinced that everyone was right, and it was my imagination. It won't take much research on your part to show that I've not been very well recently. I'm a recovering anorexic, with a history of hallucinating, so on paper don't make the best witness.'

Leon starts to move away but I wave him back. 'I don't mind if you hear this,' I say, then continue with my tale.

'Carrie came round to my house last night and asked for the money that had been raised in her name.' Neighbours will corroborate that she was seen lurking outside my house acting suspiciously before letting herself in. 'I should have just handed it over… I honestly don't know why I didn't. Call it stubbornness, intuition, I don't know, but I just found myself feeling wary. She, um—'

Leon gives me an encouraging nod. The constables lean closer.

'She suddenly got really angry. I've never seen her like that before. She told me if I didn't get her the cash, she'd kill me. I didn't believe her – not until she pushed me to the floor. I must have hit my head on the coffee table because I passed out.'

Flashes of the truth break through my carefully rehearsed fiction. Waving Carrie goodbye after sitting up all night. The stress of the last few days taking their toll as soon as I was alone, exhaustion hitting me like a sledgehammer, causing me to pass out. When I'd come to, I'd seen the cuts and bruises on my face from where I'd caught myself on the coffee table – I was lucky they were only flesh wounds, and I wasn't concussed. Instantly I'd known how they would help me.

But I can't tell the whole truth.

'She stood over me and forced me to write a message to the bank, giving notice that I'd be emptying the account in cash today. I didn't want to, but I had no choice.'

'It's okay. You must have been very frightened.' The policeman gives an encouraging smile. His colleague's pen doesn't pause.

My fingers trace lightly over the coagulated, sticky mess above my eye and down my face.

'Carrie stayed over last night to make sure that I didn't tell anybody. I was so scared I didn't sleep a wink.'

The dark circles under my eyes tell the truth of that claim.

'She had to let me go to the bank alone, though, otherwise it would have looked too suspicious. I know I should've said something to the bank manager when she asked me if everything was okay, but I kept remembering what Carrie had said about killing me.'

A mixture of genuine nerves and a smattering of acting has ensured my behaviour in the bank stood out as suspicious, and therefore memorable, just as I'd hoped while twitching and over-reacting there. Everyone in the place had seen my bruised face, too, when I pulled my hood down, so my story of being pushed over by Carrie would appear real.

'I went straight to her house with the money, as instructed. She was there, bags packed and ready to run as soon as I handed it over. I thought that would be the end of it, but then… '

I was bundled up against the cold. Only when I got inside Carrie's home did I pull down my hood, take off my hat and scarf and reveal my cuts and bruises. She'd been so eager to get her hands on the funds, she'd barely listened as I explained I'd fainted.

'What happened next?' pushes the constable.

I closed the front door, picked the scab from over my eye so that blood gushed down my face. And started screaming. Carrie's mouth sagged wide, a black hole of confusion.

But I don't say that.

'She threw herself at me. Grabbed my hair and hit my face against the door frame.' A smear of blood I'd left there would authenticate that claim. Still, the tremble in my voice now is all too real. I have to sell this fiction, or I'll be in big trouble myself. 'I started to scream. We struggled, and I kept on shouting for help, hoping someone, anyone, would hear me.'

Carrie's hand closing over my mouth. Trying to shut me up. Not understanding what was going on. My elbow in her stomach. More yells. Knowing that I'd be heard by the boys searching for Smudge by the bins behind Carrie's house, just as I'd told them to.

I feel bad for scaring them, but without their help there would have been no third party to call the police – and there needed to be independent witnesses, otherwise it might be all too easy for Carrie's version of events to be believed. I can't afford the police to dismiss me this time. Between the boys and the unexpected but painful 'bonus' of fainting and hurting myself, I feel reasonably confident that my version of events will be believed.

The front door opens and Carrie appears, wearing handcuffs. Two police officers walk behind her each with a hand on her shoulder. Her eyes lock on mine. She steps towards me, struggling against the arresting officers' grip.

'Alex, what are you doing? Why are you lying?'

Leon creates a bulwark behind which I can hide. Vigilant, the constables who were interviewing me also move. No one can shelter me from her words.

'Tell the truth, Alex!'

Still shouting my name and protesting her innocence, Carrie is bundled into a waiting squad car. I hear the slam of the door, but even through a window and three bodies, I can feel the weight of her glare pressing me down. Then an arm wraps around my shoulders. Strong, protective.

'You're safe now. Come on, let's get you to hospital,' says Leon. Sagging against him, grateful for his support, I let myself be led to the ambulance, safe in the knowledge that I've got over the first hurdle.

Carrie's story doesn't add up. Mine does.

# CHAPTER FIFTY-FIVE

## TWELVE MONTHS LATER

Alex is wringing her hands, then seems to realise and gives them a little shake before letting them drop to her side. The half an hour she's had to spend waiting in line, getting her photo ID checked, placing her valuables in a locker, then being searched, have clearly put her on edge. She hasn't spotted me yet; perhaps she doesn't recognise me now my hair has grown. It gives me the chance to watch her. She looks well – the best I've ever seen her. Glossy hair, glowing skin, more meat on her bones. I can't help but smile, and wonder simultaneously how it's possible to hate and love someone at the same time.

It's 1.45 p.m. on the dot, and visiting time has begun at Low Newton women's prison, just outside Durham. Other visitors flow around Alex, parting like a stream then rejoining, while she stands still, uncertain, looking around at the white walls and cobalt-blue carpets and matching chairs of the 1960s building. She's probably thinking it's better decorated – *nicer* – than expected, but when you're talking about sharing the same prison as Rosemary West, it's all relative.

A tremor runs through me at the thought of facing the person responsible for putting me behind bars. I clench my hands into fists to hide their shaking, just as Alex moves towards me and sits down.

'What do you want?' I ask, cutting to the chase.

'How are you doing?'

I sneer back. 'What do you want?'

'Several things.' She looks around again. Like she wants to run away. 'Um, firstly, I wanted to let you know that your friend, Wendy, has died. Her funeral was yesterday.'

Sharp pain as I bite down on my lip. Blink rapidly to hide the tears. I'd spent so long hanging around the hospital I'd decided to become a hospital visitor, figuring I might as well do some good while I lurked. Wendy and I had hit it off. A single mum to two beautiful children, she fought cancer with such stoicism, optimism and biting humour. We'd laughed long and often together.

*Poor Wendy.*

'Not much of a friend, though, was she,' I lie, my voice thick. 'She never visited.'

I don't like the look Alex is giving me. It's too knowing. She clears her throat.

'I also wanted to thank you, actually,' she says. 'Thanks to you I found the strength that had for so long abandoned me. You might have been a grifter, but I'm a better person for having met you.'

Her dark hair is longer now, past her shoulders, and the cut makes the most of her natural wave. That awful tendency to frizz seems under control, which might be down to better nutrition. Coral polish gleams on fingernails that used to be gnawed. Yeah, she looks happy. My stomach sours. I twirl a strand of my mousy, chin-length hair around my finger and stare hard. Alex shivers.

'Did you notice I've put on weight?' she tries again.

'Oh, yes, I noticed straight away, because I really give a toss.'

She ploughs on through the corrosive sarcasm of truth masquerading as dishonesty, trying to be upbeat. 'I don't have to go to the clinic any more, even as an outpatient. And do you remember that paramedic you asked to take a photograph of me? Leon? We're together now. He's sitting in the car waiting for me.'

'I'm so glad everything worked out so well for you,' I bite. Despite no longer having to vomit to keep up the pretence of chemotherapy treatment, I'm still bulimic. 'Meanwhile I've been sentenced to eighteen months in prison for a crime I didn't commit.'

'Carrie – Sophie, I mean,' Alex leans forward, voice low. I can't help remembering how surprised she'd looked at discovering every single name she'd had for me was wrong. 'You didn't commit that crime, but you committed plenty of others. You know the police suspect you of ripping off at least ten other people, but your other victims are either too embarrassed to come forward or still believe your lies, despite all evidence to the contrary.

'And you still won't tell people what happened between you and Joanne – you're lucky there's not enough left of her to find out how she died, or you could be done for murder. Don't you feel anything for her family?'

Twirl, twirl, twirl, the hair and my fingers are the only parts of me that move. It's Alex who caves first.

'I, umm, still have some questions about what happened between us. I wondered if you'd answer them. I'm happy to answer any questions you have of me.'

*Were we ever friends? Was everything an act? Why can't I answer those questions any more than you can?*

'After what you did to me and the lies you told in court, do you think I could ever believe a word that you say to me?' I ask. 'You had everyone eating out of your hand, you duplicitous bitch.'

'Please, Sophie. You know I was only acting to protect myself.'

I snort, but Alex isn't put off. She lays her hands flat on the table between us as if bracing herself, then speaks again.

'Why me? Aside from the money, I mean.'

I fight the words, but the urge to verbally punch my friend is too strong.

'Because you were the most gullible person I could find – who was worth the most. But you're right, it's not just about the money.

If it were, I'd get a job. I love the con. It's such a buzz pulling the wool over people's eyes. And anyway, don't think they don't get something out of it – the smug bastards feel the warm glow of self-satisfaction at knowing they've helped someone. Admit it, you felt good being so selfless.'

It's true – but it's not the whole truth. I'm not going to tell her the factually correct but highly embarrassing other stuff, though; the mushy crap about how the care people gave to me when they thought I had cancer made me feel loved and wanted. Why expose my soft underbelly to her, so she can kick it?

Alex shakes her head. 'So you chose me because I was easy. A born victim. Okay… Why did you send me a photograph of Joanne? You'd never have been linked to her—'

'Well, having a missing person really does help back up my claims of an abusive boyfriend who is stalking me. Even better when her bones were found. I mean, what's scarier than some psycho, who is clearly capable of murder, being after your friend, Alex? That story is definitely going to make you part with your money if nothing else does. Worked, too, didn't it?'

Boasting is idiotic of me. I clench my fists tighter. Maybe I shouldn't have used Joanne's snap, but it had made sense at the time. I shouldn't have sent that old photo of Simon, taken in happier times, either; that was sloppy of me. I'd thought it would look like 'Andy' was threatening to hurt him in order to get to me. If I'd realised my ex-boyfriend had left town, I would never have done it. I ballsed up by wearing that expensive perfume in front of Jackie, too. Hadn't realised her sister worked behind the perfume counter of a department store. I'd assumed no one would recognise my treat to myself; stupid, when I'm always so careful that my clothes are cheap. Especially stupid when Jackie had been asking questions of me even before then. In fact, she'd been the reason I'd decided the time was ripe to close my trap on Alex – that and the fact that I was getting too comfortable there.

There had been problems, admittedly, but some things had gone like a dream. Of those I was proud, from slipping a sleeping pill into Alex's Appletiser to prevent her waking when I smashed my own windscreen, to freaking her out that time I followed her in the fog.

A smirk slides onto my lips, only to slink away when faced with the prison walls surrounding me.

I can't help wondering at what point Alex realised everything was a sham. Was it that text from 'Andy' that I showed her, using my emergency second phone, that gave the game away? Or when she'd described some bloke she kept bumping into and I pretended that it sounded like Andy? Turned out it was Leon, that fool I'd persuaded into taking a photograph of Alex and me.

Opposite me, Alex shifts, sighs, frowns into our silence.

'It might not seem like it, but I do still care about you,' she says. 'I just… through all of this, I've never really understood why you did it. You're intelligent, charming, beautiful, you could be anything you wanted to be. I know I put you in here, but if you wanted me to be, I could be waiting for you out there when you come out. I could help you get over your bulimia – I'm right, you're bulimic, aren't you?'

My lips stay locked.

'Come on, let me help you. You can't tell me that our whole friendship meant nothing. What about when you asked me to come with you to America? What was that about?'

'It was easier to keep control of you that way. You were less likely to get suspicious.' At my words, Alex looks at me like a child who has been told there's no Father Christmas. He never existed for me.

'You want to lash out, hurt me, I get it,' she nods. 'We both damaged each other. We both lied until we were blue in the face. There is more to me than distortion and falsehood, though, and I think the same can be said of you.'

There is comfort in the smooth rhythm of my hair running through my fingers, round and round and round.

'Okay, want to know the truth?' I sigh finally. 'I've got a real sob story for you. A violent dad, a mum too terrified of him to have any energy left for me, time in foster care, and, yeah, actually I did have a husband that beat me up all the time.'

My lawyer had begged to use this in court to mitigate, but I'd refused. I didn't want people's pity – getting it for a lie was a very different thing than getting it for the truth. Why am I telling Alex? I don't know, so I cover it with barbs and attitude.

'I got into the habit of stealing people's identities to make me feel better. I'd become whatever they wanted me to be, in order to be popular. Or I'd see someone who was popular and emulate them, trying to fit in. It never worked. They could always tell I was a fake. But I got better at it. That's how I survived my crappy childhood, and it's how I made a living as an adult. "Look after Number One because no one else is going to" is something I learned early.'

The smirk returns as I sit back, drawn by my bravado. It gives me something to hide behind. 'But how do you know that what I've just told you is the truth, or just another shitty lie to get your sympathy?'

# CHAPTER FIFTY-SIX

Her head tilts. She studies, and sees everything.

That's why I hate Alex, because she seems to have a unique ability to see all the ambivalence, vulnerability, hurt, honesty, duplicity behind every truth and lie. Everything I try to keep hidden she lays bare.

'I know,' she says. 'I know because I can relate to bits of it.'

'Now I don't believe you.'

'Listen, I certainly don't condone what you did, but I can understand why you did that. As a kid, I mean. I was adopted. My parents loved me so much, but somehow they could never fill the hole that insecurity had dug in me. It made me vulnerable, and I made some poor choices along the way. I understand what it's like to be desperate to fit in – and to be willing to do whatever it takes to protect yourself from hurt.

'So I understand where you're coming from, Carrie—' She bites her lip. I'll always be Carrie to her. 'It explains why you've made bad choices, but it doesn't excuse your actions any more than it excuses mine. We're adults, we have to take responsibility and accept our pasts don't have to shape us for ever.

'I mean it when I say I'm here for you if you need me. I want to be your friend – I think you could do with one. I'm turning over a new leaf and moving on, and you can, too.'

This has to be a bluff. I keep my poker face in place as she continues, her words gathering pace. She's jabbing the table with her finger, creating a Morse code of emphasis.

'Remember you once said there's no fate or "meant to be"? I think you're right. But I do believe there's a reason why all of this happened between us: because we recognised core parts of our personality in one another and were drawn to each other. We've both been hurt by loved ones who should have protected us, and we've both developed lying as a way of protecting ourselves. You chose me for my vulnerability, but I share your strength – and you brought it back out in me.'

She gives a breathless shrug, an apology of the shoulders. 'I can see in your eyes that you don't trust me, and I suppose I can't blame you, after everything. But… I did tell everyone from the start that I was a liar.'

'Yes – but who believes a liar when they're telling the truth?'

I've spent all day in a bad mood as a result of Alex's visit. Shaking my head at her bleeding-heart hypocrisy, thinking of cutting remarks that I'd have said to her face if only they'd occurred to me at the time. Now that I'm locked in my cell, though, and lights off has been called, the shame I've been trying to keep at bay with annoyance seeps through me. It dampens my pillow with tears.

I keep thinking about the thing Alex said about new starts and not being shaped by lies. I remind myself once again that she's the one who put me here. She's also the closest thing I've ever had to a real friend, and the only person who's visited me. Try as I might, I can't think of an angle for her to be working.

*Maybe she actually means what she said*, a small but persistent voice pipes up inside my head. Perhaps, for the first time in my life, someone truly knows me – and loves me for myself.

Could I actually change and have a normal life? For the first time I think about everything that I've said and done. I've no regrets about leaving Dad far behind. As for Andy, after the way that he emotionally and physically abused me over a period of twelve months, I reckon taking a bunch of gay soft porn photographs of him is very mild revenge. Simple but effective, as I haven't heard so much as a peep from him since, let alone have him launch a campaign of terror against me. Every lie I've told after that was a case of survival, I tell myself.

Okay, that's not one hundred per cent true.

The patchwork of deceit unfurls, and I study it. Feel ashamed.

My lying is as compulsive as saying I've brushed my teeth when I haven't. Nothing I can say or do will ever make amends for what I have done. I've taken advantage of good people and ripped them off; I disrespected people who are genuinely sick, and deprived charities of money that has the potential to cure cancer.

No harm done. That's what I told myself, even though I knew what I was doing was despicable.

No harm until Joanne.

She'd been so easy to net. I hadn't even had to join any support groups; we'd just got chatting in the pub the day after I moved to Cromer. Grief made her talkative, and I listened patiently as she told me about her ten-year-old daughter, Alice, who had died of childhood leukaemia a handful of months before. When she heard about my terminal cancer she'd started to fill up. Gripping my hand, she told me how brave I was and that I'd beat this terrible disease. That was the moment I knew I'd got her hooked.

What with my terminal cancer, and then my evil ex stalking me, it wasn't hard to get her to cough up the money initially. The problem was that she instantly worried what her husband would do if he found out that she'd cleared out her bank account. She'd even taken out a loan for me. She begged me to give the money back. When I guilt-tripped her into backing away from that idea, she pleaded to be allowed to confide in her husband about me.

My big mistake had been choosing a target with a strong support network. I couldn't let her tell them about me. Drastic action had been needed.

But I didn't kill her. I am not a murderer – I hadn't even hurt my cat; the blood smeared on his collar had been all mine. I'd deliberately cut my leg where no one would see the wound, so Alex wouldn't put two and two together. The worst thing I've done to Smudge was put him back on the streets where he'd come from. He lives with Alex now, well-loved and looked after. See, I'm a good person really.

That little Jiminy Cricket voice pipes up again in the back of my mind. *You may not have killed Joanne, but you are responsible for her death.*

I manipulated and emotionally blackmailed her until she felt completely backed into a corner. She couldn't possibly tell her husband or anybody else what she'd done with that money because she'd be letting down a dying woman on the run. She'd be stealing my chance of finding peace in my final days. Joanne became more worked up and emotionally unstable as pressure built on her. I knew there was one thing guaranteed to push her into doing what I wanted.

'Don't worry about helping me. Honestly, I can get by begging – it's amazing how kind people are,' I'd said. 'Alice would be so proud of everything you've done for me already.'

The seed of the thought grew in Joanne's mind, and I watched it bloom into a choking weed. She was imagining her helpless daughter in my position, on the run, homeless, begging, and the drive to protect her vicariously was overwhelming. After that Joanne had promised to keep her mouth shut when I left with all her money.

I tell myself that Joanne was tormented by demons of loss, and that her desperation to be with her daughter was to blame for what happened next. I'm not sure I believe it. There was no big confrontation, no violent act, no desperation on my part. Instead, Joanne and her demons walked arm in arm into the sea's eternal embrace, where she drowned under the weight of guilt over stealing from her husband.

Anger, confusion, embarrassment, disgust, worthlessness – all that and more rips through me at the memory. How could I have let that happen?

She hadn't realised I'd been following her to see what she'd do. I'd stood on the beach and watched her final moments, frozen with disbelief and indecision. Telling myself that she'd change her mind. Any minute, she'd turn around and wade back to shore. By the time I realised she was really going through with it, it was already too late. The waves closed over her head, and she didn't come up. Kicking off my shoes, I'd bombed into the water, gasping at the cold and plunging through the rollers to reach the spot where I'd last seen her. Again and again I dived under the murky surface, coming up each time empty-handed. Coughing and spluttering and desperate, I'd screamed her name. No one heard me. Despite my best efforts I hadn't been able to save her. Every night when I close my eyes and replay that scene, that's what I tell myself.

I'm so desperately sorry for how I have affected people. I'll turn my life around and become a better person, with the help of Alex. It might take a long time for people to believe I have changed, especially as such awful manipulation came to me with such ease, but I can do it. I can become different. After all, it's what I've done my whole life.

I turn over in bed and clench my jaw in determination. I can do this!

I wish I could put my whole life out in the open, no part of me camouflaged, every lie, every indiscretion on view, so everyone can see I don't want to hide any more.

I still believe in that happy ending I've longed for.

I still believe I can make it in the end.

I still believe most people are good – and that I can be good, too. Hopefully. One day.

Or am I lying to myself?

# CHAPTER FIFTY-SEVEN

Children shout and paddle, bare legs showing beneath their coats, pink in the cold. Dogs bark, chasing waves and sniffing at things invisible to their owners. The sharp, mouthwatering smell of vinegar mingled with the salty sea air. Scattered along the beach are knots of kelp, deep green and thick as rope. Go near and smell the iodine.

Leon and I walk hand in hand along the beach, finally coming to a stop in the shadow of the church. Too cold there; I step out into the sunlight and watch my goosebumps disappear. Kick off my shoes and sink my toes into the sand. Gasp when an ice-cold wave gently laps over them. The tide is on the turn; it's time. As the waves retreat over the sand, they urge silence.

*Shhh!*

I've kept quiet for too long, though.

'Are you ready?' Leon asks.

'It's been a long time coming, but yes, I finally am.' I face the sunset-blushed sky.

The last time I saw Rosie, just after the trial two months ago, she suggested that writing a letter to my children might be a good way of saying goodbye and getting closure. Although I liked the idea, it's taken me this long to find the peace and courage inside myself to write what needs to be said.

Rosie had stuck with me during the nerve-racking run-up to the trial. Of course, she hadn't realised that the real reason I'd been nervous was because I was stitching up my friend so that she could then enjoy a fresh start. Everyone had believed my version of events without question. The evidence backed me up completely, plus it turned out that police in Norfolk had started to look at Carrie Goodwin's background to see if she was connected in any way to Joanne or Natalie.

Sophie's clean slate will be worth its tough start, I'm sure. Now it's time for me to wipe my own slate clean, and writing to my children is a huge part of that. Getting the truth down has been a huge help to me, and now I want to set it free.

'Would you do the honours, please?' I hand the glass bottle to Leon. 'You can throw it further than me,' I explain in reply to his raised eyebrow.

The start of our relationship was a baptism of fire, what with all my baggage along with his own marriage breaking up not long before we met. Luckily it means we've forged something strong. Along with everyone at the support group, which I no longer attend, he knows about Owen, Elise and Edward. Most of it, anyway.

'We don't need to bare our souls about everything immediately,' he'd said when I'd told him, guessing I was omitting some details. 'Falling in love is the easy part, it's getting to know one another and to trust that takes the time. We all have locked boxes inside us that only certain people get the keys to.'

One day I'll let the lock click open and reveal the full story of my family. Soon, I'll tell him what I did to Sophie, too. Perhaps he can help me wrestle with my conscience about whether, sometimes, it's justified to do what's wrong in order to achieve what's right. I'm certainly hoping so, which is why I visited Sophie.

For a while I wanted to hate her; it would be so much easier if I did. But I can't lose the love I had for the person I thought she was, and can't escape the fact that we're as bad as each other. Sadly, it seems she's not ready for us to face the truth together, but I'll give it another go. What I won't do, though, is keep banging my head against a brick wall – ultimately it's up to her whether she wishes to grab the lifeline of a fresh start that I've thrown her.

That's what I keep telling myself. But parents don't turn their backs on their children, and in my heart of hearts I still feel she's the daughter I never got the chance to raise. It's no coincidence that after meeting her, my image of Elise became more like Sophie, from her clothes to her character. She even started wearing Sophie's garish pink diamanté skull ring.

I'd always imagined my daughter would be straight-talking, too, and persuade some sense into me. Sophie had. Ironically, all those pep talks that she'd given me about grabbing life finally worked. She made me fight; she made me move past my problems and start living in the real world instead of my fantasy bubble. Despite everything that's happened between us, I'm better for having known her. Now I need to make her better for having known me. Together, we can find redemption. I want to do right by this 'surrogate daughter'; which is why, at some point soon, I'm going to ask both Leon and Sophie how they feel about her coming to live with us after her release. Just until she gets on her feet.

Leon has been busily rolling up his trousers while I've been lost in waves of thought. Now, he grabs my hand and we wade calf-deep into the water, gasping and giggling and doing a little dance until we acclimatise.

'Any words you want to say?'

I shake my head. 'They're all written down.'

Beside me, Leon's arm arcs back then catapults forward. The bottle flies out and lands with a splash in the sea's embrace. I say a little prayer as I watch the truth contained inside it bobbing with the waves into the distance, slightly further with each pull of the tide. Floating and glinting, then disappearing in the ocean's game of hide-and-seek.

There is a chill in the air as the sun starts to kiss the horizon, but I'm warm in Leon's embrace. We can't see the bottle any more, but still we don't move. Finally, it's Leon that stirs.

'Come on, let's go home. Smudge will be wondering where we are. I'll cook us something nice for tea, eh?'

Home. At last, I think I've found it.

# CHAPTER FIFTY-EIGHT

*Dear Elise and Edward,*

*I'm not sure how to write this letter, even though I've practised it in my head a hundred times. There are too many things to say and I'm worried it will jumble into a mess of words, so please bear with me if I meander.*

*My beautiful children, it's time for me to finally come to terms with losing you, and let you go. It doesn't mean I'll stop loving you. I'll still think about you every single day and grieve for the lives you should have had, but I can't cling to you any more – I need to let your spirits fly free. In truth, I need to so that I have the breathing space to start living again, because I've been the walking dead for too long.*

*I've met someone, and we're hoping to adopt a child. It would mean the world to think you've given your blessing to that. Leon is a good man. I've never trusted people since your father. I loved him so much, but he didn't always deserve it. There, I've admitted it, part of the shameful truth I've hidden for what feels like an eternity. The good inside him was the part that he gave to make you, though, and it's also the part of him that survives in spirit now that the three of you are together.*

*Growing up, I'd always felt insecure, knowing that from my first breath I'd been rejected by my birth parents. Poor Mum tried so hard to fill the unfillable hole in me, but none of my problems were her fault. The diffidence was inherent in me. I'd found it difficult to make friends at school, and I'd worked to fit in, even trying to smoke, though it made me cough and feel queasy. When Mum and Dad discovered a packet of cigarettes in my room they sat me down and talked everything through with me, understanding rather than lecturing – although Dad gave me a good scare about lung cancer, thanks to his knowledge as a GP. It wasn't the first time Mum told me I needed more confidence in myself and to not be so easily led, and it wouldn't be the last, but I'd got stronger as I'd grown up.*

*Yet despite all that, when I met your dad, Owen, I fell into the trap of my youth – too easily manipulated. Like so many men with a skill for emotional and physical abuse, he was a dichotomy of charm and cruelty, the switch happening so fast I often wondered if I were going mad. I remember one time in particular, we'd just got home from a lovely weekend break in Tynemouth and I'd been bending down to pick up the post from the doormat when something blurred past me and pain shot through my face. I stumbled back, and Owen reached out a steadying hand and gave that happy-go-lucky beam of his. He'd punched me, and we hadn't even been arguing. There'd been no reason. Yet I found myself wondering if I'd imagined it and was going mad, because he was smiling at me. The throbbing of my cheek was my only proof it had happened.*

*Anything could set him off. One day, he walked into the lounge and his face hardened as he saw a cup ring left on the coffee table, his laughing blue eyes narrowing to diamond-hard points. Then he punched me in the ribs, his favourite place because he knew people might ask questions if I had a black eye. Long sleeves and a high collar hide a multitude of sins. Although he was also a big fan of bending my fingers back until they snapped, leaving me unable to work. It was amazing how often I 'trapped my hand in the door'. I learned to look out for the smallest of warning signs. The tapping of the finger; the look in his eyes; the tightness of his jaw.*

*Why did I stay? I don't know. The thing is, I think he really did love me in his own way. Once, I made costumes for a theatre production that the Queen attended. There was a photograph of me meeting Her Majesty. Owen was so proud that he kept all the cuttings from the newspapers. That's the strange mixture of personalities in people who mentally abuse their partners. After each violent outburst he'd get down on his hands and knees, plead with me to forgive him. I always did. It's hard to walk out on someone you love, even when they do hit you. You think it's going to be just the once – anyone is allowed one mistake. Then one mistake becomes two, three, four, and it's harder and harder to draw the line.*

*I blamed myself for not being able to give him the one thing he wanted more than anything else in the world: children. I told myself that when we were a family he'd be happier, and his kindness would overgrow the insecure monster that squatted inside him.*

*He was so excited when I told him I was pregnant with you both. That deceptively friendly face of his breaking naturally into a constant grin. I'd been right – family life had changed him, and we'd stood in the nursery together, hand in hand, dreaming of how we would decorate. Then suddenly he'd accused me of sleeping with a stranger to get pregnant. I'd grown used to the carefully placed punches landed on my torso so that no one would see the bruises, but when he hit me that night it was utterly shocking. Do you remember how I curled up in a ball, with my arms around my bump, to protect you both? It was such a relief to feel you moving, afterwards. Of course, he said he'd never do it again. Of course, I decided to believe him once more – and only once – for your sake. I didn't want my children growing up without a father. I'd think of all the kind things he did, and the same lie I always told myself leapt to my lips: 'He's a good man. He'd never intentionally hurt me.'*

*On the day that we discovered I was having a little girl and little boy, your father and I had truly never been happier. We settled on your names, Elise and Edward, instantly. I wanted to go into town to buy clothes for you, and Owen said he'd come with me because he had a surprise for me. The station was a walkable distance, but I was already so heavy carrying the two of you that I tired easily, so we decided to drive. But on the way his mood grew darker. I knew him well enough to recognise the warning signs and tried all the tricks I'd learned over the years to calm him. They didn't work. The more I tried, the angrier he got. By the time we reached the station he was furious. We parked up, and as we prepared to walk the short distance from the car park, along the lane to the platforms, he started. Began pushing me around, ranting once again about me being unfaithful and expecting him to raise my 'bastards'.*

*Something snapped inside me then. I wouldn't let him hurt my babies. Nobody was around to help me, though; the car park and station empty and unmanned. Owen pushed me hard; I almost fell over. I was scared for your lives. All I could think of was escaping him. I didn't even notice the klaxon sounding or the lights flashing to warn of a train coming as I pushed open the wicket gate and ran through it, your father close behind. The only thought in my mind was of escaping.*

*I remember the roaring of the train, the turbulence of the air trying to drag me along, a red mist.*

*The intercity train stopped as quickly as it could, but it had been going so fast that it travelled quite a way before it was able to. It gave me time to hide and make my way back to the car and drive home, in shock. The only thought running through my mind wasn't about evading questioning, it was to get you both to safety.*

*I didn't mean to lie to the police, I really didn't, but when they came over they didn't ask me any questions, simply told me that my husband had been killed in a tragic accident. CCTV covering the station and car park didn't capture what happened on the lane – perhaps Owen, aware of the blind spot, had deliberately waited until we were in it before pushing me around. The train driver never mentioned that another person had run across the tracks before Owen; I can only assume shock played tricks with his memory, or perhaps he simply didn't see me.*

*Omission is as bad as a lie, though.*

*As a salve to Owen's parents I never told anyone the truth about what happened that day. There was no point sullying his name when it served no purpose.*

*It didn't stop me feeling responsible, though. The guilt of what happened caused me to miscarry, and losing you both felt like divine retribution for me killing my husband. It's taken me a long time to believe that even if I did deserve punishment, no divinity would have made the two of you pay the price for me, my beautiful darlings.*

*I've given away the compensation money to a cancer charity. It felt like the right thing to do. I've never been able to bring myself to spend a penny of it, and holding on to it wasn't going to help anyone. My inspiration for this grand gesture? Carrie – or rather, Sophie.*

*What I've done by covering up the truth of your father's accident is a moral grey area, and I'm not proud of it, but I accept it. When I decided to set Carrie up I opted for those cloudy shades again, telling myself that if she went to prison, she could pay for her crimes and then come out facing a fresh start – if she wanted it. I'd like to be there for her, if she'll let me. I've done some digging into her background and what I found was heartbreaking. She needs me as much as I need her.*

*One of Owen's favourite things to say to me was, 'Look what you made me do.' But I didn't make him do anything. It was all him. Just like he didn't make me do anything. I lied for self-preservation. I reacted to the circumstances before me, and can't blame anyone but myself for the decisions that made my life fall apart – just like only I can decide to put myself together again. Not Rosie, not Leon, not the friend formerly known as Carrie, not even you, Elise and Edward. Only me. I don't want to spend the rest of my life looking back, punishing myself and trying to live in an alternative universe where you're alive. Life is the here and now. Carrie once told me if I wasn't doing something every single day that I'd be proud to have on my gravestone, then I was doing something wrong, and although she may not have practised what she preached, she was right. I don't want to think 'look what you made me do', I want to think 'look what I did', and feel proud.*

*That's why I'm letting you go, my beautiful little ones, and trying finally to start a new life. With Leon. With adopted children of our own. Hopefully, with Sophie, too. That's not the same as forgetting you, though; never think that.*

*I hope my finally telling the truth sets you free, my angels.*

*Love for ever*

*Mum x*

# A LETTER FROM BARBARA

Thank you for reading my fifth psychological thriller, *The Perfect Friend*. My Uncle Norman lost his long fight with cancer at the same time as I was mulling over ideas for a new book. It's no surprise that his death coloured my thoughts, and the result is *The Perfect Friend*, the writing of which helped me immensely to work through a lot of grief.

Perhaps because of the subject matter I was hyperaware, but while writing this book, so many people around me were touched by cancer. In particular, my thoughts are with my former editor, Nick Machin, and the fabulous blogger Alison Daughtrey-Drew, whose positivity and battling spirits are inspirational, along with the lovely and incredibly private Di.

I do hope you all enjoyed reading Alex and Carrie's story. If you would like to keep up to date with my latest releases, just sign up here and I'll let you know when a new book is coming out.

www.bookouture.com/barbara-copperthwaite

If you haven't read any of my previous Bookouture books, you might enjoy *The Darkest Lies* and *Her Last Secret*.

In the meantime, why not pop over to my Facebook page, Twitter, my blog or website, for a chat? I love to hear from readers – because without you there wouldn't be any books, and hearing your thoughts helps me become a better writer. If you have time, I'd be really grateful if you could post a short review online, or tell your friends about *The Perfect Friend*. I'd love to hear what you think, and it can also help other readers discover one of my books for the first time.

Thank you so much!
Barbara x

AuthorBarbaraCopperthwaite/

BCopperthwait

barbaracopperthwaite.wordpress.com

www.barbaracopperthwaite.com

# ACKNOWLEDGEMENTS

I always start my acknowledgements with a big cheer for my partner, Paul. He's probably unaware of this because he doesn't read books! But the fact remains that he deserves the biggest thanks for his patience when I'm lost in a make-believe world and barely appear in reality to string two sentences together; his endless cups of fruit tea when I forget to eat or drink; his love, support and encouragement to push me on when I feel like giving up. My mum also deserves an award for patience and encouragement. Love you, Mum!

In researching this book, I've heard first-hand the toll anorexia takes physically and emotionally. Thank you to those who shared your stories with me. You may wish to remain anonymous, but the world can see the difference you've made to this book.

I'm so grateful to my incredible friend, Julieanne Caie, who opened up her house to me so I could have a break and find some inspiration: Ju, this is the result of my holiday in Tynemouth. Cheers for the house, the rhubarb gin and the headspace (but especially the gin!).

Keshini Naidoo, my editor, is not only brilliant with my books but also so supportive and understanding through my health difficulties. I can't thank her, and the whole of the Bookouture family, enough: my publisher, Claire Bord; managing editor, Lauren Finger; Head of Talent, Peta Nightingale; publicity and social media magicians (aka 'fingers of fire') Kim Nash and Noelle Holton; and copy editor supreme, Janette, to name but a few.

Special thanks to fellow Bookouture authors, particularly Holly Martin (your information on banks really helped) and Carol Wyer (for keeping me sane!).

The blogging community has been a huge supporter of mine, and I'm so grateful. That's thanks in no small part to Anne Cater's wonderful Book Connectors, where readers and authors can connect. Thank you also to Tracy Fenton, and everyone at TBC on Facebook; David Gilchrist and the team at UK Crime Book Club; and Shell Baker et al. on Crime Book Club.

Shell, Neats Wilson, Anne Williams, Alison Daughtrey-Drew, thank you for being there from the start, and for continuing to shout about my work (I hope you like *The Perfect Friend* as much as you've enjoyed my others). There are so many wonderful bloggers who have reviewed my books, and I can't thank you all enough.

My final thanks are the most important: they are to you, dear reader. You take the time to read, review and recommend my books. I am so incredibly grateful for all the support you show me. Thank you, thank you, thank you! One of those readers is Rosie Knight, who won a competition to have a character named after her, which is how Alex's counsellor got her name. I often run competitions across Twitter, Facebook, Instagram and my blog, so do pop by and join in the fun, or just come for a chat. I love to hear your thoughts.

Made in the USA
Columbia, SC
05 October 2018